THE RIDE TO NOWHERE

The instant Bernadine's index finger pushed the "UP" button, there was a soft whirring sound, and the elevator doors slid noiselessly open.

Come right inside, said the words in her mind.

Don't mind if I do, Bernadine thought back to them amiably.

She took two, then three steps forward, and she was inside. She turned, somewhat expectantly, and the elevator doors closed.

Comfortable? came the solicitous words. *Everything all right?*

"Fine," Bernadine said out loud, smiling a bit. "Just fine."

Look down.

She did. She looked down at her feet, and they weren't there. Only her ankles on up. Bernadine frowned. The ankles were gone now too. Bernadine frowned harder, tried to clear her mind. The knees, they disappeared next. Bernadine opened her mouth to say something in mild protest, but nothing came out. She didn't exist below the waist; there was nothing whatsoever there but empty air. Bernadine felt panic begin, somewhere inside, and her mind tore itself free. But she could see only her cleavage now. The rest was gone. Bernadine opened her mouth wide, to scream for help—

Except now there wasn't any mouth either.

There wasn't any Bernadine at all.

READ THESE BESTSELLING BLOCKBUSTERS!

EXTRATERRESTRIAL
BY JULIAN SHOCK

ZEBRA BOOKS
KENSINGTON PUBLISHING CORP.

ZEBRA BOOKS

are published by

KENSINGTON PUBLISHING CORP.
475 Park Avenue South
New York, N.Y. 10016

Printed in the United States of America

For my "pertson"

"Every society faces not merely a succession of probable futures, but an array of possible futures, and a conflict over *preferable* futures."
—Alvin Toffler

"Clearly, *intelligence* is an evolutionary survival factor . . . but it is only one of many. What we *can* assert with a degree of confidence is that it is such a *powerful* survival factor that . . . it has a good chance of surviving— assuming it does not develop a technology with which to *wipe itself out.*"
—John Grant, *The Directory of Possibilities*

finest artists, parts of the streaking light-banner phosphorescent, actinic, and ultraviolet. At its midpoint, the rainbow burst in a single burnished oval, like some lamp of Aladdin—or something meant to be hallowed.

Those beneath the light-show, who subscribed to Christian dogma but were out after midnight anyway, whispered swift, urgent prayers and would not have been unduly surprised to spy three wise men trudging over the midtown bridge in quest of the divine gold at rainbow's end.

Those who were cut from a more scientific cloth instantly drew other, equally-rushed conclusions. It was, they said as they tried to remain cool, a meteor—except no one of them had heard of a meteor which began near the earth and ascended to the zenith of the darkling sky, where it hung suspended. "Weather balloons," cried other determined skeptics; "merely an interesting astronomical phenomenon," said still others, "surely a trick of the eye." "Yes, yes!" exclaimed the like-minded; "we are actually seeing nothing more than Venus, or possibly Jupiter, from an uncustomary angle!"

And those on the wee-hour streets who were neither especially religious nor particularly scientific craned their necks and soon enunciated three letters of the alphabet which, when they were uttered, left their mouths formed in a perfect circle of clear awe: *"UFO!"* they said, unentangled by old faith or new fact. Jostling, they poked the people near them and saw a welcoming nod of agreement: "Yes, we are *seeing a UFO at last!*"

Down the street, having left a late-night bar, several people who had believed in UFOs for a long while stared up at the near-blinding luminescence with a mixture of old fact and new faith. If they had known to whom they should pray, they might have made the sign of the computer or some other exotic hint of the future. As each of the people turned to look at the others, he found the same enraptured expression on the others' faces—and the same prayerful thought: "*Space brothers*, come to save us from ourselves, to deliver us from the bomb, the Assassin, the Terrorist—*Space Brothers* from Alpha Centauri, or some wondrous and mystic corner of the universe—with pure hearts and nothing on their minds but our *salvation!*"

But aboard the shining spacecraft, in its principal cabin, other thoughts were taking shape in the minds of the travelers from afar and words were being spoken.

The male sat heavily in scorn before the instrument panel. He didn't call it that, at all, not without good reason. Progress had reached such a level, in his experience, that there were no more than a few dials, levers, and buttons to be manipulated. A child could fly this ship; indeed, as he well knew, many children from elsewhere in nearby galaxies *had* flown to earth, just to zip around and raise *hjikl*. With his expression of disgust in place, he was staring into the wide viewing screen at the people of earth who were, in turn, looking up at his ship.

"Ants," he remarked distinctly. "They look like so many ants."

"Then simply bring them closer into the screen," the female said patiently, intending to be helpful. "Sixty percent midrange magnification should be about right at this latitude."

"They're already in midrange mag," replied the male, half-turning to let her see his expression of revulsion. "I didn't mean their size, or their bodies!" he snorted. "I meant . . . *them*; human beings. All the literate ones must have read about spaceships and even the ones who cannot read surely saw newspapers or—what do they call it?"

"Television?" she prompted him.

He gave a barking laugh. "Yes, television; TV. Thousands of reports all over the world and every human being down there knows at least one other human being who has seen ships in the skies. Yet they continue to look astonished, the way their children look when they receive gifts on their natal days." He gave a grand shrug. "Ants!"

"Don't be pettish, dear," she urged him, mildly annoyed. This was an old story and she really felt it was time for him to put his old-fashioned animosities behind him. There was a task to be done, and it wasn't as if it were something new to him. Sniffing, she turned to the child and began brushing her hair. "Who shall it be this time? What is our target grouping?"

The male knew she was speaking to him and not the child. But her attitude grated on his nerves and he thought about refusing to reply. For her, dealing with the people was enough. She was extraordinarily efficient and hardworking; she was pragmatic in her decisions; she rarely carried grudges. Instead, she went about holding up her end of the business with a *sangfroid*, an easy relaxation, that bordered on the cheerful. The male was never cheerful and for the life of him he couldn't figure out whether the female functioned from a spirit of sheer, inexhaustible duty or if she really enjoyed handling human beings. She certainly never showed any of the vindictive viciousness he always displayed. Barely glancing over his shoulder, he grunted, "Ask the *Selector* if you're eager to know."

"Very well, then, I shall."

Feeling peevish—trips of a year's length always left him edgy, especially if they were coming back here; but he never seemed to understand that she was anxious to get to work also. She let the hairbrush hang in the gravity-free cabin and quickly crossed the room.

Floating in an aquarium-style glass container filled with a mottled, greenish liquid, the basic chemical of which bore a scientific resemblance to amniotic fluid, the *Selector* dreamily became aware that the female was coming. It did its best to turn, the motion a sort-of sickening end-for-end flop, and for the moment withdrew its interminably-incisive study of itself and its communion with the home planet. Its gaze steadily locking with hers, it considered the female's query, only dimly aware that she found its sad, weeping eyes utterly disgusting.

Because of what it was, the *Selector* was entirely capable of speaking aloud, however squeaky and metallic its partly-humanoid voice sounded to the ear. But it preferred exercising telepathy—speaking directly into the brains of the female, male, and child who served it. Often, they had argued the question of whether or not the *Selector* chose telepathy because it understood the concept of pain and realized that its mental communiques were exquisitely painful. The female, who was in some respects closer to pain than the male, believed in the *Selector*'s malice.

Stooping, she knew she had surprised the male by agreeing to ask the *Selector* her question. He hadn't thought she would give the damnable creature a chance to inflict its peculiar brand of internal agony. For her part, the female meant for him to see how weary she had

11

become of being a second-class *siblykron*, when her chores were the same as his, and how bored she was with his sulking ways. Hurting human beings badly was one thing; *hating* them was another, in her opinion.

She felt the words carving their way into her brain like a daggerblade shearing away gray cells and braced herself for the complete answer. It was, she thought, a kind of subversion, or rape. The *Selector* rarely entered her thoughts without locating her erotic centers and filling her with a transient urge to mate. With the being's first word, she clamped her teeth together and felt tears sting her eyes:

"It is the time," said the *Selector, "of those who place words on paper."* She turned her hands to fists, told herself that it wasn't blood she felt flowing in her skull. Only pain turned to something like liquid, or lava. *"Full instructions will be imparted on landing. Only, however, to the male. A male like me."*

"I want to kiss you, to stroke you," she said aloud, quickly, almost reaching her hands into the container to feel the *Selector*. "I want to press my lips against your—"

Her eyes flew open. *Francle striv!* she swore. She wanted nothing of the kind. The female shuddered. And there was nothing, in any case, to press her lips against. They had made the hideous thing without a means of natural procreation, without genitalia; it was no more male than *she* was!

"It is time to land," called the male, and she returned to him, looking out the viewscreen. Their destination had been programmed nearly a year ago. There was nothing to do; everything would be handled automatically.

As the minutes passed they had left the first observers

of their spacecraft behind. Now, hovering above the old building, they saw only a handful of human beings left on the streets, widely separated from one another. Still, it would not do for any of them to see the entry or the landing. To avoid the risk, that phase of the operation had also been programmed by the software installed in the craft months ago.

When the several people looking up saw the great light in the skies go out, they rubbed their eyes and instantly doubted their own senses. *"Ants!"* said the male at the control panel; and the disintegration dispersion happened on time.

Without any electric sensations, pain, or even an actual realization of the procedure being accomplished, the aliens aboard the spaceship—and the UFO itself—reassembled automatically in the immense, deserted ballroom. A quick glimpse of Sensortect told them no one at all was around. Gathering the few possessions they dared carry, they alit from the craft at once.

For a moment male, female, and child held hands and became adjusted to gravity once more. They took it all in, carefully, putting into balance the information they had laboriously studied and the actual fact of a human hall of recreation. Several tables remained in the near-darkness, huddling like monoliths across the expanse of once-polished flooring. Chairs were stacked atop the tables and the child giggled. "It looks like they're being held down, to keep them from floating away."

The male, to whom she had spoken, did not reply. To his left, he saw, a stage remained and there were crimson, velvety curtains leading into the—he paused, squinting, seeking the word—the *wings*. Delicately, he permitted

13

himself a smile. Human beings had such an interesting language. Their words, unlike his, might mean many things.

To the right was a long table which had been used for a bar. Behind it, other tables remained which had once held—he squinted again—*bottles* containing their *al-co-hol-ic* beverages. Quaint. They knew so little, these human people, yet they were so anxious to lose contact with what little knowledge they possessed!

"Did I hear right, Daddy?" demanded the child, reaching up to him eagerly. "Did the *Selector* really say it's time for 'those who place words on paper?'"

The male looked over her head at the female, smiling slightly. "I believe that is what it said. Why do you ask?"

"Because I *like* stories," she responded at once. "Will you make them tell me a story before we do our job? Will you make them be funny and clever before it's too late?"

The male gave her an absentminded but kindly glance, and patted her head. "Child," he said, "they'll do anything we tell them to do—the way they always have. *Anything at all.*"

He saw a small placard left on a nearby table and picked it up. "HOTEL HOLROYD," it said in large letters. "WHERE YOU'RE ALWAYS IN FOR THE TIME OF YOUR LIFE!"

TRANSCRIPTION ONE

"SOMETHING INCREDIBLE"

"Somewhere, something incredible is waiting
to be known."
— Carl Sagan

"There seems to be a *lot of traffic* up here."
— Astronaut Wally Schirra,
August 1, 1960

CHAPTER ONE

"Is that *it?* Is that our hotel?"

Spencer Torrence smiled at his daughter Lauren's eager expression and ran his palm through his straight red hair. "Well, it's certainly not a haunted house, however it may look from the street," he told the twelve-year-old. He glanced at the other adults around them, saw their doubtful faces. "Go on inside, princess, if that's what you want. We'll catch up."

Spence watched Lauren dart up the walk to the front of the aging building, long auburn hair streaming, clutching her ebon kitten Puck against her thin breast as she shoved at the doors with her shoulder. When she vanished inside, Spence grinned. There was nothing in the world Spence Torrence loved better than Lauren, not even his late-blooming career as a writer of nonfiction or the fine reviews he'd earned in recent years. Even before his wife April or their friends Dan and Ginger could comment on the condition of the Hotel Holroyd, Spence knew they'd stay. This would be the first real vacation he'd ever been able to give little Lauren.

"I cannot believe they'd have the audacity to ask people like Mailer and Updike to a dump like this," Dan Lloyd grumbled. The balding science expert had a death-grip on the arm of his youthful wife, Ginger, who moved on the somewhat icy walk with the grace of the fine tennis player she'd been. "I even heard reports that Michener was coming, not to mention the best writers from other fields—playwrights, TV writers of all kinds, Hollywood types, newspaper columnists like me."

"Now, Dan," Spence chided his old friend, clapping his burly shoulder. "When you've been named the very best at what you do, and you have the chance to meet all your peers, it's got to be tempting. But when they're willing to pay all your expenses for a week, no self-respecting wordsmith could pass it up. Damned few of us make enough money that we're willing to ignore such a freebee."

"I'd like to have asked you to bypass it," April said in her customarily dramatic tones. She'd been a Broadway actress before falling for Spence and never had been able to stop exaggerating things, playing scenes whenever she could. "That is, if I'd known it would be so mothering *cold*." She shuddered against Spence's side. "Or that the hotel would look like something out of an old Roger

18

Corman flick."

"Could we just stop talking about it and g-get inside?" Ginger inquired.

A week ago it had snowed again, turned bitter cold, and the warm-up was just getting under way. The result was that the humped gray patches on the ground around the old four-story Holroyd had shrunk slightly. Spence was reminded, as he held the door for the others, of the corpses of basketball players left outside to freeze beneath blankets much too short for them. He'd heard of midwestern winters but never once dreamed they could be this bad so late in March.

He followed April and their friends up the marble steps to the lobby, clapping his square hands together, then reluctantly unwinding his woolen scarf from his short, reddish neck. New York State got cold, God knew; but this midwestern winter bit deep into the skin with a vengeance that felt oddly personal, even malefic. He wouldn't have told the others even for a new five-figure contract with Macmillan or Knopf, not when Lauren was bouncing excitedly up and down in front of the registration desk; but he'd felt bad, eerie vibes of warning about coming here for weeks. And while the Hotel Holroyd was spotless, everything seemed to be functioning, he had the uneasy impression that they were being *watched*—an unnerving feeling of being stared at, or visually *inspected*—that compounded his bad vibrations. It wasn't just that the place was old, certainly close to one-hundred years, as much as it was a hunch that the Hotel Holroyd contained secrets. Joining Lauren at the desk, he tried to catch them watching—the desk clerk, perhaps, the uniformed bellmen, even the other people checking in— but they always seemed to turn away in time.

19

Or perhaps they were studying him and the others from elsewhere; unseen.

When I used to write politics on the same paper Dan writes for, Spence mused, *the guys told me I'd go paranoid someday. Start seeing bad guys even in the most unlikely places. It's the price paid by a writer with the mentality of an investigative reporter.*

Still, it was true that he was doing as well with his book-writing as he was because he'd always had a sort-of keen sixth sense about things that weren't quite . . . *right* . . . or didn't add up. He'd been talking with a senator, or the head of some corporation, drinking their booze or their coffee, everybody smiling jovially at one another; and Spence would catch that precise tone of voice, the subtly-strained emphasis on a given word, and know damned well that he was listening to a lie.

As casually as possible, waiting for Dan Lloyd to sign the register, Spence scanned the lobby, looking for the lie. The first thing he saw was the locked, metal newspaper dispenser; you put in your change, it unlocked, and you could withdraw your copy of the paper. From where he stood he could see that the legs of the thing weren't where they used to be, because an inch or so to the left he could make out the impressions in the carpet of where the gadget used to stand.

So what? he asked himself, his gaze drifting on. There were the customary artificial leather chairs in which guests could sit to read the newspapers—and the hair on the back of Spence's neck rose faintly. Again, he saw squarish impressions of where the chairs had once been placed; and now, instead of the offhand, casual positioning of the chairs, he saw they were grouped in a rough circle. *As if,* he thought, *as if someone was meant to stand in the center of the circle and speak.*

His gaze drifted up the wall, covered with a recently-cleaned wallpaper bearing a pattern that must once have been inordinately expensive, and stopped at a six-foot wide expanse of glass. Spence squinted, found he could not see through it. Now what in the devil was *that* there for? Was it possible that—?

"Old Stone Face, do you want to affix your John Hancock or go on pretending you never saw a hotel before?" Dan, holding out the slender black desk pen; Dan, with the baldness, bunched shoulders, and bulk of an Ed Asner, but with the kind blue eyes of the brilliant science writer who'd given his soft heart to a retiring tennis star.

"I was just thinking how weird this joint is," Spence replied, taking the pen. He glanced at the quiet desk clerk, finally wrote "Spencer and April Torrence" on the line beneath Dan's signature. Above it, his gaze moved over the signatures of some of the other people who'd already registered, and he whistled, impressed despite himself. He looked back up at the clerk. "Tell me, was the Holroyd closed down awhile? Has it recently reopened, or opened again for this literary soirée?"

The desk clerk was a tall, erect man in an immaculate but unusually ordinary suit. He had a high, angular head and small eyes that weren't so much furtive, Spence decided, as preoccupied, or looking inward at some more important duties. "No, sir," he answered without expression. "The Hotel Holroyd has been in use for eighty-one consecutive years. It's the oldest hotel, Mr. Torrence, in point of continuous service, in the entire state. Many of the decorations and the fixtures in the rooms, even the paintings on the walls, are the original ones installed and

21

hung when the Holroyd was opened."

Spence's eyes narrowed but he let it go. "Thank you."

"Can we go see our rooms now, Daddy?" Lauren asked, clutching his sleeve. When he didn't reply at once she turned quickly to April Torrence. "Can we, Mom?"

"Hold on a second, princess." Spence's gaze returned to the expanse of glass he had noticed before. From this angle near the registration desk he could see that, at its furthest edges, it was squared off, as if concealing a room or office on the second floor. "Dan, speak with you a moment?"

"Sure." The heavyset science writer followed him a few feet apart from the others. The women began conversing with little Lauren. "What's up?"

"I'm not sure." With calculation, Spence turned his back on the six-foot stretch of glass so that anyone standing behind it could not see his lips move. "There's something about this dump that doesn't feel right to me. I've got the old tremors along the spine, Dan."

"Hell, pal, it's just an old hotel." Dan withdrew a cigar from his pocket and, tearing away the cellophane, got it going. "Not the best one I ever saw, but only a hotel."

"Maybe." Spence sounded doubtful. "But I scanned the register when I signed in and observed that all us writers—as nearly as I can tell—have been assigned rooms in a *single* wing. The west wing."

"That's probably because they want to keep the non-paying customers separate from their usual clientele," Dan argued. A foul, heavy cloud arose from his cigar.

"Dan, seventy-five rooms have been set aside for us." Spence's gray eyes bore into his friend's blue ones. "Doesn't it occur to you that's an awful lot of people to give awards to?"

"Well, it means probably one-hundred-and-fifty total guests, and that's a helluva lot of all-expenses-paid for an old hotel to absorb," Dan said. "I suppose they plan to make it back on promotions, or maybe it's a tax write-off of some kind. But don't forget they're making presentations to novelists, poets, TV and motion picture writers, biographers, historians—the works." He chuckled. "When you're looking a gift-horse in the mouth, pally, make sure it doesn't bite off your nose!"

"That's what I'm trying to do," Spence said grimly. "The managers of this place—Mr. and Mrs. Peter Quince—are the people behind the award ceremonies, right?" He watched Dan nod. "Well, we've been around the writing business for a long while and I never heard of them before. Have you?"

Dan clamped his mouth around his stogie and thought. "The only person I ever heard of with the name 'Quince' was in Shakespeare's *Midsummer Night's Dream*, the one who keeps asking, 'Is all our company here?'"

"Do you remember any more of his lines?"

"'Here is the scroll of every man's name,'" Dan replied, making a face as he sought to remember, "'to play in our interlude.' And there's something more that comes to mind: 'You should do it too terribly you would fright the duchess and the ladies; and that were enough to hang us all.'"

Spence's brows raised. "'To hang us all,' eh? Interesting."

"Well," Dan said with a scornful expression, "you could also call the desk register a 'scroll of every man's name,' but I sure don't know why you'd begin making crazy connections like that."

April, overhearing them, came to Spence's elbow with

Ginger Lloyd following her. "If you're going to quote Shakespeare, you might as well let an old actress in on it. 'Now the hungry lions roar, And the wolf behowls the moon,'" she intoned, striking a pose. "'Now it is the time of night That the graves, all gaping wide, Every one lets forth its sprite.'"

"Whose speech is that?" Spence asked, curious. He'd felt for years that his insatiable, observant curiosity was what accounted principally for his success. He kept notes on everything. "What character said that?"

"Why, Puck," April replied, "after whom Lauren's kitten is named." She turned to the trim blonde beside her. "The boys don't like this four-story mausoleum any more than we do. You know, it reminds me of some of the hovels I was stuck with when I was seeking roles on Broadway. Only larger. You know, places with the shades of the Booths and Barrymores prowling the dark halls at night."

Ginger did not reply. Dressed in a gold-colored sweater-and-skirt combination that matched her hair, carrying her coat over an arm, the usually-conversational ex-athlete looked both lovely and strangely distant to Spence. Her mind seemed to be a million miles away, and suddenly he recalled other times in the friendship of the two couples when, inexplicably, the peppy Ginger would tend to drift away. "It's not just that the hotel is old," she said uncannily echoing Spence's thoughts. "I—I get bad vibes from it."

He stared at her, amazed. But before he could comment, he heard Lauren's squeal and spun to see what was the matter.

The twelve-year-old was a few yards away, frozen in place, staring at an apparently deserted marble staircase rising to the second floor. While Spence watched, she removed her heavy spectacles, wiped the lenses on her skirt, replaced them on her nose, and again stared at the empty stairs.

"What is it, Lauren?" he asked as they all moved toward her. "Did some clown get fresh with you?"

She turned to her father, the glasses fogging now, her bright blue eyes behind them appearing to recede to distant points. Yet he could see how startled she was, and his father's heart sensed her fear. For a moment she couldn't answer him. "It was *another girl*," she whispered, *"just my age"*—she swallowed, tried to get control of herself—"and Daddy, she *looked exactly like me!* It was like—like lookin' in the *mirror!*"

"What the hell is wrong with this place?" Dan demanded, looking at his wife. Ginger simply shut her eyes. "What's going on?"

But Spence laughed, and hugged Lauren to him. "I'll tell you one thing, princess, you'll never make a very good witness in court." He kissed her forehead. "Honey, you're so nearsighted it's a wonder you don't start pointing at old ladies and saying they look like you!"

"I mean it, Daddy!" Lauren insisted, coloring and twisting away from him. "I saw her as clear as I see you. She was my spitting image." She turned away, appealing to her mother and still obviously fearful. "And I t-think she saw *me*, too!"

"On a clear day," said her Uncle Dan, grinning amiably at her, "you can see Clare Trevor."

"It's as 'clearly', dear, not as clear," April corrected Lauren, smiling and touching her pale cheek. "I'm afraid your daddy is right. All you've done is inherit your old man's vivid imagination, baby. And maybe you've also

25

picked up a dash of creativity from the grand mistress of the stage as well!"

A busy bellman finally came and silently piled their luggage on a cart. "I like the way you put that," Spence said in an aggrieved tone. You refer to *me* as Lauren's 'old man,' while you cast yourself as the 'grand mistress of the stage.'" He gave them an elaborate sigh and winked at Dan. "Us writers are worse off than Rodney Dangerfield ever dreamed of being. We never get respect from anybody."

"That's why we have to come to dumps like this," Dan chimed in, "to honor one another!"

But as they trailed across the lobby toward the elevators, following the bellman, Spence found his familiar spinal tremors recurring. The sensation that something was badly amiss about the Hotel Holroyd had been amplified.

Because Lauren might almost have been Dan Lloyd's daughter, instead of his own, hard facts were so much to her liking. She won a steady procession of *A*'s in the practical subjects at school, such as mathematics and history, but struggled to earn *C*'s in English. Lauren had no more imagination than Puck, the kitten she was lugging awkwardly into the elevator.

For years there'd been a stupid occult theory that every living person had a duplicate somewhere in the world and Spence had once tried to track it down, learn its origin. Then, too, there were the conspiracy nuts who claimed that Franklin D. Roosevelt and John F. Kennedy had never died at all—that their doubles, for ultra-devious political reasons, had taken over as pawns for some kind of secret government. They were almost as bad as the UFO fanatics who claimed that the little green

26

bodies of spacemen were hidden at some military base in Ohio.

If I had to bet, Spence reflected, joining the others on the ancient, creaking elevator, *I'd wager twenty bucks that* whatever *Lauren thinks she's seen, she's seen.*

But there still had to be a mistake somewhere, perhaps a trick of lighting which enhanced a surface resemblance to the pretty, just-into-puberty, straighthaired and bespectacled miss whom he adored. Yes, it might be nice if the world was full of nice kids like Lauren Torrence, but duplicates showed up only in movies or conspiracy theories.

There *had* to be an explanation because what Lauren had told them was flatly impossible.

CHAPTER TWO

The tall, thin man behind Spencer and April Torrence in the line at the registration desk paused with a hint of drama, the pen in his manicured hand raised above the lined pages of the hotel book, then wrote—with a discernible flourish—"Mr. and Mrs. Seymour Glass."

"I *am* afraid that won't do, sir," said the desk clerk when he'd spun the book around, facing himself. The faint, begrudging traces of a smile moved across his bloodless lips. "It really won't, Mr. Werlin."

The guest sagged slightly with every suggestion of chagrin. "Then you recognized me," he said, casting a look at his large, bejeweled wife. She wore a virginal white dress with horizontal cords beneath the cascade of drooping and pinned gems, giving the appearance of snow. At the end of the author's long look was a definite wink, one which might have said, "I told you so"—not without enjoyment. He turned his head, alone, back to the clerk and one jetblack eyebrow lifted. "I haven't allowed myself to be photographed for many years, young man, and I thought I wouldn't be recognized. Tell me, what was your initial clue?"

"Well, sir, Seymour Glass is a character in stories by J. D. Salinger, but we're having writers in this week and I never heard of one named that." The desk clerk was prompt and knowledgeable, like a contestant in a contest for librarians. "I guess it might yet have been you, sir, except Seymour committed suicide."

"Fine day for bananafish," Harry Werlin sniffed, appraising him. Werlin had a sad hound-dog's face with Groucho Marxian brows and a condescension he attempted to restrict to his sharp middle-aged eyes. "I guess I never really got the hang of reclusion. I was willing to be a hermit, after *Mr. Ashe Made the World* won the Pulitzer, but things keep coming up. I simply *must* leave the house now and then."

"Your fans just wish you'd write another novel, Mr. Werlin," observed the desk clerk. "They don't care if you go on setting your books in the '50s."

"I don't plan on becoming a living anachronism," snapped the distinguished author, taking his wife Bernadine's arm and turning from the desk. "If my readers really want another book from me they'll simply *have* to go back to living the way they did in the '50s. It's hard enough to be profoundly philosophical for sixty-thousand words!"

Lauren tore through the doorway into their suite with the enthusiasm of a young person who has no experience from which to draw odious comparisons, and began poking into dresser drawers and darting in and out of the bathroom.

Spence and April stopped at the door, looking inside once before exchanging unhappy, resigned glances.

The rooms in the Hotel Holroyd were just as dismal as the lobby.

"At least the place is bright and sunny," Spence offered, shamefaced and looking for something to be cheerful about.

"Yes," April replied sweetly, "we can see all the faded places on the furniture and the torn patches in the wallpaper so much more *vividly* this way!"

But when the quiet bellman had put their suitcases down, he closed the curtains at the window and they realized the illumination had been naturally provided. Now the suite was amazingly dark for five o'clock in the evening. The ancient corners of the front room seemed to have ghoulish beings huddling there, snapping and gobbling up the light and leaving shadows that crept penumbrously across the aged imitation-Oriental carpeting.

Spence caught the bellman's arm, surprised by the hard muscle he encountered, and put a couple of bills in the fellow's palm. "We are definitely going to require nourishment," he muttered. "Send somebody up with rolls for the gentler sex and a fat, juicy hamburger for me." He knew both April and Lauren were dieting, as usual. "And a Pepsi for the younger lady, a decent bottle of scotch for us feebler, older people; okay?"

The bellman nodded without speaking. Spence wondered if the man was mute. Turning, as the door closed behind the bellman, Spence saw April standing at the window, her shoulders stooped and her head down. She called to him. "Look, darling!" It was her finest theatrical tone of voice. "We have one of the *first* air conditioners ever manufactured! Aren't we the fortunate ones? Should I get my camera out and take a picture of it?"

"It's too cold for air conditioning anyway," Lauren replied. She flushed the toilet and rejoined her parents. She had removed her sweater upon entering the room but pulled it back on quickly, shivering as she rebuttoned it. Behind her, the toilet continued to groan like some old, dying beast who'd had to be forcefed. "Don't they have spring in the midwest?"

"No, darling," April said at once. "Only Indians and boring races, condemned hotels and snow." She opened the closet door and rummaged in it for blankets. Paper fluttered to the floor but she ignored it. "This is called roughing it. It will make a sturdy pioneer woman of you."

Lauren swept her long hair back, to let it fall over the outside of her sweater, and uneasily lowered her weight to the cot they'd asked to be installed. "This is gonna be really neat, sleeping on a nice, lumpy cot like a real-live Army brat!" She raised her gaze, looked over at her father. "Daddy, do they really have Indians around here? Are there calvary soldiers too?"

"Shit and damnation, the word is 'cavalry,'" Spence grumbled, dropping into one of the two available chairs. Promptly, it issued an outrageous squawk of protest. "Lauren, I really thought you'd be glad to have a

31

vacation no matter where it was. You disappoint me." He drew his omnipresent notebook from an inside pocket of his jacket and flipped it open. Audibly, noisily, he released a huge sigh.

"Now you've gone and hurt the sensitive artist's feelings," April retorted, stretching out on the double bed. Wearily, she kicked off first one high-heeled shoe, then the other, letting them fall to the floor. "Lauren didn't know this would be like camping-out in the goddamn *woods*. Really, Spence, you literary types really go first cabin! If we ever take an ocean cruise, you'll probably make it a kayak and we'll all end up stranded on an ice floe or something."

"I dated a girl named Flo once, years ago, and *she* was sheer ice," he responded, bounding out of his chair and looking for a thermostat on the wall. Finding it, he fiddled with the dial and called caustically over his shoulder, "No colder than my own beloved women-folk, I must admit."

"There are no cold women, Spence, I've told you that." April, her voice mumbled beneath the blanket drawn dramatically over her face. "Only insensitive men, writers or otherwise."

"If you're going to stay under there," he snapped, "maybe I'd better put silver dollars over your eyes. They say that's the way to keep the devils from entering a corpse. Maybe it'll keep one from getting out."

"Bastard," April sang prettily.

"Now, people," Lauren said. "There's an innocent little girl in your room."

The sound of knocking came from the door. Tapping her daddy playfully on the red top of his head as she passed, Lauren went to it and admitted a man with a tray.

32

Cadaverous type, Spence thought; ought to play a butler in some oldfashioned drawingroom mystery.

He bent to pick up the scrap of paper that had fallen from the closet when April tugged her blankets free. HOTEL HOLROYD, it said in impressive, heavy letters; and beneath them, drawing a grunt from Spence, was a pair of dates: 1901-1976.

Startled, he carried the folder back to his chair so he could read it beneath an outdated floor lamp with a brown-scorched shade. To his surprise, he first noticed that a black border ran the width and length of the advertisement.

When he'd read it, as April and Lauren lent a hand to the hotel delivery man, Spence bit his lower lip. Then he hid the folder in his notebook.

He'd written comedy hit after comedy hit for Broadway. The critics used to say he was frequently corny, predictable, outrageously tasteless or sentimental, but the public virtually inhaled every word he wrote. Several of his shows had been made into motion pictures which did equally as well. Now there were those who said Adam "Pop" Cormach made half-a-million dollars a week, at the age of forty-two, whether he was presently working on a play or not.

He wasn't. Pop was standing in line in the Hotel Holroyd, waiting to get to the registration desk, and he wasn't used to it. He was uncomfortably aware that he looked both tired and disheveled and that was enough to bring out Pop's worst sarcasm. He might have handled feeling weary, if that was the bottom line; but the spray had gone out of his sparse hair, leaving it every which way but neat, and he was conscious that his breath was powerful enough to make an ox drop in its tracks. Still worse, a body odor that was pervasive for a short, slight chap like Pop Cormach had overcome his deodorant and aftershave without much of a defensive skirmish. It meant little to him, just then, that he was encircled fore and aft by prize-winning literary sharks of every kind. All he could think, just then, was how he prayed none of his friends would find him that way—especially the lovely ladies who'd played roles in his plays.

Once Pop had written some lines for a character of his to say, and they summed-up the way the playwright felt: "It's ordinary-looking fellas like me who got t'be vain about their looks, not the tall, handsome swingers. When they give the impression they've slept or doo-dooed in their clothes, they still manage to look like Bogart. When a plain guy like me loses all his polish, he resembles Lauren Bacall!"

Why couldn't he be a distinguished giant like Galbraith or look presentably rumpled like Buckley? Why couldn't he be a nice, sturdy type like Ira Levin, or Isaac Asimov, or young Stephen King—all of whom he saw patiently waiting behind him in line—instead of a middleaged shrimp with King Kong's goddamned glands?

When it was his turn, he scribbled his prestigious name in the register and virtually snatched the room keys out of the desk clerk's hand. He cupped one small hand against the side of his famous face, hiding it. Now where in the hell was the west wing and God, *please* God, let the fucking room have hot water and a mirror without ripples! If it does, I'll write your next gospels for you, I really will!

"Did you see the face on that creature?" April

demanded, looking from Lauren to Spence with an incredulous expression. "I swear, when he pushed that cart of his in here, I thought he looked like a cross between Peter Lorre and John Carradine!"

"That's a little improbable." Spence took another bite from his hamburger, wallowed it around, and made a face. It tasted lousy. "Lorre was a little-bitty guy and Carradine's over six feet."

"You know what I mean," April replied, biting into her Danish. "Lorre's hardboiled-egg eyes and sinister manner, Carradine's thinness and that perfectly *hor*rible smile he used."

"*I* thought he looked like Christopher Lee," Lauren put in. She rested her own roll in the saucer, frowned at it, and took a sip of her Pepsi. "The way he was in *The Wicker Man.*"

Spence didn't answer at once. He was taking a long pull of scotch-rocks and deciding whether to bring up what he'd discovered.

"This Danish is terrible, *ter*rible," April said, looking over at him. She was sitting cross-legged on the bed, the blanket draped Indian-style across her shoulders, and she looked as beautiful to Spence that moment as she had the first time he saw her in a Eugene O'Neill revival. "Come here and taste it."

"You've just made up your mind that everything in Holroyd stinks," Spence said firmly, "and I don't want to get up and taste your roll."

"Taste it, *taste* it!" she insisted, waving it in the air.

He sighed again and rose. "I must admit my hamburger's no good either," he confessed, sitting beside his wife on the bed. "There's a certain . . . bitterness." He took her Danish from her fingers and bit carefully

35

into it. A tic started moving in his cheek. "Odd," he said. "It tastes just like my hamburger."

"You want to taste mine, Daddy?" Lauren asked from the cot by the windows. He knew she was teasing and made a face at her.

April slid the saucer onto the bedside table and pulled the blanket tighter around her shoulders. "Honestly, Spence, if it didn't sound *utt*erly ridiculous, I'd say this dilapidated hovel of a hotel was—"

She'd stopped in mid-sentence and he touched her knee. "Was what?"

"Haunted," April replied, and shuddered. "Everything I see or smell or taste seems—reconstituted, regenerated." Suddenly she grabbed his biceps and her dark eyes rolled. "As if it had been dead, and something was bringing it back to life!"

"Nonsense," he told her flatly, gently tweaking her classic nose. "Shit and damnation, you two neurotic dames will have Old Dad seeing things that aren't there if you keep this up." He shifted his gaze to include Lauren. "Now, we certainly could leave the Holroyd and move to a better hotel. But we'd have to come back here for the meetings, and the major speeches at the end of the week, and frankly, I can't see throwing money away like that. Can you?"

April ignored him. He saw that she was looking at his notebook, poking-up from his jacket pocket. She'd clearly detected the folder he'd hidden away. "What's that?" she inquired. "What are you ferreting away this time?"

He blinked twice, shifted awkwardly beside her on the mattress. Off-handedly he caressed the calf of one silken

36

leg. "Well, it's probably nothing. Nothing much. But I guess you could call it an odd little enigma. Of sorts."

Lauren, who adored mysteries, was quickly beside them. "That's what fell out of the closet when Mom got the blankets down, isn't it?" she asked. "Tell us what it is, Daddy, maybe we can figure it out."

He gave a dry laugh. "Well, gang, it seems to be a formal notification to the permanent residents of the Hotel Holroyd," he said slowly, pulling the folder out of his notebook and handing it to April.

"What kind of a formal notifi-watcha-call-it?" Lauren demanded.

He cocked his head as he looked at her. "It's a notification that they were closing the hotel down, and everyone would have to vacate." He glanced at April, saw that she understood and shared his surprise. "Closing it, that is, back in the year 1976."

"But the room clerk looked you right in the eye and told you they had been in 'continuous service' for eighty-one years!" April declared. "I heard him."

Lauren, fascinated, strolled ruminatively toward the door leading to the corridor. Unnoticed by her parents, she opened it and looked out.

Spence gave April a nod. "Which means that the bastard told me an outright lie," he added, shutting his eyes. "Which means, in turn—I'd be willing to bet a hundred big ones—that they have *reopened* the Holroyd specifically for the purpose of inviting a bunch of bigshot writers, putting them up at their own expense, and then handing-out something like seventy-five costly awards. That sounds weirder than hell to me, beautiful."

"You're right, Mom, it is haunted." Lauren, staring out

37

the open door, spoke in a tremulous whisper. Her back was to them and the shoulders were shaking. *"But—by what?"*

Down the corridor, where it turned to the south, *the child who looked like Lauren Torrence raised her hand in a wave and the fingers wriggled. Not a sound came from her lips and she had moved away from the door, where she'd been listening, with a noiselessness Lauren considered uncanny.*

"What did you say, princess?" Spence called.

"Never mind, Pop," the little girl replied. She closed the door and leaned against it, hard. Her eyes were enormous behind the thick lenses of her spectacles. "It's just my newfound imagination again."

CHAPTER THREE

There were two extremely legible and noticeable signs mounted on the door leading into the office, one permanently affixed in the form of a plaque, the other dangling from the doorknob. The former read simply, OFFICE OF THE MANAGER; the second, in larger and more forceful black letters, said NO ADMITTANCE UNDER ANY CIRCUM-STANCES. It bore a signature which was extremely illegible and unnoticeable; modest, one might almost say.

To some extent, each sign was unnecessary. A precaution, actually, of prudent beings who strove mightily to leave nothing to chance. The manager of the Hotel

Holroyd left the day-to-day operation of his establishment in the capable hands of a trusted, quite well-paid and quite human assistant who had firm instructions not to bother him or his wife. Consequently, there was rarely any need for another employee of the hotel to discuss things with him. Those few who had, since the reopening and restaffing of the Holroyd, went away trembling and muttering to themselves about "that new weirdo manager and his weirdo wife," or went away dead. As for the matter of NO ADMITTANCE, etc., the manager's office was kept locked at all times.

Even now, when the individuals in question were in the office, standing quietly before a one-way glass.

They had a panoramic, unobstructed view of the entire lobby from that vantage point and could easily keep watch on what was happening without themselves being observed. Not that their appearance, alone, would have been cause for alarm or even suspicion on the part of the famous writers checking-in or milling about the lobby. The form of the manager and the form of his wife seemed humanoid at worst, human at best, if one merely glanced at them. It was only on a closer inspection, when one had a fatal chance to look into their eyes, that it became clear something was horribly wrong. *Different,* at least; alien.

The manager and his wife had a secondary reason for keeping the office locked every minute of the day and night, and *it* was the primary reason they had installed a one-way mirror.

After all, they had to keep the Selector *somewhere.* Since it was necessary for them to eat and to restrict that duty to their personal rooms, adjacent to the office, leaving *it* out in plain view of the humans bringing food to their suite had been unthinkable. Linens had to be changed, the whole suite needed to be cleaned on occasion, so they couldn't have kept the Selector in the bathroom or even the room in which the child slept. That left the office; and while the manager and his wife gazed at the activity in the lobby, the Selector reclined in its aquarium-like container beside them, always available for advice, always a reminder to them of their primary duties to the state.

It is to their credit that neither the male nor the female looked down at the creature in the liquid container any more often than they had to.

"It goes well, I think," said the manager, hands locked at the small of his back.

The female nodded. "What fascinates me is how unsuspecting they are," she said, more as a statement of fact than on a tone of condescension. "And these are the literary geniuses of their civilization, the—what is the phrase?—the cream of the crop."

He shrugged. "Every era, at any time and on any world in the cosmos, has its 'cream of the crop.'" His tone, as usual, was patronizing; scornful. "What fascinates me is how each succeeding civilization, even each new generation, places such an emphasis on their own silly activities and biases. On earth, for example, there were leaders among the Cro-Magnon peoples, among the Neanderthal—beings who were regarded by their peers as extremely knowledgeable because they could manufacture a simple tool, start a fire, or create an interesting myth. Yet many of these personages beneath us look back upon their own kind of five-hundred, a thousand, three-thousand years ago, and laugh merrily." A smile moved on his thin lips. "All their puny self-confidence would be dissipated at once if they knew how little they had progressed, in all the important matters, since their ancestors slithered out of the slime or swung through the trees."

"Or if they realized," the female remarked, sharing his smile, "how ridiculous and foolish they will seem to their own earth people in the future."

"Yes." He nodded. "Time is something they tend to regard as their enemy, because of personal deterioration and death; yet it is precisely what protects them from the terrible truths they do not wish to see."

The female pressed her fingertips against the glass. "This moment on this planet, Earth, is nothing but a fleeting second in the universal scheme of things. It is our understanding of that fact that makes our own tasks so easy, since we have a perspective about the value of life."

"In a thousand years, this 'advanced' civilization of theirs will appear amusing to their descendants. Quaint. In ten-thousand years," his smile broadened, "the whole pack of them will be nothing more than a footnote for scholars of the abstruse and archaic."

"Just look at them," she said, pointing, "sitting pompously in the lobby chairs, leaning avidly to one another with their little prehistoric egos positively *starving* to be accepted—to be admired—by another of their kind. What we could tell them in an hour would give the whole lot of them material for enough books to fill a new library!"

He yawned and turned away from the one-way glass. "You forget, my dear. At the end of the week, when they expect to hear speeches from their most renowned fellows, you and I shall stand in the center of that lobby"— he glanced back at her as he unlocked the first lock on the door—"and, in point of fact, tell them *everything*."

She nodded. "It's almost a shame they won't understand anything but our instructions," she said, and started to follow him.

The message bore into their minds simultaneously with the searing pain of a laser beam. The male and the female staggered, unprepared for the communication, and reached with desperation for the steadying desk.

Their eyes, watering, turned to look at the terrible creature in the aquarium.

"*Now,*" commanded the Selector, its network of pink veins throbbing in the ugly transluscent skin, staring at them with its inhuman orbs swimming in its monstrous skull. "*Start now . . .*"

Lauren carefully emptied the milk from the hotel carton into a saucer, and set Puck in front of it, a worried expression wrinkling her young forehead.

Poor old Puck hadn't behaved normally since they arrived here. Of course, that had only been an hour or two; but his herky-jerky movements, and the way he mewed incessantly, simply weren't Puck's style. This was a kitten who'd already taken on most of the dogs in the neighborhood and, if he'd come out second a few times, he'd worn the red badge of courage.

This milk Lauren had poured for Puck was the acid test. If there was anything reliable about the little black animal at all, it was his egregious appetite. Back home in Porter, New York, Puck was always on the prowl around the house, looking for something else to gorge himself with. What Spence, her daddy, considered repulsive Lauren found divinely entertaining. Instead of curling up in a ball after he'd eaten, Puck tended to sprawl immovably on his back with every suggestion of having died except for periodic, human-sounding burps that rose langorously from his tight little tummy.

Now, as Lauren watched him with earnest maternal eyes, the kitten stood stiff-legged and uneasy before his saucer, apparently not hungry at all. His small head was lifted slightly and cocked just a bit to one side, and Lauren shivered. It was as if Puck were *listening*—hearing things that Lauren and her parents could not hear at all.

"C'mon, Puck," she cried with phony enthusiasm, dipping an index finger into the milk and holding it in front of his mouth. "It's milk, honey, just like back home. Everything's all right."

His furry head drifted round with enormous deliberation until his uncanny green eyes were fixed on her.

Then, to the girl's horror, Puck looked up at the ceiling and emitted the most terrifying sound she had ever heard.

Highpitched, anguished, piercing, it lingered on the air in the hotel room like the scream of a woman falling a long way from a precipice and knowing, all the way down, that she was utterly doomed.

Oh dear Jesus, Lauren thought, shrinking away from her pet, *that wasn't a cat's noise at all—it was a* howl, *like some frightened dog baying at the moon.*

Puck leaped into her arms, then, and hooked his sharp nails into her clothing, hanging on for dear life. His tiny heart thudded against her breast, fast, and she knew what old Puck was trying to tell her.

That everything wasn't all right, at all.

"It's so *cold* in here."

44

Dan Lloyd looked up from his typewriter, then ground out his cigar in the nearby ashtray. The science writer knew that he was a workaholic and gloried in the knowledge, felt good about his constant work. He'd rather enjoyed coming to the Hotel Holroyd with the chance to meet other writers, and he felt he owed it to Ginger. After all, he'd read more than a few sports articles which had bemoaned the fact that Ginger Cavanaugh had become Ginger Lloyd and argued that she'd been only a year or two away from a Wimbledon championship when she gave it up for love. By now, Dan wasn't sure whether he was guiltier than he was grateful, or vice versa. The only things he knew for sure, at this point in his forties, were that he thanked any God that might exist for bringing a beautiful and giving woman like Ginger into his life, and that she was the final element that made his life a contented one. The way he viewed it, if he was having a rare little tiff with Ginger, he could spend a few hours with his first love—working—until she came around; and if he couldn't find exactly the data he required for a scientific piece, or if the writing of it wasn't going smoothly, he could spend a few happy hours in his wife's company.

A man just didn't have a right to ask for a whole lot more than that, in balding Dan Lloyd's sentimental book; and if he had to share a strange secret with Ginger—*about* Ginger—well, that was all right too.

Really, the only time he'd ever seen anything come close to perfection was down at NASA, where the way the space program functioned all but flawlessly—to the disheartening extent permitted by government funds— continued to fill him with awe. It was that fascination which had made his private avocation the collecting of information related to the possibility of life on other planets; because if NASA was all but perfect, the way his personal life with Ginger tended to be, the only thing Dan could imagine that was better would have to be an advanced race capable of creating a propulsion system for taking thinking beings across the limitless distances of the cosmos. If there was a measure of the religious nuts' anticipation of kindly "space brothers" lurking in Dan, he figured, at least he knew some reasons for their wanting to lend Planet Earth a helping hand. . . .

"I turned up the heat, sugar," he said placatingly, trying to think what else he could do to make her comfortable. "The wall gizmo says it's nearly eighty in here."

Ginger faced him. She had been undressing, to change clothes for dinner with the Torrences down the hall, and was clad only in a white half-bra and white bikini underpants. He could see the way the pink tops of her nipples peeked above the garment and he thought they looked like delicious candy. She was still in remarkable trim, with a narrow waist and long, slender legs. With her short-cropped, golden hair and fair complexion, she reminded Dan in her white underclothes of something herself from a distant planet—from a place where the women were all incredibly beautiful, youthful forever, with creamy complexions, dazzling intelligent eyes and the same kind of otherworldly gifts which comprised the secret he kept with her.

"I don't think it will do any good," Ginger whispered. "It's—*interior* chill, Danny, and you know what that means."

"It's goddam unhealthy for you, sugar," he argued, standing and moving toward her. "Fight it off."

"I've tried before," she said, and now her voice was distant, drifting away from him the way it had all the

46

other times, taking some vital part of her away despite their every effort. He put his big, hairy hands on her shoulders, pressing the soft flesh with his strong fingers, and her face told him that she must leave regardless of what they did. *"Hold me,"* was the last thing she said.

He enfolded her in his arms, and though he normally preferred proximity to Ginger's yielding body to anything else on his dismal planet, it was like holding a hollow shell. Her gaze, he saw, was over his brawny shoulder, fixed on the distant wall of the hotel room—

But it wasn't the wall she was seeing. He knew that.

Guys who were scientific types, who worked with cold facts and tangible hardware, who wrote columns about the advancement of technology and could take either a computer or a television apart in record time and, when they'd reassembled them, knew they'd functon better than ever, couldn't afford to talk about things like this.

Like the fact that he was married not only to a former tennis star but one of the finest amateur psychics in the world. A psychic who, never willingly, never even wanting to possess the gift, could range from psychokinesis—the movement of objects by the power of her mind alone—to precognition—seeing events develop before they'd even, in fact, begun.

He might have been able to handle it better, he thought again, patting her bare shoulder even though he knew she could not feel his touch, if she ever saw anything *cheerful* coming. Instead of knowing when her mother was going to die, or his father; instead of being able to touch a newspaper and see a stalking terrorist moving like a sneak-thief on the life of a government leader. Because she presented so many problems to him, and to Ginger herself. The couple of times he'd dared confide in Ginger's

47

prophecy because he earnestly wanted to warn people, they'd laughed in his face, and, when the tragedies struck, launched investigations against Dan and Ginger that were harrowing and grossly unfair.

Then there were the other times, when they'd told no one, and simply waited to see the scene unfold on their television screen, precisely the way Ginger described it. . . .

"Something—*horrid*—is going on here." Her shiver against him was almost electrical. At another time, he would have been instantly aroused. He saw her eyes narrowing, imagined for a moment that he could see what was happening *with* her, share her terror. But that was only loving, wishful thinking. "I see . . . the *blackness*, forming like a great, dark cloud. The deepest, most impenetrable blackness I've seen."

"Sh-h-h," he said, hugging her closer. He didn't want to hear this, Dan knew that for a certainty; he didn't want to hear this at all. "Just come back to me, sugar. Come on," he called her the way a father would summon a toddler, "come on back to your Danny."

"Thick, like molasses; but it's swirling—*parting* now, letting me *see*." Her hands came up to his waist and the nails dug into his sides through the white shirt he wore. Dan winced, held on. *"It's not death alone."* Now her eyes were wide, the pupils dilated. Sweat on her temples dampened his cheek. *"It's* worse *than death!"*

He kissed her neck, below the ear, patted her shoulder. "Now, what could be worse than that?" he asked, knowing she could not hear him.

But she seemed to answer him, anyway, as she completed her remarks. *"Oh God,* no, *I can't* stand *seeing this! I can't* stand *it!"* Abruptly she shoved herself away from

48

him. Her hands stroked the air, then became claws. Eyes wild, she raked the space between her and Dan five, six, *seven* times, and he saw the way the sweaty muscles of her arms and chest tightened to knots. "It's *coming* for us' *It's coming for us!*"

"What is, sugar?" Dan asked, taking a step forward. His heart was thundering in his burly chest. "*What's* coming for us?"

Something—not of this earth!"

CHAPTER FOUR

"That was a perfectly disgraceful and ludicrous exhibition you managed to concoct for us down in the lobby," Bernadine offered stridently when the bellman had departed. "Please, tell me, Harry, why you must always go around trying to suggest you're someone you aren't? Your reputation is probably secure enough, even if it *is* built on one shallow little book. And considering the way you keep repeddling the thing through film options, we've succeeded in keeping our heads above water. Why do you do those things, Harry? *Harry?*"

He stopped shaving with one side of his face lathered,

listening intently. Not to what Bernadine was saying, since that was bound to be uninspired and repetitive, but the way she said it. Her voice, loud enough to carry when she'd begun her quarrelsome speech, increased in volume and disapproval alike as she drew nearer and the effect reminded Harry of how she looked to him these days.

For a long while it had intrigued him the way Bernadine had of *changing size,* almost miraculously, and his writer's mind sometimes toyed with the notion that she'd unearthed the magic "Eat me" bottles Alice experimented with in Wonderland. Asleep, for example, her rotundity had a way of seeming to disperse, to spread on the whiteness of a bed like Hellman's mayonnaise on white bread. Her ampleness rose above the mattress only a foot or so at such times, his last enjoyable moments with Bernadine. And it definitely wasn't only because her big yap was shut, in sleep, but because of her flattening-out process.

Harry smiled. In a casket, he supposed, she'd manage to shrivel away to demureness and finally look petite, the way she'd always wanted to appear. Not that he was ready to conclude that he was really anxious to see such a sight; he merely wished, whenever she stood before him without her clothing, that she didn't seem to blot-out the sun. That she didn't appear so titanically unmanageable. The last time he'd made love to her, a year or so ago, the pale hillocks of her thighs looked like maneaters to him and it was Harry who shriveled away to nothingness.

Naked at the bathroom mirror, he watched his woman heave into view. Hoping she didn't see, Harry sighed. It was beyond him, these days, why he'd ever left his first wife for the S.S. Bernadine. The reason, actually, liter-

51

ally escaped him, and he'd have tried to dredge it out of his memory if he'd managed to think about Bernadine for ten minutes straight without becoming nauseated—sea-sick, on the good ship Bernadine Werlin, which was how he'd felt, perching atop her fleshy decks last year. Looking in vain for the porthole, he added to himself, stifling a snicker.

"I asked you a question, Harry, and I expect an answer."

"You do?" He was genuinely surprised. Bernadine knew perfectly well he was trying to be a recluse, at least until he thought of another idea for a book. Scraping at one cheek with his fragile swivel razor, he gave it a moment's thought. "By the nature of what a writer does," he said at last, "his visions, his opinions, become public knowledge to the readers of his work. Even a reader who's really angry about something the writer's said can't contact him the way you could visit a company and tell off the chairman of the board. It's necessary to write the publisher, get the writer's home address under some pretext or other, and *then* discover that the fellow lives on the other side of the nation."

"I don't get it," Bernadine said candidly, folding her arms across her powerful bosom.

"Well, I was always a man who *liked* to hear from people." One fanciful brown eye peeked at her from the mirror. "Even those who hated my work. The only way I had of getting the letters I wanted was by becoming a recluse, letting the world know I needed to be left alone." He shrugged his bony shoulders. When he smiled, the pinkness of his gums flashed at her. "People being what they are, everyone who reads something I've written is ready to hire the Pinkertons to track me down! Why,

Bernadine, I've received more interesting mail during the past four years than I ever got before that in my whole life!"

She stared at him another moment, unsure whether he'd made up the entire story or if he really meant it. Why she had ever married such a neurotic shrimp of a man she'd never know. Six-feet tall and maybe a hundred-and-forty pounds stripped. Which he was, most of the time, at their Larchmont home. She let her gaze pass over his body with disgust a final time, grunted, "You're impossible," and left him alone in the bathroom. When the door slammed shut she hoped the noise made him cut his throat. Just a neat slice, an inch or two long; nothing fatal.

Bored, Bernadine turned on the color TV and sank into a chair opposite it. The creaking sound of protest registered on her ears but she didn't mind. Eating, in a world one was obliged to share with a "sensitive" writer like Harry Werlin, was one of the last joys left to a woman. She propped her feet on the hassock and tried to ignore the television screen a moment longer. Remembering why she'd married Harry wasn't difficult at all. He'd had a wife whom Bernadine had despised since girlhood, one of those gushy, sweet little types who always entered the best sororities, dated the best-looking men, and wound up with a husband who was successful and rich. When she realized how susceptible Harry was, during the first Mrs. Werlin's pregnancy, she waged the campaign of her life to take Harry away and give the stuck-up little broad the first blemish on her snotty little escutcheon. And to capture a winner, just once, herself.

Which just goes to show you, Bernadine reflected, sighing, that you really can't beat city hall—or gushy, sweet little types. The ex-Mrs. Werlin rebounded to a marriage with a vice-president at ABC, and the minute she said "I do," the network took over Number One in the ratings. *And I,* Bernadine thought, *got stuck with an author who uses writer's block as an excuse for everything from impotence to bad breath and worse manners. I'd like to make the skinny bastard a recluse, all right; stick his hermit's ass on a mountain peak and watch him settle down on it!*

She realized suddenly that the channel she had on TV was the local ABC outlet and hefted herself out of her chair, ready to change the station.

Which was when she saw the eye, *looking* back *at her.*

For a second Bernadine thought it was a test pattern, or CBS, or something. Then she didn't think much of anything at all . . .

Lauren Torrence glanced at her wristwatch and frowned. She was *starving* to death by now, positively *starving,* and it began to seem to her that her parents would never get ready to go downstairs. Mom had changed her dress twice, even though she looked perfectly scrumptious in everything she wore; and now Pop was sitting on the edge of the bed in his pants and undershirt, glancing at that dumb folder he'd found and writing something in his old notebook. "A-hem," she called, emulating her mother's best theatrical tone. "A-hem! There's someone passing out from lack of nourishment over here." No response. "Ah, people, you should know, perhaps, that there is a helpless child in this suite who is suffering from malnutrition. I'm sure there're laws against child abuse in this dumb state too."

"What? What did you say?" Mom called from the bathroom. The fragrance of perfume drifted into the front room. "Be ready in just a minute, princess," Pop said, and he didn't even look up from his notebook.

Sighing, Lauren got up from the chair and ambled toward the door. She might as well see what was going on out in the hallway. Maybe there was a drunk around to liven things up, or maybe some cat burglar was in the process of—

Lauren shrieked. All ten fingers went to her mouth and she stared down, shocked.

Puck, her black kitten, had vaulted toward the door and pressed himself against it, his back arched, one paw raised threateningly with the claws showing.

She'd never seen him so mean before, not for a second, and Lauren was more startled than afraid. Reaching down, she batted him across the nose, not hard, knowing that would send him scooting.

Instead, he braced all four feet on the ground and then leaned against the door, growling deep in his throat.

He isn't mad at me, Lauren thought, her mouth dropping open. *He doesn't want me to open the door. He doesn't want me to . . . go* outside.

Bernadine Werlin turned away from her television set, leaving it on the ABC channel, straightened, and walked with dignity toward the front door.

She started walking down the corridor with an air of knowing what she was doing, where she was going, her stockinged-feet scuffing on the faded and aging carpet. A famous writer of comic plays approached from the opposite direction, hand cupped to a jaw that needed shaving. "Lo," he said, lowering his chin. Bernadine didn't answer. Stiff-legged, erect and unseeing, she marched by "Pop" Cormach without a sign of greeting or recognition and sensed nothing when his gaze followed her down the hallway.

Actually, the instructions were quite simple; elemental. There was no need to figure anything out, not even the direction of her unquestioning march. Everything was neatly imprinted on her unconscious mind, clear as crystal, just the way the instructions were shown on the television screen. All she had to do was carry them out.

There, in a *cul-de-sac* adjacent to the broom closet—decorously inconspicuous—the service elevator awaited her. Nodding, as if someone or something had addressed her, Bernadine walked slightly faster. *Get it over with*, the words took form in her mind; *nothing to it so I might as well take care of it right now.* What "it" might be, she hadn't the foggiest notion. Incurious, relaxed, feeling good, and absolutely mindless, Bernadine took the last few steps toward the service elevator and stretched out her arm.

The instant her index finger pushed the button, there was a soft *whirring* sound, and the elevator doors slid noiselessly open.

Come right inside, said the words in her mind.

Don't mind if I do, Bernadine thought back to them, as equable and agreeable as she'd ever been in her life.

She took two, then three steps forward, and she was inside. She turned, somewhat expectantly, and the elevator doors closed.

Comfortable? came the solicitous words. *Everything all right?*

"Fine," Bernadine said aloud, in the darkness, and smiled a bit. "Just fine."

Look down.

She did. She looked down at her feet, and they

56

weren't there. Only her ankles on up. Bernadine frowned. The ankles were gone now too. Bernadine frowned harder, tried to clear her mind. The knees, they disappeared next. Bernadine opened her mouth to say something in mild protest, but nothing came out. She didn't exist below the waist; there was nothing whatsoever there but empty air. Bernadine felt panic begin, somewhere inside, and her mind tore itself free. She could see only her cleavage, now, the rest was gone. Bernadine opened her mouth wide, to scream for help—

Except now there wasn't any mouth either.

There wasn't any Bernadine Werlin at all.

CHAPTER FIVE

"Are you people *ever* going to be ready to go? It's just Uncle Dan and Aunt Ginger we're eating with, for heaven's sake—not Prince Charles and Diana!"

Lauren stood boldly in her characteristic pose by the door, arms akimbo, her chin raised in a pertly challenging fashion that she knew had been cute for a long while but understood would be tolerated only for another year or so. She was a pretty child with a minor overbite, an acne-free complexion, and long, straight brown hair flowing almost to the small of her back. She wasn't nearly as pretty as she was going to get, especially when Mom and Pop got around to buying the contact lenses they'd been promising her for months.

"Some absolutely *gorg*eous babies turn grotesque on you during their teens," Mom had pointed out, back in Porter, "while other kids who aren't exceptional become ravishing beauties. It's one of nature's cute little ways of compensating. *I*, of course, retained my extraordinary good looks from the start."

She'd said it for fun, of course, but Lauren knew it was true and thought April Torrence was what every female should want to be. She'd also known, when Mom told her that, which camp she belonged in herself. There had been a broken leg that didn't heal quite right and left the tiniest residue of a limp, a struggle with braces back in the dark ages of her distant youth, and an awkward I-belong-nowhere-'cause-I'm-too-divinely-special-for-ordinary-worlds stage when Lauren had tried to impress everybody with swear words in all the wrong places.

It was only over the past couple of months that she'd begun to go into puberty, a fact Mom and she had kept from Pop awhile longer. "I'm going into puberty?" Lauren had echoed Mom, when that blackhaired beauty answered her questions. "Gee," the daughter had retorted, "is that another town in Jersey or part of the Twilight Zone?" And Mom had made a face as she winked. "Twilight Zone, kid, and you ain't seen nothin' yet," she'd cautioned her.

Not that they'd kept the news from Pop because either of them was embarrassed about it, particularly. It was because they both knew Spence Torrence wanted to think of Lauren as his precious little princess forever, if Uncle Dan would only come up with some sci-magical-drug that would stunt her development. Fortunately or unfortunately, Uncle Dan hadn't; and with the faint swelling at Lauren's bosom—concealed as well as possible by the voluminous sweaters Mom bought for her—the secret couldn't be kept much longer.

"Shit and damnation, princess," Pop grunted, finally slipping his notebook in his jacket pocket, rising and stretching, "if you're all that hungry maybe I'd better ask Dan to rig up some kind of intravenous feedings for you between lunch and dinner." He began buttoning the back of Mom's dress. "You know, t'keep body and soul together."

"Oh, *would* you?" Lauren cooed, opening the door. She'd put Puck, her kitten, in the bathroom, hoping a period of isolation from their wonderful humanness would make the black cat come to his senses. This place was flaky enough without Puck surrendering one of his nine lives to a nervous breakdown. "I'll be out in the hall, folks. Chewing the carpeting."

"But *do* stay away from the wallpaper, won't you, baby," Mama called after her without turning. "I'm not sure wallpaper-devouring is covered by our expenses-paid arrangement with the caretaker for this crypt." Pop chuckled, his shoulders moving as he finished "doing" Mom.

Lauren stuck her tongue out at them, on general principles, and then ventured into the corridor.

She'd closed the door after her. Immediately she wished she hadn't.

While there were ceiling lights gleaming from their recessed, watchful lids, they were wholly inadequate to provide enough light. Looking up, Lauren saw that some of the lights were blinking and the idea of being Out Here at the moment they all went out made her shiver. Gaunt pockets of blackness showed the full length of the hallway, like patches on the suit of a prone old man, and Lauren thought of the warnings her parents had given her about strange men with calf-length raincoats. She whistled a few bars of the theme song from a John Belushi movie, realized he'd died very young, and clamped her lips together.

Restless, now, she ambled a few yards away from the Torrence suite, staring at the smattering of paintings hanging on the walls. Prints, of course, but aged and faded prints of faces and places she'd never seen before.

One of them drew her attention and she crossed the hallway to take a closer look.

There was a castle depicted, something medieval, Lauren guessed, with a moat around it. It was a water color and the castle itself, forbidding enough with its shadowy, liquid lines and the suggestion of windows leading to God-knew-what, didn't really seem like the focal point. Lauren's gaze was drawn instead to the moat; she realized that the unknown artist had spent a remarkable amount of time getting it the way he wanted. There was depth to the water in the moat, as if *something* might be swimming silently beneath the surface, waiting for someone foolish enough to wade into it. She remembered seeing an old movie in which the hero escaped from the dungeon by swimming under the castle, and through the moat. Well, he'd never have made it through *this* moat! It looked scaly, fetid and corrupt; she could almost smell the stench of that water. Yellow slime swam along the surface and abominable, dark splotches showed here and there, as if something remotely *edible* had been thrown into the moat, to feed the waiting creature. . . .

Sound penetrated from the picture, or perhaps the

61

wall, and Lauren jumped back, eyes enormous behind her heavy spectacles. It was a *vibratory* noise, incredibly subtle and accessible only to the ears of the healthy young; but it was there, all the same, like something leaking out of the moat—something that whined, keened, and snuffled all at once, and sought to break free.

The giggle Lauren heard made her spin to confront it, her heart almost failing her.

It was the first time she'd had an opportunity to have a good look, a look of seconds' duration, and Lauren gaped open-mouthed, one small hand at her bosom.

The little girl's arms were akimbo and the grimacing smile on her lips revealed a definite overbite. Long, straight brown hair fell behind her, reaching her waist. Her complexion would have been excellent except for the fact that she was pale, her skin—where she stood at the end of the darkened hallway—oddly transluscent, giving her the distinct appearance of a ghost-child who had not so much walked to her present position as materialized *there.*

"Who—who *are* you?" Lauren asked.

When she'd spoken, Lauren wanted to scream. She sensed that her words—her necessary human breath—went out only several inches from her trembling lips before encountering some bizarre, unseen barrier. Her question died there, she thought—as if mortal words could not manage to penetrate the strangely evil, silent ambience of the second child, the Hotel Girl.

But then the Hotel Girl raised her pert little chin with the appearance of having heard Lauren's query after all, and the gesture was challenging but not—to the human Lauren—in the least bit cute. More than challenging, it *defied*, it *taunted*; it seemed to say, *I-am-you-therefore-you-aren't.*

That was when Lauren realized that the Hotel Girl was not an exact duplicate of her, after all. Because—behind the second child's thick-lensed glasses—there were eyes that seemed full of fury, even hatred, eyes that knew much more than Lauren would ever want to know, eyes that were cast-over with some filmy substance that might have been incongruous cataracts except that the substance was a hideous, flaming scarlet whenever the Hotel Girl moved, or changed expression.

"Shit and damnation!" exclaimed Lauren, imitating her Pop, fighting her fear with anger. "Tell me who you *are?*"

Words took shape in her brain at once—words that twisted, bore in, *burned* the soft cells of Lauren's *corpus collosum* and exploded into her right and left hemispheres: *Shit,* said the piercing female voice—*and Damnation!*

The Hotel Girl giggled quite clearly, clapped her small hands together, and *disappeared.*

Trembling, fighting for breath, Lauren turned with the merry noise of youthful giggling ringing in her head, and began rushing back to her parents' suite.

When her gaze fell on the painting that had drawn her attention, she gasped and ran, pell-mell, the rest of the way.

The picture hanging in the frame where the castle-and-moat had been now depicted a black hole in deepest outer space.

Harry Werlin had decided to soak awhile in the bathtub while Bernadine watched another of her interminable television programs. After he had the temperature set at a comfortable level, he let the water drip into the tub as he stretched out, closing his eyes in rest. Not that it really mattered to him what the S. S. Bernadine thought of him, these days of his self-imposed reclusion, but it annoyed him to think that if he was writing soap operas, or thinking up questions for wavyhaired and brainless masters of ceremonies to ask of the only people in the world dumber than emcees, Bernadine would respect him. He never doubted it for a minute. Why, if he'd even accepted that invitation from Johnny Carson's people, three years ago, and permitted himself to be the last guest on a program empaneled by that year's crop of sex goddesses and semi-clever wits, Bernadine would have thought he amounted to something!

Nobody understood a serious novelist, Harry moaned to himself, applying a decorous washcloth before closing his eyes. Why, the Hotel Holroyd was full to the rafters with those despicable little *genre* writers—horror and science-fiction and mystery and spy boys, nonentities who cranked-out ninety-thousand words of mere entertainment and called it a book, even when it was held-together by glue between pieces of *cardboard*, by Sam Clemens' shade! And the fact that *they* made an excellent living from their work while *he* had to make-do on royalties from additional printings and movie options was something Bernadine actually held *against* him!

He'd heard there were some compulsive category writers who knocked out a paperback in a month's time, then did it five or six more times the same year! He had to admit it was a miracle, the way they kept coming up with ideas. But odds bodkins, everybody knew you couldn't write anything *respectable* in less than a year or two— everybody who was *any*body. So what if the ordinary readers loved the junk and got their minds off their plebian problems; so *what* if the occult and western and romance authors worked at their typewriters every day, producing twenty-five thousand words or more a week! Garbage, even if there was a decade-long strike and the filthy stuff piled up at the curb on Park Avenue from midtown to the Bronx, was still garbage!

Artists, like Harry Werlin, he thought, needed to experience Life in order to gain material of enduring significance. It couldn't simply be found in the *imagination.* Serious writers were required by their dedication to get gloriously drunk now and then, support meaningful *causes,* or beat and step-out on and divorce their women, or alienate their children, or experiment with fascinating things like offbeat sex and illegal drugs and terrorist revolutions.

The recluse slept the sleep of the persecuted just.

He awakened, *colder* than he'd ever been in his life. The minute his eyes were open Harry began shaking violently. When he stared down, the skin on his shanks and fleshless thighs was beginning to turn blue; when he removed his washcloth, it looked like his frayed but precious manhood was trying to beat a panicky retreat *inside* of the prize winner.

Harry got his hands on the edge of the tub, braced, and shoved hard.

Nothing happened. He swallowed hard and tried again. Nothing. It was as if he'd frozen his arse to the floor of the bathtub.

He couldn't get out.

The sound of water flowing into the turquoise tub at a quicker rate caught his attention and he looked down at the spigot, half-believing invisible hands had turned the taps. *What's that?* Harry squinted. Something was coming *out*, now, something that wasn't water, something with a *shape* to it.

Harry screamed. He was too frightened to realize that the noise was only dispersed a few inches from his lips, before dissipating entirely against an unseen barrier. He screamed because he couldn't believe in what he was seeing, flowing into his bathtub, and because he couldn't *disbelieve* what he saw with his own eyes.

It was the hollowed, ample skin of his wife Bernadine, opaline and semitransparent, her boneless arms coming to him across the water, reaching, *the limpid, liquidized fingers* groping *for his throat! Bernadine, diaphanous in death, her skeleton removed, her broad face pale and piscatorial with the dumb eyes of a dead flounder, touching him now—her flat, pasty, lifeless lips puckered for a kiss.*

Harry tried again, manfully, to hoist himself from the tub.

But when he did, a wall of hissing *steam* lifted from the freezing water in the tub until he and the S. S. Bernadine were entirely shielded from view. There was, once more, a terrified shriek from Harry Werlin—

And slowly, like a curtain being pulled back, the steam dissipated, and was gone.

Two minutes later a maid unlocked the door to the suite and, dragging her cart of working implements behind her, walked directly into the Werlin bathroom. Humming to herself—the melody, incongruously enough given the maid's appearance, was "I Enjoy Being a Girl"—the old woman replaced the towels and washcloths with fresh ones, and then lumbered over to the tub.

Erma Jean Wicks, age sixty-eight, had been maid since she was fifteen years old and her daddy took off, never to return. Personally immaculate, though obese, she had the finicky tastes of a British duchess and tended to rank the people in the rooms she cleaned according to the traces they left behind.

"A time-waster, this one," she said, putting her hands on her considerable hips as she looked down. Disapproval lined her dark face. "Shiftless, spoiled, and even more conceited than my old daddy, rest his soul." She put her head to one side to consider it more closely, her manner that of a palmist or crystal-ball gazer involved with an especially difficult reading. "Looks down on other people, or he'd never leave a mess like that for a Christian woman to clean up after. An' when he leaves, why, it'll never occur to him to leave me so much as a note!"

Beneath Erma's gaze was scum an inch thick coating the bottom of the tub. Whoever bathed here last was unbelievably filthy, of course; but what *kind* of dirt was this? In all her years, Erma reflected, she'd never seen bathtub filth that was only dark in places. Most of this was a sort-of off-white, *honky* color, you could almost say.

Sighing, she dropped down on her pudgy, arthritic knees and emptied the rest of a container of Comet cleanser into the mess. When she began scrubbing at the tub, mopping hard with her rag, the old woman hesitated and stared into space.

Finally, she laughed. For a moment there she'd thought she heard someone *speak*. And that was nonsense, because there was no one else in the suite at all. A poor blind person could tell that.

Besides, who would be whispering a silly thing like, "Help me?"

Erma got the water scalding hot. Then she watched the

67

light-colored slime slip down the drain, and nodded her satisfaction.

When she closed the front door behind her, moments later, and shuffled on to her next room, the old maid shrugged. It didn't matter much if they remembered to leave a tip, or a polite little note of appreciation for her hard work. People who came to a hotel rarely stayed long, even more rarely made the faintest impression on Erma Jean Wicks. Most of the time, it was like they'd never been there at all.

He was one of the new breed at the network level, necessitated by the fact that they were generally in third place in the ratings and were willing to try anything.

His name, these days, was Alistair Copeland Cummings. Once they called him "Cope," his parents and sisters had called him "Al" and "Allie" respectively, and at twenty-five years of age he was the hottest screenwriter in television. Three movies-of-the-week had flowed from his typewriter, the first producing respectable ratings, the next two cracking the top ten for their respective weeks. "The next Rod Serling," they called him; "the new Sterling Silliphant with a touch of Reginald Rose's perception."

That always annoyed Alistair. He thought of himself as a Catholic Paddy Chayevsky. It was just that he knew how to play the numbers game, that you didn't get to direct too on the basis of poignant little family dramas but when you'd written screenplays that made half the nation tune-in. Really, Alistair thought, it had been surprisingly easy to get where he was. First you thought of a situation in which the sex happened naturally, but allowed you to show as much nudity and necking as the network censors would allow. You wired that into a contemporary set of circumstances that most of the nation wanted to learn more about—the drug death of a celebrity, an important marriage, something racial, the possibility of war or attack by terrorists, something *hot*.

And then, when you'd spent a day or so putting that crap together, you went back and stuck a handful of profound observations into the mouths of the leading characters. Well, *semi*-profound—and you didn't put 'em all in one scene, you scattered them through the whole screenplay to keep the audience watching. If the only worthwhile elements of the story were used up in one strong, meaningful scene, the dummies switched to another channel; but if you showed how *wise* you were, so the critics noticed your semi-profound commentaries but the People Out There in Videoland weren't asked to put two consecutive thoughts together, the sex stuff and the contemporary theme carried you right to the top.

Which is where Alistair found himself as he signed the register of the Hotel Holroyd. It was kicks to do this, to associate for a change with other guys who wrote. And it was a real perk to know that the people in the lobby undoubtedly spotted him at once. How many six-foot, seven-inch screenwriters with one-quarter Indian blood and a nose like a hawk could there be?

He met the gaze of the man behind the desk, momentarily nonplussed by an odd *frigidity* he thought he'd seen in the clerk's eyes. It was, Alistair felt, an expression of abject hatred; but how could that be when the man didn't even know him? Maybe something in his last film, about ethnic conflicts in a small midwestern town, had ticked the guy off. But he certainly didn't look like a small-town guy and suddenly Alistair wanted to hear the desk clerk speak. Ever since he was nobody but Al Cummings he'd had a hobby of identifying where a person came from by the lingering echo of his native accent. A lot of people were better at it, Al knew—Art Linkletter was the best he'd ever seen—but he was still pretty good.

"West wing, eh?" he said, prompting the clerk. "Keeping all us Scrabble stars in the same part of the hotel?"

"We find that makes it simpler, Mr. Cummings."

Hm-m, Alistair mused. He'd have to hear more. "The main speakers are on the weekend, is that right?"

The clerk's mouth twitched in what could pass for a smile. "That is correct."

Close-mouthed bastard. "Well, I hope this is what it's cracked up to be."

"I'm sure it will be, sir," replied the desk clerk, and Alistair surrendered. If he wasn't wrong, this fellow came from none of the fifty states at all. His diction was incredibly flawless and untainted. Where the hell *did* he come from then? Now the clerk was giving Alistair a broad, generous smile and the expression of the eyes—or the lack of it—didn't change at all. "I assure you, Mr. Cummings, we shall do everything in our power to make your stay absolutely . . . *unforgettable.*"

Germany? Alistair wondered, waiting for the bellman to get his bags. *Some little duchy the world's forgotten?* A bellman with emaciated form and popping white eyes began piling his suitcases on a cart. Alistair shrugged. *What the hell difference can it make where he's from, anyway?*

70

both Dan and Ginger Lloyd already ensconced. Dan was sipping a vodka martini, and tapping his omnipresent cigar on the edge of an ashtray, looking impatient. Grinning broadly at his old friends—Spence knew Dan had surely expected him to be late, since he always was— he discovered, as he took his seat, that his appetite was thriving very nicely. Spence had always been an avid trencherman but whenever he was on assignment in an unfamiliar town—researching for a book—or on vacation as he was now, some wayward, little-boy gluttony he'd managed to keep under control tended to overcome him.

Opening his large menu with alacrity, Spence saw neither the heads at the other tables, bent in hushed and questioning conversation, nor how pale his daughter Lauren had become.

Ginger did. After merely glancing at her menu, deciding on a chef's salad, she lay it aside and watched the twelve-year-old with as much nonchalance as she could muster. The instant she had seen Lauren and her parents headed toward the table, quite unasked-for some projecting filament of fright and misery emanating deep from within Lauren had drawn Ginger's attention, the way a capable dowser rapidly locates underground springs.

It wasn't hard to stare at Lauren without being noticed, Ginger realized. The poor girl's head was bowed, ostensibly in a review of her own menu, but with veiled eyes that clearly saw *other* things instead. Things, Ginger believed as she prodded for the root of the child's anxiety, that might steal away the heartiest appetite.

There are few genuine psychics who can turn the gift, or curse, off and on. Extrasensory perception, in all its aspects, takes form in somewhat the way a creative person discovers an idea: it is merely *there*, presumably forced to the surface by some bisociational connections he or she might never be able to trace on a conscious level. Some psychics can, in a period of solitude and with the assistance of personal objects used as props for tapping the unconscious or mind-right—playing cards, crystal balls, toying with numbers or astrological data—gradually shove open their wondrous inner portals.

But for the most part, sensitives—a word they tend to prefer—are obliged to wait until they are involuntarily "visited," often at the worst possible time. That made the testing of people with paranormal gifts along scientific lines exceedingly difficult but no less potentially valid. Ginger's husband Dan, learning of her own secret skills, had learned of experiments conducted by Dr. Gertrude Schmeidler in 1942, and felt that these tests were of considerable significance. Using Zener cards, which were marked with a quintet of different symbols, Dr. Schmeidler assembled test subjects who believed in "psi," whom she called *sheep*, and an equal number of people who thought it was all nonsense, whom she named *goats*. When the experiment was run, the *sheep's* score was well above the expected range while that of the goats was markedly below average. Dan had told Ginger with excitement how impossible that was, in scientific terms, and the way the test indicated that the persons who were tested had in some way *suppressed* their genuine level of "psi" ability in order to support what they consciously, rationally believed.

In Ginger's case, she was utterly helpless to prevent visions of the kind she had experienced in her hotel room but there were moments when she could manage to take a few tentative, telepathic steps intentionally into the mind of another person. These periods depended, as a rule, upon the person Ginger was "tapping" having his or her emotions at a certain level, or pitch.

When she succeeded in seeing into Lauren's young mind, it was necessary for Ginger to grasp the edge of the table in order to steady herself.

She saw a black corridor stretching to infinity, the way things can be in certain nightmares, and identified a tiny, pale light tucked-away in a corner of the hallway. Lauren herself, Ginger realized in a moment; Lauren *as she saw herself* in her moment of terror. Small, defenseless, utterly vulnerable. Along the endless corridor, which quickly became a subterranean tunnel, were framed pictures on a wall that seemed to *pulse,* almost as if the wall was nothing more than dark skin covering a throbbing heart. And at the distant end of the dark tunnel, *spinning* toward her—toward Lauren—and getting larger by the moment was a shadowy figure of such menace that Ginger had to clamp her jaws together to prevent a scream. The face of the being drawing ever closer was unclear, until it careened within yards of the psychic's watchful gaze, and then—though she had the impression that it was a member of her own sex—she grunted, slammed back against her chair, and knocked her menu off on the floor.

Because the menacing creature locked now in Lauren's terrified unconscious thoughts had no face.

"What's the matter, babe?" Spence asked from across the table. "You dizzy or something?" April put out her hand, touching Ginger with concern.

"I guess I'm emptier than I thought," the psychic replied, managing a humorless but self-deprecating laugh. She took a sip of water and glanced at Dan's anxious face. He knew, she thought; he knew what she'd done, if not what she'd seen. "I'll be fine."

"Waitress!" Spence called, raising his voice. His face was full of indignant color. "Shit and damnation, let's have a little goddam *service*—we've got a tableful of starving womenfolk here!"

Ginger ordered mechanically, through Dan, mulling it over. It was possible that what she'd seen in Lauren's mind was nothing more than a troubling nightmare she hadn't been able to lose. But Lauren was too sensible for that, too down-to-earth. Yet what she'd encountered in the child's thoughts was surely nothing more than a child's *representation* of some odd encounter, probably a gross exaggeration.

None of which helped to allay the obvious terror which she saw, even now, in Lauren's pale face. Very badly, she wanted to tell Lauren that she might be able to help. But that meant betraying the secret she shared with Dan and that, in turn, meant betraying Dan himself, embarrassing him where he really lived: in his career as an expert on science.

When the food came, they ate in silence for minutes. Then Spence Torrence threw his fork down and looked up at the others. "What the hell is the matter with this place?" he demanded angrily. "This stuff costs nearly twenty bucks and it has no more taste than that sandwich I had in my room."

"I know what you mean," April replied, nodding. She began hammering on the bottom of a Heinz A-1, lathering her entire entree with the stuff. "But at least it isn't going to cost us twenty dollars. These de*lic*ious meals are part of the *glor*ious treat arranged by the management."

"I'm beginning to think Mr. and Mrs. Peter Quince are

secretly illiterates who hate the idea that everybody else can read," Ginger said with a smile. "That they're trying to get even with you guys."

"I'll tell you this," Spence said grimly, giving his porterhouse a wry, disappointed glance. "Before this is over, I'm going to meet that bird Quince and find out what *is* going on here." Sighing, he bit into a well-buttered roll, then glanced at his oldest friend. "Hey, Dan, we haven't heard from you. How's your steak?"

Dan paused, blinking when he looked up. His mouth was full and he'd already devoured half his meal. He seemed remotely put-out at being interrupted. "Delicious," he said, trying to make a smile. "I think it's probably the finest steak I've had in ten years."

Pop Cormach had been sitting at his typewriter in his hotel room for more than two hours. His hair was sweated-out but he felt satisfied. There was a pile of pages three inches high tossed in unnumbered abandon to the nearby couch. Before he gave them to his secretary, in New York, he'd add the numbers and put them in the right order.

Stopping at last, Pop scratched his naked, inner thigh. He frequently worked in the nude because he was the kind of playwright who hurled himself into his efforts, mind and soul and body as well, and he usually perspired quite heavily. His secretary, Annie, with whom he also had sex when he'd conceived a particularly suggestive scene, kept telling him he'd wind-up with arthritis in the back of his neck unless he stopped hunching himself over the battered Underwood. Pop had always figured that if he removed his clothes first they would still be fresh and neatly pressed when he was ready to face the world.

And sometimes, when the moon was right, his naked little body made Annie ready to face him.

He hadn't really meant to work so hard or get so much done. Not this week, when he was scheduled to be one of the main speakers and still had his address to write. But something about the aging hotel itself had inspired him. When that happened—wherever Pop was at the time, and whatever else might be happening around him, including what he called "Annie's agitation"—Pop always jotted his ideas down at once. Customarily, they came with a considerable amount of detail and waiting for even an hour meant misplacing key ideas, possibly entire scenes. And that, for a comedy writer who earned as much money as Pop Cormach, rubbed him wrong almost as badly as it did appearing in public when he was unpressed and disheveled.

This afternoon, his fertile mind had seized the basic concept for a comedy with science-fiction overtones. The protagonists—Strombone, Trimpet and El-La—would be two male humanoids and a female who travel across space at a speed too *slow* for them to be seen. They'd been away from their home planet so long their memories had atrophied and they had to depend on their computer for absolutely everything. But when they finally arrived on earth, the computer developed an unnatural relationship with certain things of the unfamiliar planet: butterflies, roan horses, professional basketball, and a type of red ant found only in portions of Crete, Illinois.

According to Pop's preliminary notes, Strombone, Trimpet and El-La intended to be conquerors but weren't very good at it. Part of their problem was that they were unbelievably ancient. Each of the aliens had a life ratio to man similar to what man had to the common housefly,

77

which lives only twenty-four hours or so. The fly, not knowing any better, is content that he lives a long, fulfilling life and, when he is swatted to death, feels confident that his achievements will endure.

Man, living seventy or eighty earth years, thought much the same thing and believed—among other notions the aliens found hilarious—that UFO people like Strombone and Company had been here since the dawn of time. After all, the Bible refers to Ezekiel and his "wheel in a wheel." Actually, according to Pop Cormach's manic imagination, the aliens had been here three-and-a-half weeks come Michelmas.

The catch to allowing the computer to tell them how to take over earth was that it was against galactic rules to obliterate a race inferior to theirs by 7.6 increments on a ten-point scale. *We* scored 9.2, so they had no choice except to breed with our women in an effort to lower the increment to the level of acceptable annihilation. On their time scale, Pop typed, that would take about twenty-three minutes.

As the play developed, of course, the aliens would fall in love. We had a great deal in common. We, too, were absent-minded and let computers give us orders. Like them, we had a monetary system based on greed and took out our hostilities through sex and sports. But unlike them, we didn't even know there was an interplanetary war going on. It had been, for three-hundred-thousand of our years, but we'd been too slow to realize it. We coined the concept of an "accident" to explain it when our kind died unexpectedly, and then we coined the concept of "dying" itself—which we wouldn't have been doing if the aliens weren't waging war all this time. All the falling-in-love scenes, Pop decided, would happen when Strombone or Trimpet brought earth women aboard the UFO, much to the disgust of the jealous El-La, who'd go around singing "Lullabye of Birdland" whenever she couldn't take any more.

"What the hell is *that?*" Pop asked, aloud, half-expecting far-off Annie to provide him with information. She was so good at that, among other things.

He had thrown a hand up before his eyes because of a piercing glare that shot beneath his closed door. Irritated, blinking, he arose and crossed the room to find out what was happening. In the nick of time Pop remembered he was nude and opened the door a crack.

Nothing. Nothing but an empty, shadowy hallway so silent it was like peering into a crypt at midnight. He ventured to open the door wider and stepped delicately outside. Ghastly paintings on the walls, framed by phony gold and picturing scenes that had interested no one in fifty years. Irked, Pop stepped back inside and closed the door, ignoring the phenomenon.

There was just time for a quick shower before going down for dinner. He wanted to find out if Herbert Leiberman and Judith Rossner were in the hotel and he had a definite dinner date with Bari Wood and Sol Stein. Somewhere down the line Pop wanted to try his hand at a novel and it wouldn't hurt to talk with experts. He—

That damned light again! Glaring fiercely, illuminating the whole front room. He glanced at his TV, which he'd turned on as background to his work, and saw something strange: the light from the screen was *alternating* with the light edging beneath his door! It was peculiarly hypnotic, Pop mused, blinking again. He had to tear his gaze away from the television screen in order to go back to the front door.

This time, when he threw it wide, the illumination remained—and he cried out in actual pain, burying his face in his fingers as he sought to protect his vision. Good *God*, what *was* it! The light was like the blazing glare of a discotheque with every strobe turned to the strongest level. It was hideous, agonizing deep in the sockets of Pop's eyes, and it had given him a momentary optical illusion.

Because, right before he had to squeeze his lids shut and cover them with his hands, he'd had the absurd but distinct impression that *another* door was open, somewhere—and *he'd actually seen an Unidentified Flying Object* glittering in stoic, sinister waiting.

Pop kicked the door to, then locked it with fumbling fingers, unable to see clearly at all. The pain behind his lids pounded as he wheeled away from the door and ran stumblingly through his suite to the bathroom. He wasn't sure what he was going to do first—vomit, because he'd become aware of a monstrous nausea that threatened to rip his insides apart, or bathe his tortured eyes and cover them with a warm, wet cloth. Miniature, echoing lights continued to flicker viciously behind his lids and a headache was taking hold with the singleminded maliciousness of an Inquisition interrogator.

Good, Pop gasped, swallowing back his bile as he washed his eyes with water, *so good!* Before him, the wash basin wobbled, colorless at first because of the lingering glare but gradually assuming its genuine turquoise hue. He blinked repeatedly, bathed his eyes anew, then wiped his face on a fluffy towel. *Better,* he reassured himself, taking a deep breath. *Better now.*

Unsteady, Pop turned back to the basin, holding on with one hand. *I must look a* mess *after this*, he brooded, thinking of his important dinner companions expecting him. *I must look positively ghastly.*

He raised his head and peered into the mirror attached to the medicine cabinet.

His heart almost stopped beating. He nearly fainted. He clutched the basin beneath him as he gaped in the mirror and felt his sanity begin to slip and slide away.

Pop didn't really look ghastly. He wasn't a mess at all.

He simply didn't have *a face* any more.

At the instant he began to scream, the rest of Pop Cormach vanished from view.

CHAPTER SEVEN

"I tried to read Lauren's mind."

Dan, starting to peel off his underwear, looked at Ginger with surprise. With his undershirt bunched around his neck and the contrast of his pale back and his hairy barrel-chest, he might have been a balding turtle getting ready for bed. "You almost never do that crap intentionally."

Naked atop the covers, Ginger crossed her legs decorously and leaned back against the headboard. Her light-colored eyes were wide and she didn't know how Dan was adoring the way everything about her seemed blonde and fair, that she was so dear to him she sometimes struck him as heartbreakingly ephemeral. "Danny, that's one very frightened kid. I'm surprised you and her folks couldn't see it."

"Well, we don't happen to share any of your special attributes," he replied in mild sarcasm, scratching the black-and-gray thicket on his chest. A teddybear now that he was undressed, Dan shuffled across the floor to her and sat on the edge of the bed. His gaze at his nude young wife was both affectionate and prurient. "I remember how I had an intuition once—a really great flash of inner knowing. It was back in Toledo in Fifty. The Phillies amazed the baseball world that year by winning the National League pennant with a bunch of nobodies. And I had this fantastic feeling come over me that the Phils were going to upset the New York Yankees in the World Series." He stubbed out his cigar butt in an ashtray on the bedside table. "I was just a kid, but I put all my money on that psychic hunch. Every dime I had in the world."

"What happened?" she asked, curious.

"The Yanks won the Series, four-zip." He stretched out on his side, facing Ginger, making a comical face. "That was when I decided the scientific life was for me. No more wondrous glimpses into the future." He sighed. "Joe Page was a helluva reliever."

She made a face. "If I remember correctly, you made a bundle betting on me in my tennis matches."

He kissed her on the front of her shoulder, dropped his face a few inches and nuzzled. "I'd learned a lot about class in the intervening years. I figured anybody with form like yours couldn't miss."

Ginger squirmed, put her palms on the side of his pressing cheeks. "Are you talking about tennis form?"

"Whatever," he replied, losing his track of thought.

"Hold on a minute, will you?" she protested. His large head rose away from her with the amiable blue eyes looking surprised and disappointed. "We'll get back to your scientific explorations in a moment. I didn't tell you what I saw in Lauren's thoughts."

"Gee, that would be a terrific loss," he said, disgruntled, turning on his back to listen.

Ginger outlined what she had seen—the hotel corridor, becoming a tunnel; the faceless figure rushing toward Lauren—the way Ginger was sure Lauren was not only experiencing considerable psychic misery but had surely seen things she wasn't discussing with anyone.

"Well, hell, I can understand that," Dan put in. "She tried to tell us about seeing a little girl who looked like her in the lobby and we all jumped on her case, remember?"

"I think she really did," Ginger said in a hushed voice. "I think this place is *evil*, Danny, maybe not the way a haunted house is but by—by some alien influence. You don't think it's just my imagination, do you?"

"Not any more than I think, now, that Lauren was imagining it." He felt a shiver trickle like ice water along the back of his neck. "Although that's what Spence told her. I'm going to have to talk with him at length before long."

"So you are saying that you think Lauren feels we'll laugh at her if she tells us what else is going on?"

"Sure, wouldn't you feel that way?" He rested his palm as far down as his arm would stretch. It was like touching a patch of golden fur; it wasn't merely sensual, it was comforting to him. He turned his head to look at her. "Come to think of it, darlin', don't we both feel that way about your psychic abilities? That we don't want anybody laughing at us?"

"At me, you mean. You say it's because of your reputation but other science writers have explored the paranormal. John Fuller with his *Interrupted Journey,* Jacques Vallee with *Messengers of Deception,* Colin Wilson, John Grant, Robert Holdstock. You don't fool me a bit, Daniel Lloyd." She turned on her stomach to kiss him. "But you always include yourself in anything that might upset me."

"You're making me a lot more noble than I am," he replied, turning her back over and cupping her small, high breasts one by one. "But don't stop, I love it."

Her own hands moved to feel him. "I'm a lucky woman to give up a career just before Chrissie or Martina, or one of the hotshot new kids, could drive me out of tennis. Everyday I spend with you is like center court at Wimbledon."

"*You're* lucky?" Dan asked incredulously, trailing his hands down her firm, athletic body. His lips followed his hands, tasting the faint, soft bristle of pale hair below her navel, feeling her twist slightly in encouragement. "If God ever finds out what's happened to a middleaged bald man who wasn't smart enough to become a bonafide scientist, I will have used up all the luck I'll ever have in this world—simply by knowing you."

Within seconds Ginger was starting to writhe on the bed, an arm out-flung, panting and ready for him. Looking up, he saw with wonder how her already-flat belly was sucked in—how the tips of her icecream-cone breasts had raised, and how her beloved head was thrown back in feminine need.

And no matter how much I want her, Danny thought miserably, hollowly, *I've just gone impotent for the first time in my life.* A great puzzlement mingled with sadness and embarrassment as he sat up, slowly, looking down at himself with disgust.

Sensing his problem, Ginger began gently manipulating him. When that did no good, she sat nimbly up in bed, kissed his mouth, and bowed her head over him.

At the instant her lips touched Dan he heard—so plainly, so distinctly he believed that someone was in the bedroom with them—the taunting, tinkling sound of childish laughter.

Crying out, his chest heaving, Dan was on his bare feet at once. He cast his angry, frustrated gaze from one corner of the room to the other, fists doubled.

"Danny, what *is* it?"

He didn't, he *couldn't* answer her. He walked around the bedroom, opened the closet door, glanced into the bathroom—

And finally returned to the bed, redfaced, shaking his large head. Ginger was incredibly beautiful. She still had that wanting look of a woman whose flesh tightens and gleams with sweat like some expensive oil had been applied the length of her trim body. And she was as inaccessible to him as if he'd never met her.

"I heard a kid," he said shortly. "Obviously, you didn't. So just as obviously, it's all in my head. My unconscious mind has doubtlessly provided me with an excuse for becoming an old man all at once."

"You aren't *old*," she argued, reaching up to him. "I'm sure I can—"

Miserable, he turned away from her and trudged his way into the bathroom. For a moment it did not occur to him that he might actually have heard the hurtful hilarity of a young girl. He'd trained himself to be

86

pragmatic, down-to-earth, his entire life. Only Ginger was permitted to experience anything exceptional, anything out of the normal—into the paranormal.

But eventually his well-trained mind seized upon the question: Why *now*, why *here?* Why, when he'd never had that kind of problem before, had it happened during a vacation period in a different town? He belched, compounding his embarrassment as he knew Ginger must have heard it; *turning dyspeptic on you, babe, sometimes the guts are the first thing to go.* The taste in his mouth, though, was odd, damned peculiar; it wasn't like the bilious taste you generally got with indigestion. It was, in a way, more like—like something *chemical,* concocted in a laboratory.

What next, Dan? he asked himself, standing with a sigh and flushing the toilet. *How about a nice heart attack to really screw things up for everybody?*

He turned on the water faucet with one hand and used the other to lean on the wall by the basin.

When he did, Dan Lloyd gasped in terror.

He left the hand there, because it wasn't a sensation of pain he'd felt—*but the wall was throbbing, pulsing, as if some mad alien heart lay against the other side of the wall, beating maniacally, and* . . . waiting.

"Ginger," he said in a small voice that didn't carry.

He took a few steps to the other side of the bathroom, rested his hand against the wall there. Again, *pulsing,* the fast but obvious beat of a *living heart!*

"Ginger," he called again, loud enough to be heard. The sounds of bedclothes rustling told him she was coming. Breathing quickly, now, filled with weird images that sizzled like electrical impulses through his brain, Dan moved to the bathtub and reached across it to touch the distant, half-tiled wall.

The pulses were no longer steady. They came at intervals, almost as if they were purposive, as if a code—a message—was being driven into his fingertips.

"What is it?"

He looked over his hirsute shoulder. Ginger had pulled on a robe against the late-winter chill, and the coldness of this bizarre suite, but left it open. The sheer, familiar, normal beauty of her nudity where the robe gapped made something in Dan twist with yearning. He felt absurd with his bare, bristly bottom tooting-out but made himself leave his hands where they were, his arms stretched over the immaculate and ordinary bathtub. *If I concentrate,* he reflected, more afraid than he'd ever been before, *I could figure out what the pulses are saying.* "Feel the wall," he whispered, as if fearing to break the contact. "Just—feel the wall!"

Eyes wide, she did as he asked, fingertips grazing the area beside the wash basin. She shook her head, clearly not understanding. "Here," he said roughly, inclining his head; "over *here.*"

She joined him at the tub, scarcely able to reach the tiling, standing on tiptoes. They stood that way for a long moment, two unclothed people side by side, palms flat against the bathroom wall as if some nocturnal policeman had wished to frisk them. A second later, tears came into her light eyes. "What am I supposed to f-feel, Danny?" she whispered.

So. Inhaling, he straightened, slowly drew Ginger back with him. He nodded, frowning, part of his mind wondering if he looked wild-eyed, like some looney-tune showing himself to small children. *So they* were *messages I was feeling,* he thought, knowing how wild it all was, hating

88

himself for drawing such a ludicrous and altogether frightening conclusion. *But what . . . Somebody . . . is communicating—it's meant only for the* writers *in this sanitorium. . . .*

Worried, almost beside herself, Ginger threw herself into his strong, short arms and pressed full-length against him. He was reminded, again, of what a marvel she was; how, with her slightly greater height, everything fitted perfectly when they stood like this.

Dan knew, then, because of what was happening to them—the bridge that was rising to her moist and gentle banks—that he could take her back to bed, and that they would enjoy marvelous sex.

Except that he also knew he didn't *dare*, and that he wouldn't touch Ginger again while they were in the Hotel Holroyd.

Because, once again, with his wife close in his arms, he heard the teasing, infuriating, impossible *giggle* of an unseen child.

The male and the female were sitting at their dining room table, drinking coffee. They were utterly relaxed, so poised in the unfamiliar world that anyone seeing them—and knowing *what* they were—might have believed a conquest had already been achieved.

"I'm becoming more accustomed to life here," said the female, putting her cup in the saucer. "There are surface similarities. They help."

But he was lost in his own thoughts and her remarks did not register. "They all came," he reported. "Every last one we invited."

"That's unusual, isn't it?" she asked, falling into his conversation with practiced ease. "Sometimes there are stragglers, ones who aren't interested enough. Or those who are too busy to come."

"These journalists, novelists, poets and playwrights," he said, the object between his eyes wrinkling in disgust, "enjoy believing they are different from their fellows. Special earth people. The Selector was correct in approaching it this way. They've come together the way Neanderthals gathered around the fire in a cave."

"I think installing them in one wing was a sound concept," she murmured. "It makes disposing of them simpler, tidier, doesn't it?"

He nodded. "Even when they come with friends, the way the Torrences did, there is still a preference for privacy. Until the day comes when they expect to hear their little speeches, they'll spend considerable time alone. Which makes it so much easier to . . . *get them*, one by one."

"Do you ever grow weary of it?" she inquired. "All the destruction?"

"Never!" he exclaimed, astounded. He poured them more coffee from a silver service and studied her face. "Do you?"

She beamed and shook her head. "Not for a moment, husband." She hesitated, deciding how to put it. "It is our responsibility, but it is *my* joy."

Behind them, the door opened and a child entered the room.

The male looked at her sternly. "Did you do your duty?"

She nodded, and helped herself to food from the table. "The next step is the bat."

"*Cat*," he corrected her. "A bat is something quite different." He picked up a platter from the table. "Before you do anything else, take this to the Selector. I'm certain it's hungry."

The child obeyed. The bones on the platter would make such a nice midnight snack for the Selector. She paused, one hand on the door leading to the office, where the alien creature floated in its aquarium tank. "Why do earth people have to sleep?" she asked.

"Because their brains are exhausted from trying to think all day," replied the male, glancing at the woman.

"You're always so needlessly scornful," she said flatly, and turned to the child with a maternal expression. "They are able to use only a small section of their brains. Even their scientists know that; approximately one-third and never, in the case of any human being, more than fifty percent. The only way they can get in touch with the rest of themselves is through dreaming—do you remember what we told you about dreams?—when they can mildly engage their sleeping segments. And those, of course, are primarily made of fantasy content."

"It is nearly enough to make one feel pity for them," the child said thoughtfully, frowning. Then she brightened, something that might have been a smile passing her lips. "But not quite," she said. "Not quite."

"There's my good princess," said the male, watching the door close behind his daughter.

Lauren awoke with pressure on her chest. Startled, she almost cried out.

Then she saw it was only old Puck, his whiskery mouth tickling her chin, his otherworldly green eyes melding with her own sleepy gaze.

"Go 'way, you dumb cat," she complained, shoving

him off her and turning heavily on her side. "Can't you see somebody's sleepin'?"

In a single, lithe bound, he was back. His muzzle drooped above her shoulder, questioningly. Lauren squinted up at the familiar, furry face, trying not to give him the satisfaction of laughing. "Leave me alone, dammit!" she wailed. "Go use your litter box."

But Puck waited, weightlessly. He seemed hung above her like a black marionette dangling from someone else's strings.

Lauren sighed massively, tucked her pet under one arm, and threw her p-j covered legs over the side of the bed. "All right, all right then, I'll take you for your durned old walk."

She glanced at the Westclox alarm on Pop's table: almost two o'clock. Pop and Mom were zonked out and Pop was making the dreadful snoring sound he always swore, awake, that he didn't make. If Lauren knew anything at all about the way they worried over perverts and assorted creepos prowling around in the middle of the night, neither parent would authorize what she proposed to do. *Can only authors authorize?* she mused. But the alternative seemed to be Puck jumping up and down on her the rest of the night, or, as the kitten was wont to do when his wishes were denied, waking-up in the morning with the stench of cat urine acrid in her nostrils. And Lauren knew who'd be blamed for *that*.

She slipped into her shoes, then found her coat, Puck watching her expectantly as she yawned. Mouse-quiet, she tiptoed through the suite to the front room, the cat at her heels. At the last second she realized the door would lock automatically after her, so she ransacked through Spence Torrence's things—piled on the writing desk—

and finally located the room key. Puck went under her arm again; she gripped him tightly, protectively, as she went outside.

This late at night the Hotel Holroyd was not only clothed in stealthy black shadows, elongating the corridor which led eventually, to the elevator, but indescribably still. Pop had told her of being in hotels where Shrine conventions were going-on and complained about the way celebrants made a racket all night. Where Lauren walked, her heart and Puck's blending as she darted worried glances from side to side, it felt like she and the kitten were the only human beings left alive on the earth. People—other writers and their families—were doubtlessly asleep behind the doors she was passing, Lauren told herself; but she couldn't shake her impression that the hotel was deserted.

At least, *some* of the rooms. Deserted of living, or human, creatures.

She averted her gaze from the painting that had, earlier in the day, appeared to change. Spotting it, however, she accelerated her pace. She had the notion that a *third* painting hung in the same, old frame, and that peculiar *eyes* were watching her. When she finally began running, Lauren's pace faltered and she was full of uncharacteristic indecision. More than anything, she wanted to get on the elevator and reach the reasonably-bright hotel lobby, where people might be. But she also was growing increasingly fearful that she'd round a corner and run directly into the red-eyed Hotel Girl.

Relieved when no one else was using the elevator, Lauren and Puck rode downstairs with a rising feeling of new security.

The lobby wasn't brightly lit. There was light from the

registration desk, a chandelier that Lauren thought installed when Abraham Lincoln was president glowed faintly from the middle of the ceiling, and that was it. One or two very old men sat stiffly in leather chairs, beneath the ceiling light. They would have looked dead, mummified, except for the way pens and pencils in their big-knuckled hands drifted silently across paper. *Midnight messages*, Lauren thought, hugging Puck closer; *what terrible things do they write in the blackness of night?*

She was surprised when a body moved, behind the registration desk, and jumped. "Hi," she said. It was a woman with a vast uncertainty of years, barely looking up from some papers before her, only her sallow lips parting to indicate that she'd heard Lauren. Ahead of her, a bellman, dwarfish and stunted in the shadows by the marble steps leading outside, opened one cold eye to see her pass.

Lauren jogged down the steps and, as the hotel doors shushed behind her, couldn't keep from gasping.

Several inches of snow lay on the ground around the Hotel Holroyd and, when Lauren looked up, she saw that the night sky was turned white by descending flakes. It might have been January or February, instead of late March, and the girl shuddered, wishing she'd put on something warmer beneath her coat than the flimsy p-js.

Puck slipped away, alighting soundlessly on all fours, and took off. "Puck!" she called, annoyed. "Where are you going?"

The kitten was sliding black coal as he disappeared around the corner of the building, and Lauren ran after him, slipping in the wet slush beneath her feet. She saw Puck dash into the parking lot, prayed there were no cars leaving then, and hurried after him. When he cut a

94

corner again, the panting girl continued her pursuit.

The top floor of the Hotel Holroyd, at the back of the building, was nothing but a dazzling glare of light. Stunningly white, at first, it changed before Lauren's blinking eyes to an alternating series of colors—a blue the color of the sky hanging low above a distant star, an emerald-green glittering like tinted glass, a crimson so blazingly red that Lauren cried out and took a step back from its supernatural intensity.

Machinery, Lauren thought—some kind of incredible machinery never seen by human eyes. But what in heaven was it that toiled with such brilliance in the middle of the night; what terrible deeds were being performed at this secret time when the rest of the city slept?

The curling, cruel, prolonged howl filled Lauren's ears and she covered them as best she could with her small hands, wincing away from the shriek and dislodging the sticking snow that clung already to her head and face. She had never heard such a ghastly yowl. It might have been the last agonized cry of something tortured beyond endurance, beyond the human ken; it might have been human, once, or the piercing pain of an animal trying to absorb what its limited senses could not conceivably accept.

Lauren shouted. *Something* was dislodged, from a height above her; something was dropping to the snow-shrouded concrete, and *running* toward her. Before she could move, it was vaulting toward her—*hurtling* itself into Lauren's arms—

And she sobbed, at first with relief, with familiarity, as she snuggled her kitten Puck against her trembling, freezing cheek.

Until she saw that Puck, the black cat, from behind his head to his terrified tail, *had turned totally white.*

TRANSCRIPTION TWO

"RITUALIZED PLACES"

"Time is not the fourth dimension, and should not be so identified. Time is only a relative observation."

—R. Buckminster Fuller

"Applied to the world as representatives of *all* the world, facts become superstitions. . . . Like the entrails of animals or the flights of birds, such scientific superstitions become the preserved *ritualized places* where we may read out the past and future of man, and hear the answers that can authorize our actions."

—Julian Jaynes, *Origin of Consciousness in the Breakdown of the Bicameral Mind* amicable, April would answer them and take good notes. She would go to the door when someone knocked, handle her household chores, and generally give him the impression that life was running smoothly enough that he could snooze another twenty minutes or so.

It hadn't always been that way, his absolute confidence in April. When they married, somewhat more than thirteen years ago, they'd both found themselves in the circumstances of countless newlyweds. Instead of having been old neighbors and lifelong sweethearts, or putting up with an endless year's engagement, the way Spence's and April's peers had tended to be, they'd had a whirlwind courtship and stepped before a Justice of the Peace without really knowing one another at all. And, for awhile, it looked perfectly clear that they'd made a mistake and it wouldn't work out.

Spence, for his part, had wanted April to put her dreams of Broadway stardom behind her and be satisfied with life as a housewife or homemaker. April tried, she really did; but there were times when Spence would find her slumped in a chair, a newspaper listing of auditions dangling from her limp hand.

For her part, April hadn't liked the feast-or-famine life as the wife of a book writer on the way up. Several times she'd hinted that he should try to get his old newspaper job back and write his hardhitting nonfiction books as a sideline. He tried, for six months. He didn't give up his regained vocational position until just about the time April decided she could make the marriage work if he would only permit her to act in amateur productions in and around Porter, New York. That rainy night was, both of them felt, when their marriage began in earnest, a time when each of them confessed to frustration and

100

unhappiness and started growing together. While it was sometimes necessary for Spence to make trips to Guatemala, Libya, and El Salvador, and for April to spend two weeks rehearsing for a role in *Annie* or *Applause,* they discovered that it wasn't, for them, so much the quantity of time they spent together as the quality of their shared moments. When he could, Spence took April with him on his journeys and attended her plays. This trip, when they would associate with other writers, was actually important to both of them since they'd been apart nearly a month before leaving Porter for the midwest.

Now, however, Spence saw April's nightgowned form dozing within easy reach of his arm and realized that it wasn't her presence he sensed.

Worse, there was a harrowing moment when he wasn't quite sure where he was, at all. He had the disconcerting impression that their heads were at a different direction, the bed felt unfamiliar, the light pouring in through the window should have been either at his back or on their feet. He sat up in bed swiftly with a feeling that the world had gone awry, and turned to see who was stirring.

Lauren, strangely wearing her overcoat over her p-js, sat immovably on the floor just inside the bedroom door. She was exceedingly quiet except for her subdued weeping, and her gaze seemed to be rigidly focussed on a small, motionless figure in a box at her feet. Spence frowned. Why had she dragged Puck and his bed in here? Was the animal ill?

He lifted himself from the bed as softly as he could, careful to avoid waking April, and padded barefoot across the floor. Lauren didn't appear to hear him coming, and he knelt down beside her, worried, touching her cheek with his gentle fingertips. His eyes questioned her with

101

anxiety and sympathy.

"They did something awful to Puck," Lauren whispered when she realized Pop was there.

"They *who?*" he asked, puzzled.

"I don't know," she said, making a face. She pointed. *"Look."*

He did, and rocked back on his heels with a gasp. Cowering in a corner of his bed, all the fight gone out of him, Lauren's kitten seemed to be barely breathing and did not even look up at him. The thought that leaped to Spence's mind was on his lips before he stopped it: *Is that really Puck?*

Because there was a beautiful white streak down the tiny animal's back, reaching from behind the head to the limp tail. Puck had been the blackest cat Spence ever saw. In addition, he realized, the pet's muzzle was flecked with spittle and one hindleg was trembling.

"What in the world happened?" he asked as he stared at Lauren.

She told him the best she could, succinctly, breaking into noiseless tears only when she reached the end of her story and described the way Puck, terror stricken, had vaulted into her arms. "I've been sittin' here with him ever since. He shook *so* badly for a long while. But he's c-calmer now."

"I don't understand," Spence commented, stroking Puck's head and scratching behind his ears. "Do you think the light you saw did this to him, accidentally, or the people who were controlling the light?"

Lauren shook her head helplessly. "I don't know, Pop." She bit her lip. "All I care about is that Puck gets a-all right."

"We'll do what we can," he promised her, kissing her

102

forehead and straightening.

He located the yellow pages in a desk drawer and turned to Veterinarians. Selecting one at random, he dialed the number and waited. *Lauren has never been a neurotic child. If she saw a light like that, well, she saw it.* He told the receptionist who answered the nature of his question. Flustered, she said shakily that she'd put Doctor Caladi on the phone. Spence tapped his fingers impatiently. "Yes?" a voice inquired and he repeated the bizarre story, watching Lauren from the corner of his eye.

"That, sir," reported Doctor Caladi, an Italian accent filling the line like syrup," is simply impossible. Absolutely impossible."

"Well, shit and damnation, it happened." Spence leaned forward into the conversation. "My daughter had a young black cat yesterday and today he's a two-tone job."

"No."

"Look, doc, I've heard of *people* who have had such a bad fright that their hair turns white overnight. Why not cats?"

"It never happens to people either," snapped Caladi, then paused and hedged his bets. "Perhaps, on rare occasion, the terror has been so monstrous or the person's age and health so . . . unfortunate . . . there may be some recorded instances. But cats, no. Their nervous-a systems are different. I have personally observed very small cats confronted by two or more large-a dogs, knowing they will be badly injured—but they've never turned white." The man inhaled. "It's-a superstitious nonsense, your daughter got back the wrong cat!"

The phone went dead. Spence raised his gaze. "That

103

was Chico Marx on the phone, I think," Spence said with deceptive mildness. "He says-a it's impossible."

"Shit and damnation," Lauren said clearly, glaring.

"Exactly," agreed her father.

April awakened moments later, full of plans for sight-seeing. It astonished Spence the way she could be sleeping like the dead one instant and volubly alert the next. For his part he preferred arising to tomblike silence and saying nothing whatever until he'd had two cups of coffee. April was so enthused about seeing the city that she only glanced at Lauren and him before bounding out of bed and, chattering all the while, virtually skipped toward the bathroom.

Enroute, she looked out the window and cried, "Oh, shit and damnation!"

"Of all the words I've worked so hard to create," Spence sighed, "the only thing I'll be remembered for is a curse I heard my grandfather use once. What's the matter?"

She turned to him, outraged. Her blue nightgown bodice barely covered her full breasts and the curving pressure of them against the material was a sight Spence never grew tired of. "It *snowed* last night!" she cried, gesturing with a dramatic arm. "That white shit is kneedeep on the walk and the ground, and it's still coming down!"

He stopped fiddling with the telephone and went over to see for himself. "I'm sure you're exaggerating," he said as he walked. Then he saw, and blinked. "You're right! It's late March, the start of spring, and it *is* knee-deep out there—or close to it. Did anybody dream of a white Easter?"

"It's not a bit funny!" April sniffed, disappearing into

the bathroom. "We can't go outside in that mess. This damnable hotel is *miles* from the heart of downtown and it wouldn't be anything but misery to go out there." The toilet lid flipped up with a loud slap. "We're *trapped* in here!"

"Well, that's putting it strongly," he argued, stripping off his pajamas and starting to get dressed. "I hardly think Mr. and Mrs. Quince *ordered* the snow."

"*I do.*"

He turned, zipping up, startled. It was Lauren. Her expression was so serious it was solemn. She clearly believed precisely what she said.

"Where are you going?" April asked, emerging from the bathroom in her underwear. For a moment Spence wished they hadn't brought Lauren with them.

"It's a little late for breakfast," he replied, thinking how fluently, with what well-trained grace his wife moved. "I thought we'd have a big lunch in an hour or two. In the meanwhile, I'll go downstairs and talk to some of the other guests." He decided to skip a tie and slipped into a somewhat gaudy sports jacket, his face grim. "If I can, babe, I'm going to locate weird Mr. Peter Quince or his wife and discover what the hell is happening at the Holroyd."

April, her skirt zipped, was halfway into a blouse. She stopped buttoning to stare at him. "Is something wrong?"

He laughed without merriment. "Take a look at Puck," he said as lightly as he could, gesturing as he passed Lauren and her kitten, and opened the door. "I think you're in for a little surprise."

Halfway down the corridor, he stopped at the Lloyd's room and rapped on the door. There was no immediate

105

reply and he thought, for a moment, they had gone out.

Then the door opened a crack and Dan's right eye peered somberly at him. "Morning," Spence offered, wondering why Dan didn't ask him in. "Want to go down to the lobby and help me ask some brilliant investigative questions?"

"I'm not up to playing Mike Wallace this morning." A heavy brow drooped over the right eye which, Spence saw, looked red-rimmed and weary. "Bad night."

"Well, suit yourself. Will we see you guys later in the day?"

Dan hesitated. "I'm not sure. Right this minute, buddy, I'm thinking about getting us on a big bird and flying back to Porter. While there's time."

"Take a look out the window," Spence said shortly, moving away from the door. "Big Bird's grounded. You may have to hop back with Kermit."

He was riding downstairs in the elevator when he realized what Dan had said. That they were thinking about leaving—*while there was time.*

Spence squared his shoulders, smoothed back his red hair, and headed directly for the check-in desk. Across the lobby he could see the marble steps leading down to the front doors and, beyond them, the whistling, white fury of a snowstorm. The man who'd been at the desk yesterday, when they registered, gave Spence a frosty glance. "Good morning, Mr. Torrence."

"I hadn't noticed," he snapped, grabbing the check-in register before the other man could stop him and spinning it to face him. "I just want to look through this thing to find the names of a few writers I know. Locate their rooms."

"That information is confidential," the clerk said

smoothly, slipping the book out from beneath Spence's fingers with a dexterity for which he wouldn't have given the fellow credit. "The management realizes that many of our guests are gifted artists, celebrities who are customarily bothered more than they wish to be. If you will remember the invitation we sent you, Mr. Torrence, you'll recall that we pledged absolute privacy."

He'd said the word British-style—"*priv*-acy"—and it compounded Spence's irritation. "Where will I find either Peter Quince or his wife?"

"That is difficult to say." A fine brow arched. "The management has much to do in preparation for the speeches to be made over the weekend. I should imagine Mr. and Mrs. Quince are involved." The brow lowered. "And unavailable."

"Very well." Spence's fingernails drummed the top of the desk. "I want you to leave word that I want to discuss some matters with them at their earliest opportunity. Got that? Have either of them ring me anytime, and they can come up to my room or I'll meet them at their office. Okay?"

"I shall be delighted to convey the message, sir."

The man was like a younger version of Sir John Gielgud in *Arthur*. Spence, starting to leave the desk, changed his mind and pivoted back to it. "Where is their office, by the way? Can you point it out to me?"

"Of course." The desk clerk, his eyes slits now, angled his body and lifted both his gaze and an imperious arm. "Do you see that mirroring on the second floor, sir? That's customarily where one would find Mr. and Mrs. Quince."

I was right when we checked in, Spence thought, looking up. The lighting in the lobby, on a gloomy day, looked halfhearted and morose, and the mirror seemed cloudy. *We* were *being observed. But why?* "Thanks very much," he said as amiably as he could. "You won't forget to tell your boss, right?"

Working on a pleasant smile, Spence began an apparently idle, directionless tour of the lobby. He was surprised to see that it was relatively deserted. It didn't seem likely, the way most literary folk tended to live sedentary lives, that they'd all gone sightseeing. Perhaps they were sleeping late.

A handful of writers he didn't recognize were holding court in the leather chairs at the center of the lobby and Spence caught the phrase "outmoded existentialism is no excuse" as he sidled by, and stopped. Looking back, he saw that the chairs had been carefully replaced, that the imprints he'd seen yesterday were now covered. *Or did I imagine it?* he wondered, conscious of a nervous tingling sensation along his legs.

When he stopped at the newspaper dispenser he found that the day's edition either hadn't come in yet or was already sold out. For a second he felt a twinge of alarm scoot along the back of his neck. He saw by his wristwatch that it was 11:30, reminded himself that it wasn't unusual for a newspaper to be gone by that hour. *Torrence, you're getting more paranoid by the minute.*

He paused to light a Pall Mall and glance at the registration desk. The clerk had his back to him, presumably slipping a message in the manager's letter-box. For the first time Spence allowed himself to wonder, fleetingly, why several lines in the registration book had been deleted by glaring streaks of Liquid Paper. Had the clerk made an error, had some of the writers checked out, or what was the Hotel Holroyd hiding?

A moment later he was darting silently up the curving, carpeted stairway leading to the second story, and the manager's office. At the back of his writer's mind Spence knew that, if Quince and his wife really weren't around, he planned to search the office for clues. He'd done that once at Idi Amin's headquarters and nearly died, quite literally, when a mammoth black colonel materialized behind him. By now Spence couldn't even remember what lie he'd designed to save him. But he'd never forget the bloodlust in the man's eyes or the magnum strapped to his waist.

To Spence's right on the landing he saw two corridors converged. A black maid with a cart bearing clean linens had her broad back to him and was humming a tune he recognized as "I Enjoy Being a Girl," and Spence smiled.

Three steps to his left, the smile vanished.

A glass-fronted door barred his way. Through it, several yards down the hall, there was another door with a sign indicating it was the manager's office. But when he tried to shove the glass-fronted door open, he found it absolutely immobilized. Locked tight; and if he didn't miss his guess, it was bulletproof glass.

Spence reflected. Somebody had to get into the manager's office to empty wastebaskets and generally clean-up. Which meant that the hotel employees surely had keys to the door.

He ran down the first corridor, on tiptoe, and caught the heavyset maid before she disappeared into a room. "Pardon me, ma'am," he said with his old, engagingly boyish smile. It always amazed him how he could depend upon his imagination to conceive the rapid lie. "My photographer and I have instructions to take pictures of Mr. Quince's office for a story we're doing. You know, a

109

nice little gesture to repay him in part for his generosity. But I can't get through that glass door."

Suspicion hardened the woman's eyes until they seemed acorns. "Ain't nobody allowed in there 'cept Mr. and Mrs. Quince."

"Well, I have an appointment with them at noon," he said, nodding. "For the interview itself. We just need a few pictures of the office. For background."

"I don' see no photographer," she said, scowling.

"He'll be along in a minute." Spence realized he was starting to perspire. "If you'll just unlock the door, and leave it open for my partner, I'm certain Mr. and Mrs. Quince will appreciate your thoughtfulness." A bribe was next.

Her head swiveled on her neckless shoulders. "Ain't got no key. Couldn't let you in if'n I wanted to. Never had no key and don't have no key to that door now."

He stared into her unblinking eyes and gradually came to the conclusion that she was telling him the truth. "One thing, all right? I don't want to miss them, when they come. Could you tell me what the Quinces look like?"

"Uh-*uh*," she replied, shaking her head again. "Can't do that."

"Can't," he prodded her, frowning, feeling in his pocket for his billfold, "or won't?"

"Mistah," the obese maid said stolidly, incuriously, "I don't know those people from Adam and Eve. I never saw 'em in my life."

He was several steps down the corridor when the idea occurred to him and he turned back to her. "Ma'am? How long have you worked for the Hotel Holroyd?"

She peeped back at him from around the edge of the

110

hotel room. "Evah since it reopened," she called back to him, "just a little while ago." And closed the door behind her.

By bedtime, Lauren was enormously relieved to see Puck venturing out of his bed. When she tried to feed him, he ate—slowly, as if it might hurt for him to swallow—but he curled up at the foot of her cot with every appearance of being the same old Puck.

Except, Lauren brooded, for the white stripe in his fur.

She fell asleep almost the second her young face touched the pillow . . .

Everyone Lauren Torrence had ever met in her dozen years of life was lined up in a series of neat columns. The memory loses nothing, forgets nothing; the conscious mind merely finds it difficult, on occasion, to bring to mind a given face, a certain name. They were all there, Lauren's parents, her grandparents and her cousins, Puck, a puppy she'd had once which died of some mystical version of canine crib death. There, too, were her schoolmates and neighbors in Porter, New York, second in rank behind the people who meant the most to her. And behind them, trailing into an infinity depicted by massive gray-and-pink clouds, were the teachers, doctors, dentists, drugstore and grocery and department store clerks—everyone Lauren had ever encountered, however fleetingly.

On the breast of each one was a name-card and, as her dream unfolded, she strove to read them, one by one, conscious of feeling frantic, of being given an impossible task. She was moving into the third row of relative strangers when she knew, in the special certitude of the nightmare world, that someone was behind her.

Faceless, garbed in peculiar clothing Lauren had never seen, stood three people in a descending rank of sizes. They said nothing to her, they did not even appear to realize she was there.

They simply lifted their arms to reveal odd tubular constructions which lay in the palms of their hands—and began firing them. No sound accompanied the violent gesture. There was only a feeling Lauren had that something was being discharged from the tubes, something powerful and destructive . . . and the certainty that her family, friends, and acquaintances were being killed!

She cried out, shouted at them to stop; but then something very peculiar happened: Instead of Pop, and Mom, and the others dropping in the gracelessness of death, Lauren became aware that an exact number of people stood in the distance—and as the noiseless, devastating tubular fire struck her loved ones and acquaintances, the OTHER people, draped in shadows, began to explode and disappear!

She tried to awaken, then, to open her eyes and sit up.

But she couldn't do it until she saw the mammoth, gleaming UFO on the horizon climb slowly into the black sky, hover above her for a terrifying instant, and then careen silently into the far depths of space.

Before she struggled to consciousness, she realized she was entirely alone on the planet earth. . . .

Everyone Ginger Lloyd had met in her life was neatly lined up. Everybody was there, from Dan and her parents to Spence, April and Lauren Torrence; from the girls she had competed against in tennis to chance acquaintances. Each person wore a name-card but Ginger could not make

112

them all out and squirmed against her Danny, in bed, faintly whimpering. She began panting heavily when she saw three faceless figures behind her, each of them raising a tubular weapon and firing pointblank at her world of associates and companions. *Other* people, on the sidelines, fell to the earth and vanished. Ginger cried out, and Dan began to shake her.

Even with his arms around her, with her eyes wide open, she saw every detail of the glittering spacecraft as it soared into the sky. "I'm going to be left," she screamed, "left *alone!*" She clung to his neck with the abandoned emotions of a small child. "Don't go, Danny—*don't go!*"

CHAPTER NINE

Henry Clurge had enjoyed reading science-fiction when he was a boy and a young man. He'd read the grand masters—Bradbury, Arthur C. Clarke, Fredric Brown, Richard Matheson and others—and found to his surprise a rather sludgy imagination opening a crack in his mind. Watching "Twilight Zone" and "Star Trek" on television, the crack had spread and, when he was eighteen years old, Henry Clurge began writing science-fiction stories.

They were, without exception, wretched things. Ham-handed, contrived, ludicrously implausible things with so little appreciation of science that magazine editors who were obliged to read them tended to skip lunch, down a bubbling Bromo, and fire the accursed manuscripts back to Henry. There was a point in the young man's life when, if he'd saved his rejection slips instead of angrily wadding them into balls or ripping them into shreds, he might have papered his walls with them.

By the time a decade had passed—sometime around Henry's twenty-eighth birthday—he bit the bullet, or laser gun. He gave up his great flirtation with that special Medusa-headed muse who flutters her lashes and whispers the siren call of time travel, swords and sorcery, parallel worlds, and futuristic societies. He booted her out and, creaking like the door in a haunted house, his inadequate imagination slammed shut. So far as Henry Clurge knew, it was closed, locked, and bolted for good, never to be reopened again.

Possessing rather limited career options by then, after the extensive expenditure of his time and effort on the writing of unprintable tales, Henry resorted to a friend's connections to get himself a job in a hotel. To his credit, Henry persevered; he learned the business. And four years later he found himself not only an efficient desk clerk, with the haughty airs and sniffing-nose characteristics of many men in his profession, but—to his utter astonishment—right back in the world of science-fiction.

Only this time, he'd realized with shock and more than a few moments of trepidation, the s-f was entirely *real*. There was no "f-for-fiction" to it.

Because Henry Clurge had become a desk clerk at the Hotel Holroyd.

Oh, it wasn't that Mr. and Mrs. Peter Quince flew through the corridors, passed through walls, or any of the other things Henry had once written—not, at least, in his presence. Everything functioned on a businesslike plane. He knew better than to mention to the Quinces that he'd caught a glimpse of their spacecraft and recognized it for what it was. What disturbed Henry was that he knew *they* knew he knew, and, concommitantly, he did *not* know what extraterrestrials wanted with an old hotel.

Alone in his own room, at night, when a woman named Martha Runyan came on duty, there were periods when Henry tried very hard to piece things together. Resorting to the same imagination that had proved inadequate for magazine acceptance, he'd sat at his desk with a pen and a stack of hotel stationery, scrawling possibilities and then burning the pages to ash. According to all the old stories and films, when an ordinary human being "knew too much," he had to be eliminated. But some of the same storylines suggested that if the human being could *get something* on the extraterrestrials, he might be able to blackmail his way to survival.

There was also the neat question of whether or not Henry was engaged in anything seditious or treasonable. While it was true that he didn't know what the Quince family was doing on his planet, some peculiar, *sinister* air exuded from them and he was reasonably sure they were up to no good. Remembering a whole range of stories about strange beings who occupied shadowy rooms in the houses of ordinary people, he could discern the problems with that style of approach and toyed with the idea that the Quinces were planning a country-wide hotel chain. That would be a vastly more practical way of bringing their kind into the cities. It would permit them, as well, to have places for mass numbers of aliens to stay and live

116

the way they chose to. But the condition of the Holroyd, whether it had been refurbished or not, certainly did not argue for it as a "flag ship" for a whole fleet of hotels.

He'd considered, for several reflective evenings, the notion that the unobtrusive Quinces simply chose not to view the hotel *as* a hotel but saw it in their own bizarre terms. Maybe it was, to them, a living laboratory and they did not intend to perform any ghastly experiments on human beings but only wished to conduct a scientific study of the way human beings lived when they were away from home. God knew, Henry thought with disgust, a great many people seemed to forget the simplest rudiments of good manners when they stayed at a hotel. The "Star Trek" concept that an advanced world would probably be under strict orders not to interfere in the affairs of lesser beings always had sounded wonderfully *civilized*, to Henry Clurge—a fine, optimistic view indicating that people grew increasingly gentle and cultured, as they evolved.

For awhile, the desk clerk had watched people checking into the Holroyd, studying their faces to see if they might be extraterrestrials like the Quinces. He'd almost convinced himself that the place was being used as a prison for criminals, troublemakers. When a girl he'd known during his high school years checked in, during that period of Henry's careful guesswork, he'd abandoned that particular explanation without realizing that he had moved precisely one small step toward an understanding of the Quinces' intentions.

Then, when they dreamed-up an award week for writers like that nosy Spencer Torrence, Henry Clurge had become completely nonplussed. He wasn't too ignorant to realize that this was the primary reason the

Quinces had reopened the Hotel Holroyd. But why they had purposely set out to surround themselves with some of the most creative and penetrating, curious and investigative minds in the United States made him throw up his hands in confusion and despair.

Still, he mused as he hurried to catch up with "Mr. Quince" before the manager could unlock his glass-fronted door and disappear behind it, there were elements of delight in this new turn of events. Acceptance of himself as a writer had been Henry's primary *raison d'être* for ten years and he'd failed. The literary community hadn't wanted him. Now it was *he* who was on the inside and knew some of the secrets. If he played his cards right and kept his nose clean, someday when the mysterious activities at the Holroyd were over and the Quinces went back to wherever they came from, he might write a book that would make the whole literary establishment notice him. And if a few of these pompous writers were . . . *injured* . . . in the process, because of what Peter Quince was doing, that was something Henry Clurge felt he could live with.

"Yes? What is it?"

Henry saw the look of impatience on Quince's face, how cold the eyes were, and swallowed. "I was asked to deliver a message to you, sir," he said with titanic deference. "One of the guests—a Mr. Spencer Torrence—insists upon meeting you or . . . your wife. He said he'd be glad to come to your office or ask you to his room." Henry shrugged helplessly. "I didn't know what else to do but tell him I'd inform you of his wishes."

"Damnable temerity," the manager said beneath his breath, scowling.

"What was that, sir?"

The face of Peter Quince went blank. "Never mind; let it go. You did the right thing in notifying me of his intrusion. Good work, Clurge." He started to turn away but realized that the clerk was standing on the steps, staring up at him. He sighed. "Well, what is it? Is there more?"

"I need to know what to tell him if he asks again," Henry gulped.

"Tell him you delivered his message, of course," Quince snapped. What happened next froze the clerk where he stood, one hand clutching the railing for support. In an almost-rubbery flexing of muscles, without the telltale glint in the human eye that suggests a person has seen the humor in a situation, a smile clicked into place on the manager's face. Deep inside there came a dreadful *"ug-ug-ug"* sound that might have served as laughter, and the noise and the terrible smile drained Henry's face of color. When Quince's hand reached out to touch his shoulder, Henry needed to brace himself to keep from pulling spasmodically away. "So this Mr. Torrence desires to meet my wife and me, does he? Well, well, Henry,'" the awful smile widened. "I think we shall accommodate him. Eventually."

"I'll inform him, sir," the clerk replied, bobbing his head and darting back down the stairs. All the way across the lobby he felt Quince's remorseless, steady gaze boring into his back.

Why in the name of God didn't I notice that before? he thought as he raised a polished, wooden leaf and dove behind his desk. *Odd, odd, odd!* He looked up, when he dared, and the manager was no longer standing like an icon on the stairway. As idly as he could, Henry turned his head to peer up at the one-way mirror fronting

119

Quince's office, and shuddered. Now, the manager's face, its image, was clear in Henry's mind; dominant, and frightening. He knew he'd never forget it again. *This is the damnedest thing I've ever seen in my life.* He began sorting mail, his hands trembling. *And why should it be this way? Why, and how?*

For the next hour, deep in his tortured, private thoughts, Henry Clurge tried to come up with a way in which Spence Torrence, a resident of Porter, New York, might have a relative in the person of an extraterrestrial from God-knew-where. . . .

By that Wednesday afternoon, Ginger Lloyd was almost as bored and restless as she was apprehensive. For twenty minutes she had been sitting in a chair by the hotel window, staring outside at the dismally quiet, continuing fall of snow. With everything else happening, it lacked reality for her; it seemed so unlikely with the month of April less than a week away. Some of the stuff had drifted on the ice-cold hands of a periodic whining wind until a hillock of glistening white reached halfway up the wall of the Holroyd toward her hotel room. It was easy to believe that there was something *purposeful* about it, that the damned crap was forming a mountain that someone could climb to get at her. Anywhere she looked, below the window, there was more than a foot of packed snow; and nowhere Ginger looked could she see either footprints or the tread of a determined vehicle.

Danny, thank God, appeared to have recovered from his strange behavior. He'd stopped talking about the pulsating walls, and muttering about messages being sent to influence writers, and gone out with Spence to attend a few informal get-togethers in other writers' rooms. It was, Ginger reflected, not the nicest thing she'd ever done to disbelieve what Danny was saying when he'd always been so nice about her own gifts as a sensitive. But unless he'd lied to her, which she doubted he ever had, even once, Danny's life was utterly devoid of psychic experiences. There was just no *basis* for him to begin receiving otherworldly messages when she, herself, had been incapable of detecting anything odd about the walls.

Clearly, she ruminated, not without tenderness and concern, it was only a peculiar reaction to his moment of impotency. Poor, sweet, romantic Danny, she sighed. Ever since she was a girl Ginger had heard that men in their middle years began to suffer a decline in their sexual proficiency. It wasn't surprising, or in any way meaningful, Ginger decided, for Danny to fall prey to the same human condition that they all must face. And if he couldn't do it any longer, well, she could live with that. It was the whole Dan Lloyd she loved, not just his sexuality. Men always made so much of making love that it was ridiculous.

Why didn't he notice how *cold* it was, she thought as she arose and walked to the television set, instead of babbling about the hotel taking away his manhood and sending Morse code or something through the walls? She drew her robe closer around her shoulders and tried the TV again.

Since they'd arrived, Monday night, the darned contraption had been on the blink with half the other things in the Hotel Holroyd. Ginger wasn't an ardent TV fan but it irked her that she was unable to watch it when she wanted to. Fine tuning, to the best of her ability, she saw the snowy freckles on the screen begin to part and smiled her pleasure. It wasn't a great picture, and the sound was so soft she needed to kneel in front of the set to hear; but it was *some* contact with the outer world, and, she realized, it was a news program.

A moonfaced, affable man with shiny eyes—the caption at the bottom of the screen identified him as Bob Gregory—was standing before a weather board. The picture was one of such normality Ginger could have cried out with joy.

"Well, it's been another beautiful spring day in town," he said, beaming on his audience, "as I'm sure you've noticed. Temperature in the upper sixties and no precipitation of any kind to mar your outdoors pleasure."

Ginger's mouth opened. *Beautiful spring day? Upper sixties? Outdoors pleasure?* She reached for Monday's newspaper, leaving the TV on, and hurriedly located the television log. Perhaps this was an out-of-town weather forecast, she thought, a program from Cincinatti or Louisville.

But there was a photograph of Bob Gregory beneath the log. And the number of his channel was the same as that to which she'd turned the hotel television. Disoriented, she glanced at the window and saw the enormous flakes continued to drift by.

"But there's a rare anomaly in one part of town," Bob Gregory said. Ginger pressed her ear against the set, listening harder than she'd ever listened before. "To the amazement of the weather bureau and, I must admit, the amazement of forecasters and meteorologists all around the city, *snow is falling on one block of town.* Yes, there's a considerable accumulation—nearly sixteen inches, we're told—in the square on which the Gallows picture framing store, the B. Dalton book store, the Hotel Holroyd, and the Hook's Drug Store are trying valiantly

122

to do business. It's heavy with ice, as well, and reports inform us that few people are getting in and out of those establishments at all."

Ginger gaped at the screen, detected the puzzled emotions of the pleasant fellow at the weatherboard. The notion that the snowfall was somehow *deliberate*—that *someone or something was trying to keep them all from leaving the hotel*—became so irresistibly convincing that she knew, in her psychic's terrified heart, that it was true.

"Got to admit we're at a loss right now to explain it, folks," Bob admitted ruefully. Then, incredibly, he took a step toward the camera and winked. "But my hat is doffed to Jack Frost or whatever little wintry gremlins brought this last-ditch snowy dump to the good people over at the Holroyd. I'm going to accept it as Snowfall Number 51 for this winter—and that brings my annual prediction to within one of a perfect score!"

Almost in tears, Ginger switched off the set. "Damn you," she whispered, looking at the window. "Damn you!"

As gently and quietly as a casket-lid being lowered, the snow continued to fall.

April Torrence was in the bathroom, putting up her long, dark hair. Lauren glanced toward the room, saw her mother's slender legs, heard her humming to herself. Lauren growled, "Shit and damnation," and got up to go out to the front room.

It hadn't meant much to Mom that poor old Puck wasn't the same anymore. She had hugged Lauren, given her a bunch of sympathetic looks. But she'd also laughed at the importance of the matter. "Your kitten is up and

123

around, feeling in fine fettle," she'd said. "Frankly, honeybunch, I think Puck looks prettier with that nice white streak."

Lauren hadn't expressed her own impression—that her cat looked more to her now like a skunk, than a kitten—or tried again to convince Mom that what she'd said about the intense, glaring light was true. What was it about grown-ups anyway? They sold little kids a bill of goods about Santa Claus, and wanted 'em to believe whatever they said about religion. They told kids a million times not to lie, and reassured them that they could *always* come to Mom and Pop with a problem of any kind. But when *you* believed something different, when you were a kid—when you'd seen strange things with your own eyes and told them the exact *truth*—they treated you like bein' locked up was the next logical step. She'd gone to Mom and Pop with her problems of a very different kind, even produced a real-life *cat* as proof, and it just made her look weird.

Well, the truth was that Lauren believed Pop *sort-of* bought her story. Not everything, because he couldn't tie it all up with his own beliefs and the things he'd known and seen in his life; but enough to know how scared she was.

But instead of trying to figure it out, he'd just asked a few questions and this afternoon, when Uncle Dan showed up, the two of 'em forgot the whole thing and went off to talk writer stuff. Writer crap; Lauren made a face as she headed for the door. Writer shit-and-damnation.

She thought she'd go down to the gift shop and browse around. After all, she'd promised Grandma Torrence she'd bring back a souvenir and they'd only be here in this stuffy hotel another few days. If she didn't want Grandma to think she was a liar, too, she'd better go see if she could find something decent for four dollars or less.

Clutching her purse, Lauren opened the door leading to the corridor.

The Hotel Girl—the look-alike child—was an inch away! Except for the flecks of red in her pupils, which showed when she turned her head, she was even more like Lauren than she'd believed she was at a distance. But Lauren couldn't ever remember having an expression like the one on the Hotel Girl's face. An expression that was . . . hungry, malicious, and insulting. An expression of hatred that made Lauren want to slam the door and go hide under the bed.

"Who *are* you?" Lauren asked, scarcely able to project her voice across the eons of universal distance that seemed to separate them despite their physical proximity. She licked her lips, finding them dry, unwilling to form the words. "What d-do you *want?*"

"*You,*" replied the Hotel Girl. The index finger of her pale right hand shot forward, striking Lauren between her budding breasts. A small but distinct electrical shock flowed from the finger into Lauren's bosom and she cried out with pain. The Hotel Girl, imitating her, licked her own lips and they shone with spittle as she leaned forward as if she meant to kiss Lauren. "You're *mine!*"

Lauren slammed the door.

From the other side she heard the sound of childish laughter, a maniacal, *killing* sound that filtered through the heavy door and rang like the hilarity of a torturer in Lauren's ears.

She saw Puck, cowering at her feet.

He was snow-white from head to tail.

CHAPTER TEN

Lie quietly upon your bed, alone, and watch the sun come up, slipping like a harem maiden through the drapes at your window. If you have slept well—if you have forgotten your nightmares, the random turnings and twistings of night—you are linked to other elements of a special moment. All the adhesive traces of your yesterdays remain but you find sleep has slipped them into files of perspective, and you do not yet have the obligation—it is so early—to draw them out and begin your worry.

Parting from the warm embrace of sleep, your senses

are only beginning to come alert this Thursday morning and yet, having slept in peace, you do not think to question whether they will or not. You know they will; there is no doubt. You possess, in this instant shared with so much more, a confidence of oneness with your world. As the sun has risen, again, and day becomes your transient mate, there is a part of you that admits—ruefully, almost, for you are part of this time, on this planet of skepticism—that just as the sun and moon always rise, so will you.

Now, you do not think of yourself as anything extraordinary, unless it is some special distinction of your individual achievement, some excellence you've been granted or have developed. It is enough to be integral, an element in the cosmos; it is enough to be mind, now, instead of brain; it is enough to sense that while there is a "you" in occupancy of your unseen thoughts, something precious and unpriced and liberated, in a larger sense the brain beneath your mind, and the body beneath that heavy brain, are linked inextricably to a vastness that will be forgotten and rendered insignificant the moment you stir, and sit. A second longer you float above the ocean of the commonplace, at peace.

The Selector floats stoically in its glass container, face down. It does not have to concern itself about drowning because its existence is sustained by a complicated variety of means ranging from the mammalian and piscean to the harder connecting tissue of wire and mechanical cell. It has not slept well for it has not slept at all, never has and never will. For the Selector there are no clinging traces of yesterday because it knows the moment, alone; only the moment.

It does not worry, and will not, because everything the

127

Selector wishes to do, to know, or be, has already been perfectly achieved.

There is no fear of this day, or of tomorrow; because its life is artificial except for a low, throbbing echo of parts that were once vital and vibrant. There is no fear of death, because that which is not totally alive cannot totally die.

It has seen the sun rise on many planets, and many suns rise on the same planet. It has felt the rays of a dozen moons lambent in a night sky that endures for years, and it has never been moved to song. Unlike you, it is not a part of anything except others of its kind and lacks the experience to know loneliness or apartness. But it knows it will rise, today and all other days. All that it has is its individual accomplishment, a feat of receiving the murmuring messages that permeate the universe; for it knows that the ether Man once believed slid like syrup throughout space is nothing more than *data*—the collected thoughts of beings who were just born, and those who were born, and died, millenia ago.

A second longer the Selector floats above the ocean of the cosmos, at war.

Despite what Lauren believed, that he had conducted a futilely brief and cursory investigation of the peculiar events occurring at the Hotel Holroyd, Spence Torrence had actually continued to seek information on Tuesday and again on Wednesday.

On the latter day, filled with misgivings about bringing-up matters beyond the normal, he'd discussed the subject at several gatherings of writers. Dan Lloyd pitched in his help, after the Tuesday when he'd remained with Ginger in his suite, even though Spence felt there was something

128

Dan was keeping from him. There was, of course; his inexplicable impotency and the heartbeat *throbbing* activity Dan had felt from behind the walls. Knowing nothing of these matters, Spence was both gratified and surprised when the hefty science writer who'd been his companion for so many years—who had always served as Spence's conscience of reality, of fact—spoke with candor and persuasiveness.

Wherever they went in the hotel, however, both on Tuesday and Wednesday, it proved to be ultimately fruitless with only a few exceptions. Reminded of how old the place was, and seeing how matters were affecting Spence and Dan, mystery writers remarked how fine a building this would be for murder. Romance novelists got dreamy-eyed conceiving love affairs between young women and reincarnated lovers from earlier existences; horror writers became glassy-eyed as they considered how atmospheric was the refurbished hotel, and how grand a place it would be to slay a dozen or two of their helpless characters. But in terms of believing that odd, unexplained things were going on, the peers of Spence and Dan politely changed the subject.

In other groups they visited, writers with a formal theological bent scoffed at the idea of any kind of unseen threat, whether the formerly-dead or the visiting alien; while Dan's peers in science brushed them off with their concretized denial of anything remotely paranormal or otherworldly. A tall and distinguished gentleman named Max Saperstein, who wrote both books and columns for the public explaining psychology in terms of urging a conscious selection of our obsessions as an avenue to achievement, found Danny and Spence privately interesting. He listened to everything they had to say. When he surreptitiously brought out a pen and notebook, and asked them "What do *you* think?" they left the room with embarrassment and alacrity.

Yet there *were* two events, on Wednesday morning, that provided support for the concern Spence and Dan were voicing. While they were listening to a muscular middle-aged man with bushy silver hair speaking animatedly about a protegé who was both murderous and "incredibly talented," a heavyset man sitting nearby— identifying himself as a dramatist and translator—asked them if they had seen the fabled "Pop" Cormach. "I'd almost swear I saw him signing in," the fellow stated with obvious worry, "but I haven't seen him since and the desk clerk claims he never arrived."

Then, sitting on the outskirts of a genteel political dialogue involving a loquacious, versatile, and pencil-tapping conservative and a southern socialist whom Spence and Dan didn't recognize, they saw an overly made-up but stunningly striking female poet motioning for them to join her in the corridor outside. "I believe you're onto something," she stated without preamble. Her full lips pressed together and she seemed pale. Spence, observing the courage battling with fear in her brown eyes, thought they must be ordinarily lovely beyond compare. "Harry Werlin was here, I'd swear it," she continued. "I'd know that pretender to genius any-where and I saw Werlin and his wife on the elevator." She shivered. "But they say at the registration desk that the Werlins remained in seclusion. I made a few inquiries after that, gentlemen, and it seems to me that they've disappeared."

Disappeared. A frightening word, when you stopped to think of it. Spence tried to tune-out his family and friends this Thursday morning. He understood that they were conversing lightly and amiably because it wasn't natural to live in fear and they wanted to block out what was happening. But what the beautiful poet said to Spence brought the problem into perspective for him, gave him something to analyze. While he hadn't eaten breakfast yesterday morning, he had stopped at the restaurant and had the inspiration to take a head count of the writers who were present then.

After all, the truth of the matter was that most people who shoved words around for a living were either ill-paid or obliged periodically to exist on a "feast or famine" basis. When the royalty check came in, usually more than a year after publication of a book, or a sizeable advance for a new sale, there might be plenty of cash to go around. But when publishers were obliged to delay the processing of a check, writers working full-time at their craft sometimes struggled through literally penniless episodes. Free meals, three times a day, were definitely part of the attraction when invitations to the Hotel Holroyd awards were received. And it seemed to Spence that the writers who'd come were not likely to pass up an unlimited, cost-free breakfast, whether it tasted bland the way it seemed to him or delicious as Dan Lloyd oddly appeared to consider it.

Yet yesterday morning, when Spence glanced around the hotel restaurant, he had been startled to see that the number of writers and their companions coming to breakfast was strangely *diminishing*.

Now he tried to begin piecing it together. Each table, he noted, sat up to six people. He and Danny had estimated that at least seventy-five members of the writing community came to town, and that each of them

131

was accompanied by at least *one* second person. One-hundred and fifty guests, therefore, were presumably present in the restaurant on Day One, Tuesday morning. There were twenty-five tables available and they'd been crammed.

But Wednesday, the second morning—yesterday— Spence had seen that four tables weren't being used at all. Twenty-four people *not* present and accounted for.

Feeling Ginger's watchful eyes on his face, but knowing nothing of her psychic gifts, Spence looked around the restaurant now as casually as he could.

He barely stifled a gasp.

No one at all *was sitting at ten of the dining tables.*

He counted methodically in his head, found himself so worried that he had to start over. There were, by actual count, *sixty-six human beings* present in the hotel dining room this morning.

Where the hell had everybody else *gone?*

Alistair Copeland Cummings couldn't say that he'd enjoyed his stay at the Hotel Holroyd to date. It wasn't so much that he was accustomed to much finer things, since the young part-Indian's success was still recent enough that he could recall his humble beginnings without a mammoth memory-stretch.

But he wanted, very much indeed, to forget the past entirely and the gloomy, cavernous, almost-institutional hotel in which he found himself stuck for most of a week reminded him with no trouble at all of how close he remained to the nobody he'd been.

Wednesday afternoon, as a consequence, Al Cummings had permitted his insecurity-motivated, compulsive desire to work its head. He'd crammed his six-foot,

132

seven-inch bulk into a singularly uncomfortable chair before the desk, opened the case of his electric typewriter and plugged it in, then began laying out a storyline for his next TV motion picture.

It seemed to the hawk-nosed screenwriter that a controversial major issue was taking shape involving the increasing number of strikes in professional sport. Athletes meant plenty of ways to work-in titillating sexual scenes, when it came time for that. But at the outset he felt he should establish his own viewpoint, one that he could utilize to "hook" an audience. And as easily as that he realized that huge numbers of people resented the fact that athletes tended to earn more than one-hundred-thousand dollars a year.

Okay, he'd said with excitement, agreeing with himself, *this bigshot athlete signs a fantastic contract, but he has this sweet little grayhaired mom in Indianapolis or Duluth or somewhere, and he doesn't help her, he lets her live on social security. But he has this gorgeous actress-groupie he wants to marry—and she's out of his class, socially, so we get lots of conflict going . . .*

He'd worked hard and enthusiastically until after midnight, gobbled down some tasteless food he called down for, and slept the sleep of the industrious, the just, the creative. An undefiled work-machine of sheer originality.

But this morning when he awakened, Al didn't feel undefiled. He felt as if he'd gotten drunk at the big party scene he was planning for his teleplay—huge-headed, sore all over, vaguely nauseated. He dressed, including a suit and tie, largely to impress Alistair Copeland Cummings with what a mature and dignified guy he was. He'd worked under worse handicaps than those. He'd finish the storyline in rough, then go downstairs for some chow. Freddie Silversmith was supposed to be in this joint and he could buy Freddie another cup of coffee and maybe talk a little business. But first, he had to have the whole story in his head. And that meant another hour or two of early-morning work.

When he switched on his electric typewriter Al noticed that he'd caught the tip of his twenty-dollar tie in the roll bar and raised a brow in surprise. He'd been pounding at keyboards since he was a kid and this was the first time that had happened. Annoyed, he put out his right hand to roll his tie free.

But when he turned it, toward him, there was something wrong with the operation of the machine. Instead of freeing his tie, the darned thing tugged at him and brought his face forward a good two inches.

Absurd thing to happen, Al mused, and yanked at his tie. It held fast. He decided to turn off the power on the typewriter and hit the switch, but nothing happened except that the machine made a loud, angry sound. Now what the hell?

Out of the corner of his eye he saw his scissors resting on the edge of the desk. Al always did a lot of pasteups as he worked. When a page of work was three-quarters the way he wanted it, he felt it was wasting time to type the whole thing over. Instead, he'd revise the remaining quarter on a second piece of paper, then paste or Scotch tape it onto the original. If he could reach the scissors, well, he'd just cut the tie in two in order to get back to work.

But before he could implement his plan Al felt the roll bar *lurch*, sickeningly, and saw the carriage shoot to the left—as it yanked his face forward, and pressed his large nose against the typing paper. He cried out, both in irritation and something else: fear. It had just occurred to him that if he didn't extricate himself from this ludicrous snare, the damned typewriter and the electrical current which powered it might conceivably break his neck . . .

If there had been, at the core of Al Cummings' being, a greater detachment from ego—or a closer commitment to the regulations of reality, and the imperative of the impossible—he might have saved himself. What had begun to happen to him, in a certain sense on the higher planes of actuality, could not happen at all. But in common with most people, Al believed absolutely that which he saw with his own eyes and, in particular, he believed wholly in the pain he felt—a pain created by his willingness to acknowledge the way his neck seemed unnaturally bent. That was the genuine hold which the extraterrestrial "Peter Quince" held over Al, and the others staying at the Hotel Holroyd: that even educated or creative people, whatever they said, were not yet sure on planet earth, what was possible and what was impossible at any given time. It was the secret of magic all magicians, all shamans, all science-fiction writers and all authors of fantasy and horror, sensed from the moment they began their work—the precious, amazing secret that, if you involved another person intimately after you had set matters askew and made the bold proposal of an alternate universe, you could tell them anything and they would believe it. The secret was nothing more nor less than the way a gifted man could turn illusion into an acceptance of reality.

Looking about for a way to save himself, Al rejoiced. The telephone, the cord within reach of his long legs! He had written corny scenes like this, watched the fictitious kidnap victim, twined in rope, use his foot to kick over the telephone and mumble a hasty plea for help. Sure,

135

when he yelled for assistance and they came up to his room, it would become a richly embarrassing situation. But unlike Harry Werlin, Al Cummings didn't have a lot of pride. He only wanted this ended so he could get back to work and again be the small-town part-Indian boy who saw a play he'd written on the television screen. Al lashed out with his right leg—

And the typewriter, muttering fiercely to itself, yanked— hard.

Instant pain lurched from the back of his neck, at the top of the spine, pulling a liquid, anguished scream from Al Cummings' throat. His head was forced at an almost impossible angle, one temple jammed between the tape cartridges; and the pressure was nearly enough to suffocate him. The tie felt like a second Adam's apple; it cut like wire. For a moment he saw black spots before his eyes and faced the fact that he might well *die* in this silly position.

Yet a part of Al that might well have been the latent Indian element reasoned with him that a man who'd come as far and as fast as he had should be able to devise a way of not being killed by a goddamned *machine!* Tugging in a breath, ignoring the agony in his neck and throat, he formulated an emergency plan: He would raise the typewriter in his arms and struggle over to where the cord was plugged into the wall, then curl his toe beneath it and pull the cord from the wall, shutting off the current. When that was done, he'd take off down the hall looking for assistance; for somebody who could cut his tie in two.

He wrapped his long arms round the typewriter, grunting, and forgetting a crucial fact: Just as it was a dumb magician who gave away the secret to his magic, it was a dumb magician's volunteer who told the magician

136

everything he needed to know. And Al already had seen evidence that what he was thinking was being heard.

That was when his head suddenly began being *sucked* into the roll bar!

There wasn't even enough time to shout or scream again.

For quite a while the typewriter churned, apparently never having been placed under an injunction not to speak with its mouth full. To anyone who'd been there to hear it might have sounded, at first, as if it were *chewing*. The bar continued turning, the way a fisherman reels-in his line; and then it was over. *Other* sounds emerged, reminiscent of digestion occurring; and the keys began typing of their own accord.

It wasn't a lengthy communication. When it stopped, when the power died at last, there were only two words typed on the page Al had inserted into the typewriter: THE END.

Silence came. Alistair Cummings' suite was empty.

CHAPTER ELEVEN

Lauren ate her breakfast quietly, without looking up. It didn't taste good, and she was worried about Puck, and she couldn't stop thinking about the Hotel Girl telling her "You're mine!" but she didn't want to make a ruckus—Mom liked to call it that, sometimes, and Pop once had drawn a sketch of a comical monster which he labeled "The Ruckus"—since nobody quite believed her anyway.

But out of the corner of her eye she could see Aunt Ginger's pretty face, and how drawn it looked. Both of them saw how hard Pop was working, ignoring his morning coffee and scribbling all over napkins, even the menu; and neither one of them wanted to disturb him. Perhaps he'd found out more than Lauren knew; maybe he'd figured out a way to break free the snowy walls that continued to press against the hotel and over the icy streets to the airport. Right then, Lauren wanted to go back home, to Porter, more than she'd ever wanted anything in the world. *You're mine.* What had the look-alike meant? In what *way* was she the property of the Hotel Girl? What did the Hotel Girl intend to *do* with her property?

Lauren turned her head to stare across the dining room at the windows. The day was colorless, but it was more than that. There was something *waiting to be said,* and it rose like skeletal bones from the mountains of snow; something evil, and it had to do with all the writers like Pop and Uncle Dan in the hotel, with the way the food tasted bad, with poor Puck turning white along the top and the terrible nightmares she was having and the light they'd seen—and with the Hotel Girl who looked like Lauren, and who certainly was involved in the colorless, pregnant evil at the windows.

She saw Aunt Ginger look where she was looking, across the room at the frosted windows, and for a tiny moment—for a flickering instant Lauren *knew* was real, and genuine, however impossible it seemed—she sensed some kind of *mind contact* with her lovely blonde make-believe Aunt. It was an odd feeling, really; like being naked, completely exposed to another human being; except she knew Aunt Ginger liked her and she didn't mind, somehow. Instead, she sensed that Aunt Ginger also had things on her mind—and something she wanted to say when Pop stopped his scribbling. . . .

139

It looked to Spence as if eighty-two people had not shown up for the day's free breakfast. But okay, he thought, nodding to himself and no longer realizing that the others had stopped conversing and were watching him, let's draw a few logical assumptions. Let's say that of the one-hundred-and-fifty people who came to the Holroyd for awards week, four became so fed-up with the conditions and the food they used their own resources to move to another hotel. He'd considered it, except that beginning this afternoon there'd be a few formal meetings and he hadn't wanted to commute. Let's say, Spence reflected, another two people became ill and left the Holroyd—either to go to the hospital, or to go home. It certainly made sense that Quince, the manager, wouldn't want to make a point of it. Hotel operators weren't eager to let their patrons think something about their hotels might cause illness. And throw in another two people who had some kind of urgent business to take care of at home, matters that developed unexpectedly after they had already come: sick people at home; rush contracts for new books; a royalty check coming-in which they couldn't wait to get. That made a total of eight people who'd left the Holroyd of their own volition and could not take advantage of the gratuitous meals.

That still left—his right hand described circles, from the wrist, as he calculated—that still left *seventy-four* of the one-hundred-and-fifty people who appeared to be gone! Spence inhaled sharply. Seventy-four people who had—

Had *what?* Been kidnapped? Vanished into thin air? . . . Dear God, *died?*

And if so, if they *had* died, what had they died *from?* Unless there was a resurgence of the Black Death, the bubonic plague, there wasn't a group of one-hundred-and-fifty people anywhere which would be cut in *half* by natural death in only a few days—not if they were all eighty years old and up!

"Are you all right?"

Close to surprised thåt anyone else was around, Spence blinked at April, grew aware of her slender hand pressing the top of his. "Sure," he said shortly. "I'm great." *But for how long?* he added in his mind.

"Spence, honey, what is it?" She was whispering, more for the sake of propriety than to keep Lauren, Dan and Ginger from hearing. She leaned close to him. "What have you been doing? What's wrong?"

"Let it be a bit longer, all right?" He kissed her cheek. "Let me just think this over another moment."

In roughly three days that they'd all had rooms at the Hotel Holroyd, seventy-four people were . . . *gone*, disappeared. That was an average of about twenty-five each day. At the present attrition rate, with approximately seventy-six people remaining, and two days left before the closing ceremonies—*why, there'd be almost nobody left at all by Saturday night!*

The nation's finest writers, in every conceivable field of expression, would vanish from sight *as if they had never come to the Holroyd at all!* Writers, Spence thought as his heart filled with horror, and those with them. People like April and Lauren Torrence, Dan and Ginger Lloyd.

"What are you doin', pal?" It was Dan, his long-time, beloved friend Dan. For an instant Spence could see the balding man in his coffin, the perpetual cigar gone out forever, the puffy, affable features he knew so well sinking into the earth inside a lead-lined box. Spence's eyes stung with sudden tears, not only for Dan but

141

because it had just occurred to him that *he* would never see Dan's descent into the ground—because he'd be nearby, in another casket. "Are you finally planning that novel you always wanted to write?"

Spence looked up. April was applying fresh lipstick, her plate of bacon and eggs pushed back, half-eaten. Ginger and Lauren were locked in conversation. He winked at Dan, shook his head slightly to warn him of his desire for secrecy. "Just noodling, Danny. Look, you and I'll be taking in a lot of fine seminars this afternoon. I'm sure already I'd like to get some feedback from you. How about setting-up an appointment for our own rap session in the lounge, say, at nine o'clock tonight?" He watched April and Ginger tune back in to what he was saying. "You don't mind, do you ladies, if a coupla old pals have a few drinks together?"

April gave him a grin. "You're just trying to get even with me for that night in New York when Mike Nichols asked a few other people and me to his apartment for a gabfest. Actors only." She squeezed his hand. "You're safe with the science expert, pal. Dan'll let you know when you've had too much."

Dan turned to Ginger. "What about you, babe? Any objection to Spence and me downing a few tonight for old time's sake?" His glance met Spence's. Something was up, he was sure of that, and he couldn't wait to hear what his friend had to say. "You'll know where we are since we're trapped in this crazy house by the snow."

"No, you're not," Ginger blurted out.

"What did you say?" April asked, looking with surprise at the other woman. "Did you hear a weatherman say the snow would all melt away this afternoon?"

Ginger looked at the brunette, then slowly swiveled

142

her head to take them all in. *"I heard a weatherman say it's a beautiful spring day."*

When they permitted her to continue, she explained to them what she had heard on the news program. They gaped at her, stunned.

"Then it can't be real snow," Spence exclaimed, frowning. "It must be an illusion of some kind. Things like that don't happen."

"That isn't exactly true," said Dan, lighting a fresh cigar. "Just when meteorologists think they've figured all the angles out, when they've just spent half-a-million dollars for the shiniest new equipment, freak storms go right on happening. Take the famous great blizzard that hit the eastern seaboard in March of '88. It was supposed to be a fairly tough storm, sure, but nobody anywhere predicted what happened. There were four-hundred people killed by that freak snowfall." He blew out the match, dropped it in the glass tray. "A little over a year later was when the Johnstown Flood hit Pennsylvania. Over two-thousand people lost their lives in that baby."

"But that's not the same as snowfalls limited to a single block or two," Spence argued, leaning back in his chair and tapping his fingers on the table. "Is it?"

"No, but it's happened nonetheless." Dan shrugged. "I can't give you facts and figures off the top of my head. But my guess is, the snow is genuine."

"One thing about that, Danny," Ginger put in, touching his wrist.

"What's that?"

"The snow might be entirely real," she replied, lowering her gaze, "but still *caused*. Induced, created, by—someone else."

"But why?" April asked. "Why would anybody *want*

to make snow kneedeep around the Hotel Holroyd?"

"That's an easy one that doesn't require a scientist," Spence answered. "For the very fact that's happened: To keep us all from leaving the hotel." He looked at Dan and saw a faint nod, even a tremor of anxiety. "To *trap* us, and keep us here as long as they want."

He didn't add, aloud, the way his thought ended. *To trap and pick us off, one-by-one, until nobody's left come Saturday.*

He waited another five minutes, to make sure Lauren was really sound asleep, and then opened the bathroom door. Wide.

Left that way, with he and April at the foot of the bed, Lauren couldn't see what he wanted to do with her mother.

"Just hold me for a few minutes," April whispered to him, a totally uncharacteristic whimper in her voice. Both of them were naked under the covers and she was shivering with the cold, her long legs touching him, chilly against his skin. But he knew that being cold wasn't why she asked him to hold her. "I've t-tried so hard not to let my imagination run away with me, but I c-can't help the way I feel. Spence, I think something terrible is happening in this place. I think s-somebody doesn't like writers and their families."

He lay her head on his shoulder and knew at once that it was a mistake. It always had been, because April wore her hair long and it unfailingly tickled his neck and cheeks. But he wanted to comfort her, and he liked her close to him that way. "It's hard to know how much of it is our imagination and how much of it is really . . . inexplicable."

"I don't think it's 'inexplicable' at all!" she exclaimed, raising her voice. "I think someone is behind it. Someone very malicious. If we could get to him, this might yet turn out to be a pleasant week."

In the dark, Spence smiled. One of the things he liked about April was her shifting sense of proportions. When she was under the spell of one mood, she was convinced that they were all going to die. When the mood shifted, the slightest fraction of an emotional inch, she could suddenly become just as worried that their vacation might be ruined.

Through the years, of course, he had helped her learn to get control of her tendency to over-dramatize matters. That was what she had meant by saying how hard she'd tried not to let her imagination run away. By now, Spence suspected, unless someone put a million dollars in April's palm or pointed a gun at her, he wasn't sure she *knew* when to be happy and when to be unhappy. Everything about her, he realized, hugging her, was a series of contradictions. On one level she was still the talented, aspiring actress, as self-involved as any sex-kitten starlet; on another, she could be the calmest, most reasonable of wives and mothers.

"I have a few things to discuss with Dan, if you'll remember," he said slowly, wanting neither to alarm nor encourage her. "Some notions. If we compare notes, maybe we can come up with an answer or two." He hesitated, grimacing. "God knows I got nothing useful out of this afternoon's seminars. I don't know whether it's because writers all look at a matter from their own professional bias, and can't allow their ideas to blend with those of other writers, or merely that meetings of all kinds are a monumental waste of time."

145

"Don't go," she said in her afternoon voice. With her training, it surely carried. "Don't leave Lauren and me alone up here!"

"Sh-h," he cautioned her, turning on his side to her and putting his palm over her left breast. "There's no other choice. Honey, I—I think some of the writers here have gone home or something."

"Gone home?" she asked, her dark eyes inches from his face. "You mean—disappeared. Unaccounted for?"

"Well, accounted for by *me*," he replied, stressing the syllable. "That's what I want to check out with Dan. See if he had any ideas to explain it. Run one of mine by him." He kissed her mouth, felt her wide lips open for him. "You'll be okay for an hour or two. Just don't allow anyone in, anyone at all."

"Should I allow you in?" she giggled. "Now?"

"Try to keep me out," he said with a low chuckle.

But something *did* stop him. Conscious of wanting her, experiencing the same sensations he'd always known when he made love to April, he found himself failing to become aroused.

"Let me," she whispered, perceiving his problem.

A moment later she rose above him, a sight that had never failed to stimulate Spence. With her long, dark hair down her bare back, the lower section of her body hot against him, he'd always loved reaching up for her full breasts, cupping and gently squeezing them. They were, he thought, at their most beautiful in the shadows of night, above his line of vision with their smoothly-rounded underside making them look enormous and their dark-blackened broad nipples deliciously protruding.

As usual, he let his hands track down her sides, the

146

thumbs meeting at the hollow of her navel, dropping into the moist, furry nest of April, seeing—always with something like awe—the way their bodies converged. But this time, despite the excitement he found as fresh as it had been thirteen years ago, there was no way to build a bridge for their need, for their convergence as one. "Shit and damnation," he grumbled. "Shit! Dam*nation!*"

She drooped forward across his chest without her lower body leaving him, kissing his cheeks, his eyelids, his mouth. "It's just your worry," she soothed him. "It's only how afraid you are for us."

When she vanished from view and he felt her tongue lapping kitten-like the length of his chest, he knew the kindness she intended, and he knew it would do neither of them any good. Gently, he pushed her away and sat up. Head bowed, feeling useless and worse, feeling strangely *invaded,* he sighed and then arose to go into the bathroom.

The tile floor was chilly on his bare feet. He glanced into the mirror over the medicine cabinet, made a face at himself. "Old man," his lips formed the words, putting no sound to the phrase; "dried-up old man." He looked down on the counter extending from the turquoise tub, locating a glass still wrapped in its sanitary covering, and his glance fell on the wall.

The wall seemed . . . swollen, *pushed* outward—*and then, it retreated; and then, again, pushed* toward *him again as if it were made of skin.* Spence stared, then rubbed his eyes, and once more saw the bizarre process occur. It was as if the wall were *breathing*, as if it had become the chestwall of a massive hotel-beast and he, the prize-winning author, had somehow been—*swallowed.*

Touching it, carefully, ready to pull his hand back

CHAPTER TWELVE

Strolling quietly into the Hotel Holroyd cocktail lounge, Spence worked hard at trying to get his thoughts into some kind of functioning order. It was difficult to put behind him the extraordinary pulsations of the walls in his bathroom, and to ignore the cold fact of his impotency; and when he'd walked through the shadow-strewn west wing to the elevator, he'd had the eerie feeling of being observed—of *eyes* peeping out from the faded pictures on the walls lining the corridor. If he was wrong about the hotel, and the things that had occurred here were nothing more than freak incidents to be idly

149

discussed in an article some distant day in the future, his mental condition was no laughing matter. He'd truly gone paranoid and he'd probably spend his declining years on a psychiatrist's couch.

But after he had taken a step into the lounge, his old, warning tentacles of the Big Lie being boldly told him began to quiver and Spence found himself heading for the bar with all his senses alert.

At a glance, nothing about the place proclaimed its difference from any other hotel lounge in the country. Overworked waitresses in tiny skirts and mesh hose labored to keep a sparkle in their eyes and a smile on their lips. The noise of bottles and glasses lightly clinking was a familiar, unthreatening sound, and the plush red carpeting beneath his feet offered comfort. Even the relative darkness of the lounge was as it should be—

Unless you were an investigative author whose imagination was boundless, and who genuinely believed that he could almost *smell* a situation that wasn't quite as it should be.

This lounge, Spence decided, contained a darkness that seemed to seep up from subterranean caverns deep in the bowels of the earth. If Hell itself had a cocktail lounge, this was the way it would seem. Because it wasn't so much a case of *repressing* light, or the ordinary blackness of nine o'clock at night, as it was a matter of unnatural darkness *entering* the large room. A small distinction, maybe, he told himself, but it was there. In one's own bedroom, upon retiring, there was a dismissal of illumination. But in the Holroyd lounge, the blackness of night seemed to rush up from below the feet and virtually *overcome* the few pale bulbs glowing futilely here and there.

150

This hotel is haunted, he admitted grimly to himself, spotting Dan Lloyd's broad shoulders and wending his way to his friend; *and Lauren was right to wonder what is haunting it*.

"Y'took your time getting here," Dan grunted, scarcely looking up.

"Sorry." Spence slid onto the stool beside Dan, caught the bartender's eye. "I had a few little—personal problems."

Dan's round head swiveled. His almost sweet blue eyes opened just a bit and Dan plugged the gap in his mouth with his perpetual cigar. Then he took it out again and tapped off a nonexistent ash. "You couldn't get it up," he said.

"How the hell did you know that?" Spence demanded, startled.

"Because I had the same problem." The balding writer looked down at the drink in his chubby hands and sighed. "First time in my whole life."

"It can't be a coincidence," Spence observed, smoothing back his red hair. The bartender was there, startling him; broadshouldered, colorless eyes, attentive but noncommital; silent. "Vodka martini, please." The bartender took his silence away. Spence followed the man with his eyes, wondering how far the alienness of the hotel went, wondering if the broadshouldered bartender and even the attractive waitresses in their abbreviated costumes were part of it. Part of what was going on. "I don't know whether our problem is permanent or not, but I have this hunch that it's nothing more than a side effect."

"Damned nuisance of a side effect, if you ask me," Dan grumbled. He took a huge gulp from his glass. "We have the best-looking women in all of New York State and suddenly they find out they're married to two old dodos who've lost the lead in their pencils."

"Better that than—*vanishing.*"

For a moment Dan didn't reply, Spence had said it so offhandedly. Then he glanced up, shivering. "What was that you said?"

Methodically, detailing it and citing the figures, Spence told his friend what he had learned about the gradual attrition of writers in the hotel dining room for breakfast. "We're . . . *going,* Danny, one by one. They're picking us off at the pace they prefer and by Saturday night, there'll be no one left."

"Jesus, pal, that's a little much," Dan protested.

"Explain it, then. Where have the others gone? Look around you." He gestured with his hand. "There can't be more than eighteen or twenty guys in this lounge at nine-fifteen in the evening and I'll lay you odds that half of them are from the other wings of the hotel. Nonwriting types. And there are damned few of them, so few I almost think the Holroyd discouraged business other than us literary types this week."

Dan squinted into the darkness. The headdress of beaded perspiration ringing his head made him look like an aging Jewish Indian. "I don't see anyone I recognize at all," he confessed with a nod. "Not a soul."

"Not one." Spence stopped speaking when the bartender returned, putting a glass on a napkin before him. The big man's gaze met Spence's, held briefly. It wasn't threatening; it said nothing, nothing at all. He moved down the bar and presumably out of earshot. "Yesterday, if you'll recall, we talked for forty-five minutes with one of the biggest and most talented lushes in the business.

152

The Irish guy, remember—the one who thinks he's possessed by Dylan Thomas or somebody? Dan, can you imagine his not being here in the lounge tonight?"

"No." Dan shook his head a little. He looked tired. "I can't."

"What's that line from John Millington Synge? 'He's gone now, God spare us, and we'll not see him again.' I think that's the upshot of it. We'll not see him again, or any of the others who've—been taken."

"But taken *where? Why?*"

"Sh-h, keep your voice down." Spence frowned, sipped his martini and squirmed until he nearly faced the science writer. "We can't be sure who's in on it and who isn't."

"My God," Dan said under his breath, making a face, "and I'm the guy who always pooh-poohed all the conspiracy theories! The one who argued that the world was pretty much the place it seemed to be. The guy who didn't *dig* the notion of wild-eyed assassins and secret governments, of people living at the center of the earth, of the Abominable Snowman and the Loch Ness monster and— and extraterrestrials visiting us in their goddamned impossible flying saucers!" He snorted. "The silliest thing I ever heard was all that claptrap about *invasions* by little green men, bug-eyed monsters lurking under every psychotic's bed!"

"Yeah, I know," Spence said, nodding. "Space brothers in immaculate white robes like some sort of cosmic christs are the other half of the equation— weirdos with flowing, golden hair and messages of peace." He shut his eyes, then asked, very deliberately, "But I've read a lot about UFOs and it's pretty hard to dismiss out of hand."

153

"What is?"

"The sheer number of them that have been seen over the years. Seen, in countless cases, by people who shouldn't be fooled: pilots, engineers, astronomers, guys who monitor radar and keep running into blips on their screens which they can't explain away. Seen," Spence continued, "by people who are so respectable that calling them liars or hoaxers amounts both to nonsense and libel. Jimmy Carter, before he was elected to the presidency."

"I remember that," Dan said, nodding. "He promised a complete investigation after he assumed office."

"And we didn't get one, did we?" Spence mused. "I wonder why not. Dan d'you remember years ago when we'd lie around the apartment getting smashed? And rap about the—the unguessable possibilities, the mysteries, in the universe?"

"We were a helluva lot younger then," Dan replied. He finished his drink and motioned to the bartender with the colorless eyes for a refill. He waited until he had it before continuing. "You kept running this oddball damned data past me, some stuff you'd found in old books by Charles Fort. And I'd use my knowledge of science to shoot you down wherever I could." He glanced at the redhead, then patted at his perspiring forehead with a handkerchief. "I'm afraid my bright, incisive, inquiring scientist's mind became a little closed—sealed—over the years. That happens to a lot of us scientific types."

"Let's play the game again for a few minutes," Spence said softly.

"What's your hunch?" Dan asked. He looked intrigued despite himself. "Obviously, you have some kind

154

of notion about what's happening here. You aren't going to try ghosts on me again, are you?"

"Not haunting in the *usual* sense of the word," Spence said. "But I'm tempted. T. C. Lethbridge wrote a book called *Ghost and Ghoul* back in '61 and he wasn't exactly the type who received automatic writing from St. Peter, you'll recall."

"I know Lethbridge," Dan acknowledged. "He conducted archeological investigations for the Cambridge antiquarians and the University Museum of Archeology and Ethnology in Britain, right?"

Spence nodded. "Lethbridge believed that everything conforms to natural laws, even if we haven't developed a theory to explain a phenomenon. And he suggested that there was an entirely natural force, akin to electromagnetism, which explains places that are haunted."

"I do seem to remember reading something about that," Dan averred.

"The point is that Lethbridge believed certain places, especially those near water and those on ley lines, somehow *record* powerful incidents—incidents of tragedy, sudden loss, agonizing death—and what we are seeing as haunting is, to quote him, 'no more and no less than television pictures.'"

"Well, at least there's a scientific basis for his notion," Dan admitted.

"Here, I jotted down a fascinating quotation from his book. I've been carrying it around in my billfold." He drew it out, but the lounge was so murky he had to hold up his cigarette lighter in order to read it. "Lethbridge says 'the real *you* is only being shown a film *for your education*,' and that '*you* are something quite outside the hurly-burly which appears to be going on in the world.'

155

He equates the mind with the soul, you see, and recognizes that it is apart from the purely physical brain."

"He's not alone in that," Dan remarked. "He has good company. Go on."

"He wrote, 'You belong to another *altogether*, and when the film comes to an end, you presumably come *out* of the cinema and get on with your real job.' Heartening idea. Now, I'm not telling you that's what we have happening here," Spence continued. "I'm only saying that we have somehow become entangled with somebody *else's* brand of reality, and that the film we're watching isn't ours—that it amounts to a haunting because it is spooky, uncanny, involving other natural laws."

"Other natural laws?" Dan was sober-faced but just as clearly he didn't believe the redhead. "You think it's what I mentioned, don't you? You actually think—"

"I actually think that *an invasion from outer space has begun at the Hotel Holroyd,*" Spence said firmly, "but that it *feels* like a haunting to us because we are being subjected to an alternate reality belonging to *another, dominant people.*"

"Come on," Dan retorted mildly.

"You read all the experts, Dan, right? Scientific expertise? But ever since quasars were found in outer space two decades ago, your people have been absolutely *astounded* by the amount of energy they radiate! Correct?"

"Well, there's some recent analysis from the Very Large Array radio telescope in Socorro, New Mexico, indicating that quasars are a lot like radio galaxies. That quasars may be galaxies engaged in violent infancy. But—"

"But you aren't sure, right?" Spence prodded. "Dan, look at my theory logically and fairly, okay? What are your authorities saying about the possibility of life on other planets these days—intelligent life?"

Dan caught his breath, decided to remain his affable self. "It's true that Carl Sagan multiplied the probabilities of intelligent life and concluded there could be as many as one-million advanced civilizations in the Milky Way alone."

"Wow! That's pretty impressive."

"Yes, but it merely scratches the surface." Dan pursed his lips. "Because current, very competent estimates speak of probably *one-hundred-billion galaxies* like the Milky Way."

"My God!"

"Mathematically, the laws of probability show that it is more logical to assume there is life on other planets than it is to assume we're the only ones in the universe." Dan's tone was grudging. He lifted a cautionary finger. "*But* Michael Hart, the astronomer at Trinity University in Texas, believes there are no intelligent folk hanging around *this* galaxy—and since we lack the propulsion system to conquer the boundless distances of our own galaxy, in any meaningful way, there is no reason to assume that intelligent life elsewhere—in another, very distant galaxy—knows how to travel as far as this planet. Spence, I won't insult your intelligence by telling you what kind of light-years we're dealing with. Our best hope, according to Hart, is to colonize this galaxy ourselves and he thinks we will do it within two-million years or so. When we've done that, he says, 'interstellar travel won't seem so intimidating!' "

"What about the fantastic telescopes we've developed?" Spence asked. "The ones attempting to make contact like Project Ozma, back in '60?"

Dan made a face. "Frank Drake, the astronomer there, says that if there *are* a million advanced worlds in the galaxy, we'd have to examine at least two-hundred thousand stars before we found a signal—or get incredibly lucky. Not that I'm *against* you, Spence. Making contact with another species would be, as Bruce Murray of the Jet Propulsion Lab in Pasadena stated, 'the greatest event in the history of science.' I agree with that. You just don't grasp the problem with the numbers. Besides, why would another world *want* to invade us? Why wouldn't its representatives contact our representatives and set-up mutually productive meetings?" He wadded up his cocktail napkin with angry fingers. "What the hell have *we* got that people from an advanced world could conceivably care about?"

Spence shrugged. "Some of the scientists brave enough to study UFOs have pointed out that we foolish little human beings did something pretty significant back in the '40s, significant, perhaps, by the standards of advanced peoples. We split the atom; we invented the bomb. It's felt that we may be threatening to break some intergalactic laws by decimating ourselves, that they might well object if we sent Earth out of orbit. Some of these educated, brilliant, dedicated people claim there are observers here already, from distant civilizations, who will wait patiently until we're ready to instigate World War III—hoping all along we'll find a way not to do it—who will step in at the last moment and *stop* us. By whatever means they have."

"Bullshit," Dan blurted. "We can't look for outsiders

to help us. It's up to us to grow up and face our responsibilities."

Spence ignored him. "And there are other people," he said ruminatively, "who believe this has all happened *before*. Two or three times, perhaps. After all, archeologists go right on finding bones that send the origin of man back fifty-thousand years, almost every year or so. Which would explain why we find artifacts—such as electrical batteries which can be *made to work*—from thousands of years back, when, according to logic, they weren't 'invented' until modern times." He hoisted his martini and peered, almost dreamily, at the fluid. "I sometimes believe, Danny boy, that there will come a time when we find—deep inside the earth, and on the ocean floor—clear evidence that civilizations far more advanced than ours, but drastically different, ruled this planet a million years ago. And that they destroyed themselves." He glanced at Dan. "But that we won't be *permitted* to destroy ourselves again—because we have an energy force, a power, so great that there can never be a scientist of the future who uncovers *our* artifacts."

"Pal, I just can't handle much more of this groundless speculation," Dan Lloyd muttered. His cigar had gone out. He relit it with a match that flashed with his gesture of irritation. "Just tell me *exactly* what you think is happening at the Hotel Holroyd."

"Okay. Okay, I will." Spence paused. He'd seen that he was getting a trifle thick-tongued and licked his lips before proceeding with care. "Explorers in the past invaded civilizations on earth which were beneath them in advancement, and the rest of the world didn't even hear about it for years. Even peaceful folk like mis-

159

sionaries go to natives in the jungle and quietly rear-
range their lifestyles *forever*. An invasion doesn't have to
be mammoth, or begin at the top. Some invasions begin,
I'll remind you, *by infiltration*."

"Go on."

"Danny boy, an ordinary, rundown old hotel like this
would be a terrific place to begin an invasion. Who else
would notice besides the helpless men and women
staying at the hotel?"

Dan was surprised when a shiver worked its way down
his spine. He hunched his shoulders, frowning, and
leaned toward Spence. "But why a hotel?" he demanded.

"It's pretty obvious, I think," the redhead said slowly.
"All kinds of people come to a hotel. Even if they repre-
sent one work—writers—we come from most of the
states in the union, from different walks of life, with
different needs, views, beliefs, and levels of achievement.
Maybe the extraterrestrials have found a *better* way than
hopping all over the United States in UFOs."

"What do you mean?" Dan inquired, whispering now.

"At a place like the Holroyd," Spence replied, "they
can set up a command post"—he raised one auburn
brow—"and let the people, the *specimens*, simply *come to
them*."

and it was striving to understand the nature of the unwelcome influence, and adjust to it.

Alone in the darkened manager's office and quiet as death in the dwindling hours of night, the Selector allowed some unguessable, inner chemistry its release. A series of yellow-green, oddly caked bubbles drifted from its orifice to the surface of its fluid and spread like so many stench-filled seeds. The belch made the Selector feel somewhat better, physically. It did nothing at all, however, for its state of mind. While the software of information flooded its brain, while it remained in subtle contact with the personages calling themselves Mr. and Mrs. Peter Quince, and while it attempted to make its coldly rational decisions and select those who would be next, a key section of cells—thinking, sentient cells that were all the Selector possessed in the line of personality—continued trying to determine the nature of the troublesome influence it sensed.

Life, throughout the universe, was formed as a spiral, the Selector knew. It tended to curl in upon itself, encountering anew data and events that seemed to be a part of the past. There was, of course, no such thing—no past, no future. Only the present. But nothing about the psychological imperatives of this lively world registered upon it as familiar. Briefly, what could have been excitement bestirred the Selector and it lifted its head in a rare instant of wonder: Was it theoretically possible that the beings of Earth were . . . *different?* That they were an altogether new breed the Selector had never encountered before, despite the nature of its mission? If that were so, it realized, then the spiral had not turned fully in upon itself after all; or the geometry of life was even more complex than it had previously concluded.

Objectively, the Selector knew, it was itself a replication—a reencountering—of the miasmic life that began on most planets with Earth's chemical propensities. In the dawn of time here, as elsewhere, creatures had swum in turbulent liquids choked with the initiatory substance of altering life. But after studying for an eternity, even the Selector had never learned *where* the chemistry of life began, or *what motivated* the others like it to wriggle onto the bank and change a planet's history forever. The Selector, of course, was brilliant, incomparably informed, certainly a mammoth advancement over the dank, fishtailing predecessors here and elsewhere. Yet there were times, like now, when it longed to sprawl upon the riverbank and contemplate its own change of being—to climb a tree, to swing from branches, even—though it realized such thoughts were heresy—to climb down again and stand upright in the guise of Man.

And so it was that the Selector was able, at last, to identify the source of its psychic trauma on the planet Earth. *Feelings*, it said, intellectually tasting the word and finding it somewhat frightening; *emotions*. They covered the face of Earth, unseen, like the plasmatic oceans linking the stars; they suffused the mind, clouded it, confused and qualified the crystal clarity of one's intellect. They asked questions never voiced by the Selector, or those who accompanied it here; they quested, yearned, believed, and—strangest of all—loved. The complexity of the feeling sickened the swimming thing, caused its intricate internal machinery to clog. Pictures of human beings holding hands, making love— it groaned; that was what they called it, as if it could somehow be *manufactured!*—made the Selector tremble its full length. Pictures of elderly people, called parents, and youthful people, called children, complicated the issue. Pictures of the multiplicity of love caroomed in zigzag patterns through its brain—love of the Creator, love of country, love of neighborhood, love of friend— *friend?* it asked—these feelingful beings loved *everything!* Their labors, their shelters, even domesticated beasts!

Why? it demanded, plunging deeply into its spinning cranium; *how?*

And the word surfaced, *Caring,* it came to the Selector; and the creature turned it round and round, peered with absolute scientific detachment at the alien thought-patterns, adjusted and readjusted the precious microscopes of its incomparable brain centers—*there is that which they call* Caring *but I have no reference points, no data with which to perceive the nature of its component parts.*

When it realized it was confronted more by mystery, by mysticism, than by rational enigma, the Selector sensed its own helplessness growing at a terrifying rate. Splashing, gulping, heaving and thrashing itself upon its back, it squinted up at the shadowed ceiling of the manager's office and—for one daring moment, in one surge of curiosity that might almost have been deemed courageous—it *opened* itself to the emotion-things battering at every corner of its being from this structure called a hotel.

The *shrieks*—telepathically received, of course, felt with intense pain inside their minds—brought "Peter Quince" and the woman running. Tears instantly streamed down their cheeks, not in empathy or affection but anguish.

And wincing with the torturous misery the uncaring Selector brought them, they stooped over the proximate aquarium, seeking to soothe their monster. At once the female saw the way it was flapping, saw the seed-like yellow-green regurgitation oozing on the surface of the fluid, and shuddered. She looked at the male; he picked up the net and skimmed, cleansing the pool.

Then the female reached inside. Almost maternally, she began stroking the thing the length of its nightmare body. "Sh-h," she said sweetly, trying hard to ignore the pain in her mind, confronting it. The male inclined his head solicitously, the way a father might peer down at a nightmare-laden child, murmured, "Tsk, tsk."

And the Selector, looking with blind malice at them spoke. It entered both their minds at once, lancing into them with the agonizing plunge of a dental drill: *"Kill them,"* it commanded. *"Kill them!"*

"Which ones?" "Peter Quince" bent to the thing, willing to commit any act to placate it before it destroyed them. "Which ones are *next?*"

"All of them—swiftly!" The Selector scored them with its jealous, unknowing power. Each Quince shuddered with the cutting force of the communication. The monster kicked out, released another string of bubbly bile, increased the volume of its command until the others dropped to their knees in pain. "Kill *all* their souls—*as quickly as you can!*"

It was midnight. The hotel lounge would close in another hour. A parade of glasses lined the bar in front of the two human men. Each of them held yet another glass in his hand.

"There is a ver' reasonable argument 'gainst the idea of invasion from outer space," Dan Lloyd said, concentrating. His speech was growing thick, he knew, but he

165

didn't much care. Spence was beginning to get to him with his nonsense about extraterrestrials and it was important to get the upper hand. If he didn't soon, Dan realized, he might begin to believe it. "You know what it is?"

"No." Spence shook his head. His red hair was unruly, drooping over his wide forehead like a despairing flag. "You tell me."

"Okay." Dan inhaled, steadied himself. "For extra-terrest'ls to come here from another planet, presumably from a galaxy hundreds of light-years away, they would need to be *extreme*ly intelligent people. *Advanced* people. Right?" He glanced at Spence, who'd become an unclear image recently, and thought his friend nodded. "S'okay. The best minds on *this* planet believe that our war-like ways are a hangover from our past, a racial memory, even a *habit* we haven't outgrown. They believe—'n I agree—that the more brilliant people get, the more advanced, the more *civilized* that people will become. An' civilized, advanced people don' go around *killing* each other."

Spence nodded. He was still understanding what Dan said, because he had to. But the precise meaning of it was dawning on him, because of all he'd drunk, a good strong beat later than usual. He felt like he was *replaying* Dan's words, a second or two after they'd been uttered; but he was trying valiantly to keep up. "Gotcha."

"Well, this should the'retically hold true anywhere in the cosmos; right?" Dan sipped his drink. "The more advanced the world becomes, the more moral it is, the more likely it is to have *sanctions* 'gainst killing—especially wars. That is a natural outcome of—of immeasurable progress of the kind it'd take to travel across the universe. With learning, we think, comes a preference for peaceableness, a *banning* of war 'n other forms of violence—whatever the hell 'Star Wars' says. So y'see, pal, if they're a million years ahead of us, their weaponry would also have b'come so advanced that the average guy on the street would know how to wipe out civilization. Logically, then, *if* a place of progress like that exists in the universe, they *must* have abandoned all idea of killing—or we'd have a *contradiction in facts*, a paradox."

"I saw a paradox on the lake when we were flyin' in," Spence said. He giggled. "Quack, quack."

Dan looked at Spence, hard. "You're gettin' drunk."

"I am not!" Spence shook his head, and it made him dizzy. He laughed. "I *am* drunk."

"Look, Spence, there are a thousand reasons why the Hotel Holroyd hasn't been invaded by extraterres'tls. We're one of the youngest civilizations, when you stop t'think of it. Put yourself inna position of a world only a thousand years older'n us and ask what we'd have to offer? We'd be so *backward!* If you could go back in time and talk to your own grandfather, when he was a young man, you'd have almost nothing in common with him. He wouldn't *believe* the world was the way you'd describe it to him! He couldn't *accept* the changes that have taken place—and that's only a handful of decades. What if you were trying to talk, instead, to an ancestor of yours during the days of the Celts?" Dan fumbled with his cigar, relit it a last time, and looked patronizingly at Spence. "Add five-thousand years to that—twenty, *fifty*-thousand years—a *million* years—and you couldn't even *communicate* with a being that far back." He puffed twice, and slipped off the stool. "Somethin' may be wrong here but the possibility of ghosts makes more sense t'me

167

than extraterres'tls!"

"The walls," Spence said clearly, distinctly, holding his breath. He stared straight ahead of him at the end of the bar, where a pretty, exhausted waitress was stacking coins on the counter, toting-up her tips for the night. Dan wouldn't believe this, it would mark him forever as a fool in Dan's eyes; but he had to tell him the rest of it. "The goddamned walls—*throb. Pulsate.*"

Dan froze. "*You* felt that?"

"Yep. Yep, yep, yep." Spence nodded, then glared defensively at his old friend. "I know it sounds crazy as batshit but don't try to convince me it was only my imagination." He took his empty cigarette pack and angrily tore it in two. "Shit and damnation, Dan, I *saw* it happen—I *felt* the walls vibrate, and move, with my own two hands."

"Easy," Dan said soothingly. He got back on the barstool and sighed. He stared at the redhead with his eyes opened wide. Sobriety came back into them, and fear. "I was relieved when you admitted you couldn't make love to April. Figured it was the food, or the water, and maybe it'd just go away when we left here next Sunday. But I don't feel exactly relieved by this. Spence, it happened to me too." He nodded. "It was like some kind of mechanical *heart* was behind the walls, breathing. Breathing *hard.*"

"It's out to get us, y'know?" Spence said. "All right, science expert—give me one serious explanation for it. Tell me what's a better theory than extraterrestrials trying to invade us."

Dan leaned closer to him. Out of the corner of his eye he sought the broad-shouldered bartender, finally saw the man washing glasses and preparing to close the

168

lounge for the night. "Let's collect all the data," he said. "Did April see it happen? Or Lauren?"

Spence finished his drink, clapped the empty glass on the bar, and stood. He wobbled slightly but drew himself up with dignity. "Just me. Apparently you and I are the crazy men in this mess. The paranoids."

"It must be happening to others, as well," Dan remarked, "but they know how it would sound if they mentioned it to us." He crumpled the remains of his cigar in the tray. He sighed again, and whispered: "Ginger didn't see it or feel it either. You realize what this has to mean?"

"Shall we say it in unison?" Spence asked, straightening his shoulders. "*What*ever it is—*whoever* is sending these messages—is trying to influence the writers for some reason."

"It may be only the men," Dan observed.

"Uh-uh." Spence shook his head. "I ran into our friend, the lady poet, earlier today. She confessed to me it had happened to her. And I'll tell you, Danny boy, what I make of it in my unscientific fashion: If we don't figure out what's going on very, very soon—and stop it— among the *next* writers who disappear from the Hotel Holroyd—"

Dan finished it, his blue eyes blinking with worry. "Will be Spencer Torrence and Daniel Lloyd."

"I'm going to bed," Spence said heavily.

He undressed in the bathroom, trying to be quiet. He didn't want to awaken his family. His thoughts churned, they felt turgid and heavy with the weight of the fear he and Dan had given them, yet gossamer and ephemeral, too—because the ideas they had shared were beyond the

169

norm, and because he was still trying to shake off the effect of the alcohol he'd consumed. When he inadvertently struck his knee against the bathroom door, making a jarring sound, he swore; but when he was thrown off-balance toward the walls of the room he grabbed desperately at the wash basin to avoid touching them.

No subliminal messages tonight, he told himself, aware his heart was beating heavily: stay away from the damned impossible *walls*.

Padding barefoot across the bedroom toward April, something he'd thought caught at the fringes of his mind and wouldn't let go. Something that had to do with the expression he'd used to himself—"beyond the norm." While he couldn't quite pinpoint the idea he'd had, he felt more sober—more clearheaded and defensively alert—than he'd ever felt before when he reached the sleeping April.

Turning away from her, he stood at the side of his bed looking over at his daughter. She was on her back, sleeping quietly, innocently. Prone, she still looked so *tiny*, he thought. She was so clearly helpless and vulnerable, that he wanted to rush to her and take Lauren in his arms—protect her with his own medium-sized, adult bulk. *I've seen big men in caskets*, he ruminated, feeling old and all-knowing, *and the biggest of them take up so little room. The thickness of the most powerful man's chest isn't much more than a foot. People, we earthlings, Lord, we pride ourselves on our prowess—consider ourselves a race of giants—and there's so damned little of the best of us! The average tree is taller, sturdier, lives longer than a Mr. America . . .*

He saw Puck, curled on the cot, at Lauren's feet, playing 'possum. Spence didn't blame him; Puck had gone

170

through more than any of them and his basic catty self had paid the price by being altered. While its extraordinary eyes were shut, Puck's ears were tilted, listening. Spence wondered if Puck would forget what had happened to him; he wished the kitten could tell them exactly what it saw. And he wondered if *any* of them, should they live through this nightmare, would ever forget the dark events of the Hotel Holroyd.

Across the way the bogus snow was still drifting noiselessly past the window and Spence shuddered. How did they do that; and who the hell was "they?" He stretched out beside April, again striving to be silent, and muttered under his breath when the betraying springs squeaked. April stirred faintly, sprawling on her back, and he inhaled. Apparently she wasn't cold any longer because she had removed both her nightgown and her brassiere and wore only her panties. In the black-streaked room, the uptilted and firm breasts of the woman he loved looked delectable, like snowy cones topped with some kind of exotic fruit. In her sleep, restless and probably apprehensive, she kicked off her sheet. She lifted a knee, making a small, groaning sound. Spence looked down at her, loved the way her body descended from the sharp hillock of her bosom to the nipped-in waist, saw the softness of her yielding lower belly from which his beloved Lauren had miraculously emerged; and he yearned for April, longed to awaken her with kisses, and enjoy—be comforted, *reassured* by—the complex delicacies of her femaleness, her precious difference from him.

But Spence didn't dare try, again, and fail. He knew that. There were only so many blows a guy could take to his pride, so many ways his vanity and his most precious individual intellect could suffer before—

171

Beyond the norm. His brows knitted in the dark. Always, repeatedly, they were showing Spence and the others in the west wing things that were beyond the norm.

Was *that* how it was done, was it mandatory to do it this way to Dan and him? Did they, perhaps, find it necessary both to confuse the bodies and the minds of the men in the Hotel Holroyd in order to weaken them enough to allow an effective victorious attack?

Dan, of course, knew science well, the facts. And the possibilities of extraterrestrials visiting the planet, let alone invading it by means of reopening an old hotel, were unquestionably very low. Especially when Dan had said what he said in the lounge: "The more advanced the world becomes, the more *moral* it is, the more likely it is to have *sanctions* against killing." But did that add up, *really* add up? Wasn't Earth vastly more advanced in all technological ingredients of progress since the 1880s, the 1780s, the 1680s? Was *it* more moral than before—was Earth a *better* place according to the parameters of morality?

And what was that other thing Danny said? "Their weaponry would have become so advanced the average man on the street would know how to wipe out civilizations." Okay, Spence nodded in the dark; he could follow the reasoning of that theme. Since the advanced world did exist (according to the premise), or it could not have sent out invaders, the logical hypothesis of a brilliant factory-worker or check-out girl or teenaged athlete being able to manufacture deadly weapons meant that the people of that world *had* to have outlawed all forms of violence.

Spence sat up, breathing hard. His fists doubled. He

172

looked at the open bathroom door without seeing it, struck forcibly by his sudden thought:

If peace was literally mandatory, *then all the normal people—all the decent, law-abiding, ordinary beings which walked the distant planet—would obey the law. But what if that world still contained a criminal element? What if they hadn't been able to eradicate the men and women humanoids who refused to abide by the mandatory laws—who ignored the mandate, the guiding principle, of the respectable folk?*

He drew a cigarette from the bedside table with fluttering fingers and lit it. *What if actual madness had not been effectively dealt with—what if, on that incredibly progressive and peaceful planet of Danny Lloyd's, there remained the terrifying problem of lunatics—homicidal maniacs—and they strolled the streets, continuing to plague the decent people, and had in their power, too, the common knowledge of how to destroy the world?*

For God's sake, what would a civilization that wouldn't kill under any circumstances, could not kill by their own essential laws, decide to do about its psychotic mass-murderers?

Spence burned his fingers on the match before he remembered to shake it out, but he didn't notice it.

What if the Hotel Holroyd were full of them?

TRANSCRIPTION THREE

"NO CONSTRAINTS"

"There are no constraints on the activities of a very advanced civilization. They could prevent their star from exploding or they could cause a supernova explosion. They could alter the orbit of their star in the galaxy."
— Nikolai Kardashev,
Soviet theorist

"I was thinking this globe enough
till there sprang out so noiseless around me
myriads of other globes."
— Walt Whitman

CHAPTER FOURTEEN

Georgei Ivanovitch Gurdjieff, who taught a scientific system of self-exploration, was a Greek-American who believed that people are fundamentally *asleep*, even when they think they are fully conscious. He valued highly the content of dreams.

When Gurdjieff was twenty years old, a man he would never meet—Professor V. Hilprecht of the American University of Pennsylvania—was attempting to decipher a cuneiform inscription from two miniature agate fragments. Sleeping in an exhausted state, he dreamed that a long-dead Nippur priest took him to a treasure chamber and showed him that the fragments belonged together. They were earrings from a votive cylinder, and when they were fitted, the message would become clear. A third piece, however, was missing. When Hilprecht arose, he was able to fit the pieces together precisely as the priest of his dreams instructed him. And several months later, visiting a museum in Constantinople, Hilprecht was astonished to find . . . a *third* fragment. It fitted perfectly with the others, and the message became clear.

Two people dreamed that Thursday night in the Holroyd, one of them a small female child with hair that reached to the small of her back. Since coming to the hotel Lauren had experienced such a bizarre series of events that, in her confusion, she was sometimes unable to know any more whether she was asleep or dreaming. And when Puck jumped to the floor of the bedroom and little Lauren sat up, she could not tell whether the dream she was having had ended or if she remained unconscious. Scarcely glancing at her sleeping parents across the darkened room, moving with the uncanny grace of the somnambulist, she followed her pet to the front door, and opened it.

Somewhere, Georgei Ivanovitch Gurdjieff bestowed a benign smile. . . .

Puck was her focal point, nothing else. Sure of foot, graceful in the snug direction of her youthful brain's creative right hemisphere, Lauren began walking down the ill-lit, deeply-shadowed corridor of the Hotel Holroyd, unafraid for the first time in days.

She was beyond the ability to detect that her altered kitten, with the snowy white streak down its frail back, was no more in control of his faculties than she. Stiff-legged, moving at a deliberate but unhurried pace, Puck trotted forward without the knowledge that his mistress accompanied him. Sleepwalkers both, they passed beneath the transmogrifying picture in the hallway, heedless as a bumpkin in a country graveyard, until—*the figure materialized ahead of them.*

Glowing with light, it was not tall, it was not of itself forbidding. Because it was in full control of the situation—because it had commanded these nocturnal circumstances to *Be*—its customary malice was banked, like searing flames that had, only a whisper of time ago, blazed across a wilderness of alien thought. *The Hotel Girl took shape in the light: the child who resembled Lauren looked down the corridor at the human girl, and raised her arm*—beckoningly.

"Come," she ordered Lauren and the small, furry animal who had become her focus, as well. *"Come— and I shall show you tomorrow."*

In the deep molasses muddle of Lauren Torrence's sleep-drugged, shrinking mind there was a microscopic reaction. Pausing, only for a moment, she blinked her eyes behind her heavy spectacles and shook her head. Only Puck heard what she said: *"No. No, please . . ."*

And then she followed her pet, who followed the Hotel Girl, and a door rose before Lauren which she had not seen before and of a kind she had never known existed. Several yards behind the look-alike, Lauren frowned, sought control of her own thoughts, tried to achieve that which Gurdjieff claimed was nothing more than an altered and relatively insignificant version of her sleeping condition. She did not like what she saw, ahead; it frightened her in its extraneousness. The door seemed enwrapped in a vivid swirl of cotton-candy lighting, not a genuine door of the solid kind one rapped upon for admittance, but a disorienting portal which slipped and slid from shape to amorphous shape in a consternation of bewildering geometric proportions. When it opened, even that was not true, or possible, and Lauren gasped: The door simply existed no longer. There was only the yawning doorway filled with a brighter illumination of the otherworldly, a cascading and shimmering aura of diffused hues in the center of which the Hotel Girl paused, waiting; beckoning.

Nearest her, Puck obediently leaped into the arms of the look-alike. Lauren protested deep in her throat, then closed the distance between them, stepping with trepidation across the threshold into another reality....

The flight of stairs was brief. With each step up Lauren felt a *give*, a disconcerting *yielding* beneath her weight as if the steps accommodated her, sought to give her a confounding, light gracefulness of motion. The ascendance was so buoyant it might, to a person mature enough to think in those terms, have implied a dimunition of gravitational force. Only now beginning to gain control of her own thoughts, Lauren saw the door close behind her, and trembled. She barely discerned the way the walls on either side of the narrow chamber of steps *hissed* and *bent*—as if some truly terrible, transient life had been invested in them and some unhuman heartbeat shot alien blood along the encroaching arteries of the short tunnel, and began to bridge the ventricular passage of two disparate worlds.

What Lauren saw next wrenched a breath of fresh surprise from her, not because it was so alien but because it was not: She was moving into an old, deserted dance ballroom, no antechamber of hell or of distant space people, but a high-ceilinged, gaily-painted, shiny-floored hall in which people no different from her—except for their age; except for the fact they had danced here many years before Lauren's birth—had swept, and dipped, and tripped the light fantastic. Still yards from the Hotel Girl, for she could not totally seem to close the gap, Lauren sensed a feeling of relief and momentarily closed her eyes. There, by the little rising wall to a platform, dancing people had shut their eyes in the grasp of a romantic waltz, a perky two-step; and on the platform four or five tuxedoed sidemen had rippled the keys of a piano, raised horns to a range of notes always heard only in their aspiring heads, and a rhythmic drummer had cracked his stick on crisp rimshots and jangling, golden cymbals.

Here, in Lauren's shadows just inside the entranceway to the old ballroom, fond couples had clung as one until they heard, as Lauren imagined she heard now herself, the sweet, seductive, plaintive promise of "Good Night, Sweetheart."

The Hotel Girl had vanished.

She knew it before she opened her eyes; she experienced the look-alike's absence as an awareness of departing peculiarity—and she knew, too, that her pet Puck remained in the Hotel Girl's arms.

Silence, so oppressive it was a cousin of excess heat, oven heat that crept round the edges and stealthily clad one in a cocoon of sweltering blanketry, stalked the deserted ballroom and rudely brushed-away the nostalgic memory-traces of harmless, human dancers and happy, human music. The place was no more illumined in shifting patterns of light; only a single, scary corona of illumination remained and it hung upon the ballroom floor like a glaring white shadow, or something darting from a laserbeam. Lauren froze where she was, half-crouched, unwilling to breathe more loudly than was absolutely necessary—fearful that the tiniest sound she made, in this crazily-cloistered room, might bring from the distant decrepit walls or the vacuous, empty stage, a gabbling babble of mindless, resentful rage and a devouring, extraplanetary viciousness.

Surely there had never been a place so quiet before on Earth, not a desert, not a wooded forest primeval. If music spilled-out now from unseen trumpets and silver saxophones, it would be a fiendish cacophony—some melodic accompaniment for hordes of bug-eyed beings with a million crawling tentacles and another billion wiggling antennae. Lauren thought it was as if some powerful brute-thing with an acute, extraordinary sensitivity to even the most miniature movement had not only corralled the corrupt silence but magically *drawn-out* of the ballroom every being or object which might announce its tenuous existence. She felt that way, herself, about herself, then—eerily, the quietude attested to her transient and groping appearance on the stage of living things, thrust upon her the cold notion that she accept wholeheartedly her own lifespan's tentative temporariness. Perhaps it was that which moved her.

For the unbent steel of her youthful spine brought the words to her lips. She did not shout—nothing, *nobody* could have shouted in that vast and sinister arena—but she spoke: "I am *me*," she said, little more than a whisper. "I am Lauren Louise Torrence."

The reply peeling from the walls in a soprano shriek,

was deafening: "And *this* is *your future!*" it cried.

Unobserved lights flashed on. Panels of mirroring that had concealed *it* sibilated into undiscoverable partitions. Droning, a reverberation snapped the aphonic stillness and slowly built, became a rumbling tintinnabulation and leveled-off to a purr of silken machinery which rested on a discordant level heard only in the crawling nerves beneath shrinking human flesh. At once shrill and sordine, the hum sporadically coughed as if developing some fantastic power of which human beings could only surmise, or dream.

Then the panoply of its illumined brilliance broke through the interdimensional barricades and Lauren, *seeing it,* jitterbugged back several steps, felt the sharp tears come to her eyes in the glittering face of what she was seeing, and covered her gasping mouth with her shaking hands.

The spacecraft—the Unidentified Flying Object—filled most of the deserted ballroom with its sonorous, sepulchral, moonbean might. Like the aurora of a new morning in time, it caught and trapped light from unbeknownst sources and generously gave it back in a convex coruscation of alien irradiation. For a moment it was impossible for Lauren to see its shape, so bedazzled she was by the sheer silver sparkle of the UFO; and then she detected, beneath her tremorous cupped palm, the oft-sketched familiarity of its twin-pieplate construction, and double rows of small windows winking from within. She gasped when she thought it was hovering, ready to rise; then she saw the hard projecting triangulated steel legs supporting the astounding craft and, at the throbbing midsection, another enigmatic, curving door . . . to inside. At all times it gave off an actinic fluctuation of impossibly brilliant colors

183

that ran the gamut of man's sight and flashed-off into ultraviolet hues of which Lauren had only the sense of something blinding, some imponderable phosphorescence that might in itself power the spacecraft. She shook before its majesty, its mystical marvelousness. Something primitive in her knees wished to bend, to make her bow.

I must tell Mom and Pop, Lauren decided, the desire for communication drawing her alert and erect, turning her toward the inexplicable stairway up which she had come to the anything-but-deserted ballroom. *They must know.*

"They must *not!*" shrieked the soprano command of the Hotel Girl; and though Lauren could not see her, the words were not within her mind but badgered her hearing as they battered her ears. "You *must not* tell them—*ever!*"

Lauren spun, her anguished eyes trying to locate her look-alike. She brushed her hair back from her eyes, strove to avoid the mesmeric glitter of the massive UFO. "I *must!*" she insisted. "I *must!*"

Laughter collided against the walls of the room and shattered on Lauren's eardrums. "You fool, they would not *believe* you! You *know* that, don't you? Because you can never find your way here, never in millenia, they will *not* believe such a preposterous story!" And the giggle, simultaneously childish and a manic sound older than the sorry history of humankind, pelted Lauren's hearing like pellets of hard ice. "You *know* that!"

She read my mind, Lauren thought; and, *She is right, they* won't *believe me!*

"But who *are* you?" she shouted, turning round and round in her effort to see the Hotel Girl again. Her heart was in her throat; it was mammoth, it was thumping in cannonades. "And—*what* are you?"

The alien door at the midcenter of the spacecraft snapped into position and the girl who looked like Lauren Torrence stood in the aperture, enwreathed in a crimson shroud of light. Something was in her arms and she clutched it tightly, held it to her as if she might never let go. *"You shall find out what we are, and what we* want, *soon enough! Soon enough, sister!"*

The Hotel Girl threw the object from her arms. Lauren screamed. The object came across the floor toward her with projectile force, carried as if by magic.

And when it landed at Lauren's feet, she screamed again.

It was Puck, her pet kitten.

He no longer had a white streak down his back. *He had turned white* all over, *every whisker, every scrap of fur standing on end in the final terror of poor little Puck's brief life was* whiter than snow—

And he was stiff as a board. Very, very dead.

The alien spacecraft's door snapped shut with the sound of wristbones breaking, and all the lights in the ballroom went *out.*

The second human soul which dreamed, that Thursday night, belonged to Ginger Lloyd.

Dan had dropped to the bed after removing only his shirt and shoes and, exhausted with unique mysteries and all that he had drunk, fallen asleep at once.

Possibly it was the proximity of a new, living life beside Ginger that caused her unconscious mind to shift, seek, and dream; perhaps it was her natural tele-pathy that sensed, even without bringing her back the

185

whole story, her little friend Lauren's nightmare visitation.

She saw, in her mind's eye, something soaring across the skies at midday, a flash of gold-and-silver light at dazzling heights, traveling at more-dazzling speeds. At first, in her dream, she believed it was an experimental plane—some fine, expensive new jet liner, perhaps, even a rare glimpse of the metallic "junk" with which the Americans and Russians had begun to litter space.

But the gold-and-silver light *stopped*, hanging for a moment like a second sun suspended overhead, and that was impossible. The sleeping Ginger stared in curiosity at it, tried to figure it out.

That was when it began an intricate series of darting, ninety-degree turns which could not be achieved by any flying machine of man without splattering the helpless pilot or astronaut against the walls of the craft like tureens of soup stupidly hurled by a poltergeist.

Why, it's a UFO, marveled the dreaming Ginger, squinting up at it with wonder, even a pleased fascination. *I've always wanted to see one!*

Which was when it *plummeted* at once—dropped like a great boulder in a Fortean rainfall of wild implausibility—cutting the afternoon sky like a carving knife, and began heading toward *her*. Asleep, Ginger tried to scream, sought to run; but nothing happened to help her.

It did not collide with her. At the last moment, the UFO stopped, hung above an aging human structure like some dark Bethlehem star citing the birth of an antichrist. She saw the name human people had given the structure, saw it spread before her like a banner headline printed across the front of a newspaper:

186

HOTEL HOLROYD, it said; and beneath that, WELCOME MR. & MRS. PETER QUINCE.

Then she was inside the hotel, squirming because she felt, in her dream, that she might be discovered. She saw two humanoid figures carrying *something* into a large, high-ceilinged room; saw that the something *splashed* as the humanoids walked. *I don't want a close-up*, Ginger thought; *I do not want to* see *it.*

And with perversity of one's nightmares, the "camera" that was sleeping Ginger Lloyd dollied forward, swept silently across the large room; and though she attempted to shut her eyes against the vision, she was helpless, she could only wait, and stare.

The creature in the tank flopped onto its back and, meeting her hypnotized gaze, *smiled* at Ginger. Hideously . . .

At last she could cry out and her screams brought Dan, her precious Danny, awake. Instantly he held her close in his arms, the curling hairs of his matted chest a hirsute blanket. Sobbing, she clung to him, sought to absorb his cool, masculine strength, his sturdy, scientific sanity—

And saw the tears standing in his affectionate blue eyes. "It's *extraterrestrials*, isn't it?" he asked simply. "Genuine? From outer space?"

She nodded, held back her own tears, shaken by the change in him. "I saw a—a *thing* called the *Selector*," she said softly, touching his cheek, seeing that he was uncharacteristically unshaven. Despite herself, she shuddered. "It's . . . awful. Indescribably ugly; awful."

"It's going to eliminate all of us?" he asked. Again she saw the fear in his eyes, his startling acceptance of all that she saw. But there was something else, too, in her Danny's eyes. Was it—*resolve?* When she did not reply, he shook her gently in his big paws. "Not just the writers, but *all* of us?"

Slowly, Ginger nodded. "I think so," she whispered. "Or m-maybe the nonwriters are only . . . in the way."

Danny sighed. He said, "Okay," in as mild an agreement with something as she had ever heard from her balding bear of a husband, and got up. He kissed her mouth and, for a moment, held the back of her golden head in his hand. His eyes seemed so sad. "Right," he said.

From the bed she stared at his departing figure. Even Danny's back was an intricate tangle of black hair. Never actually fit, he still gave Ginger the impression of a rare, husbanded, indomitable strength. Never once had she felt a tingle of fear, with Danny around, until they came to the Holroyd. She realized he sensed those facts, knew he despised them.

He closed the bathroom door after him. She heard water running.

Ginger hugged her bare knees against her breast, tried to think what she should do, *could* do to help them all. For an awful instant she'd believed Danny was going to take a desperate action, do something fantastically brave and dangerous; but he had only gone to the bathroom. Her heart went out to him. *Perhaps*, she reflected, *he is only crying*.

Dan Lloyd walked over to the wash basin in his stocking feet, turned on the cold faucet, and bathed his broad, full-moon face. Absently, he patted it dry with a fuzzy hotel towel bearing the place's accursed name. He thought how normal it seemed in there, but only on

188

the surface, only if you didn't observe the peculiar off-white glare of the lights in the bathroom and the way—he was sure of it—the angles of the place were all wrong, uneven and awry. Sighing, he saw that his aftershave was there, in the medicine cabinet. Until three years ago, he'd refused to use the stuff, thought it was for sissies. He'd even told Ginger once, in his frank, hearty way, "Men are supposed to stink." Then Lauren, his best friend's daughter, had given him a bottle of aftershave for Christmas and now he thought aftershave was just swell. He slapped some on, inhaling the fresh aroma, feeling heartened—just a bit—by its application.

Then he turned to the wall nearest him, and looked at it. Right then nobody could have told it was a god-damned nightmare place, this hotel bathroom; nobody would have seen the small *surge* of the wall, unless he were looking for it.

Dan was.

Inhaling, he closed his eyes, raised his arms, and dropped his bulk forward, on his hands. Immediately his fingers *tingled,* as if something electrical coursed up from the wall and through them. A second later he felt his biceps, then his shoulders, his neck, and his sensitive spine absorb the tingling sensation. *Please, let me be enough,* okay? he muttered, his voice scarcely audible. *Take me and leave Ginger alone. Let my wife, and my friends, and that little girl out of it, okay?* There was no immediate answer.

Twenty seconds later, the real throbbing began, the wall *breathed* against him, and the domineering alien messages of the extraterrestrials seeped into Dan Lloyd's nervous system.

CHAPTER FIFTEEN

The Torrence family reached the hotel dining room first, that Friday morning, and unconsciously pulled their chairs somewhat more closely together than usual. Theirs was the comfort of some unarmed, naked family of prehistoric times cuddled around a dying fire and, just as early man feared but two things—exposure to the cold and starvation—the Torrences feared the equally unseen Mr. and Mrs. Peter Quince.

All three of them had dressed silently, except for mumbled little exchanges, before taking the elevator downstairs. No one had occupied it with them. Now

Spence brooded, as he took his seat and prepared to go through the motions of breakfast, that they were beginning to acquire the mind-set of people in Germany before Adolf Hitler's storm troopers came. They were only acknowledging old routines, handling their necessary tasks, eating meals with regularity. He realized that they all knew, at the back of their minds, it was only a question of time until someone they'd never met cold-bloodedly pulled their names out of a hat. When that happened, he saw, they'd be no more able to protect themselves than persecuted people had ever been.

Staring across the half-empty room at the long, vertical, narrow windows, April Torrence thought that the persistent, soft flutter of streaming snow represented bars on a jail cell—that they were, in their way, more hopelessly confined in this aged hotel than they would have been in a real prison. She ran a nervous, artistic hand through her dark hair and realized that she hadn't washed it in two days. She hadn't bathed that morning. Her sigh was tremulous, something greater than a sound of fear; hadn't she read somewhere that the first sign of breakdown in a woman was when she began to let herself go?

Neither April nor Spence noticed the distraught expression on Lauren's face. They had no idea that she had left their suite last night and followed Puck, her pet, to the shining, petrifying threshold of another world. They were so clearly lost in their own anxieties that Lauren couldn't bring herself to tell them what had happened. Part of the reason for her silence was that she believed the Hotel Girl was right, that Mom and Pop wouldn't accept her word for what occurred in the deserted ballroom. But beyond that, her own nerves

191

were so raw, so vulnerably exposed, that Lauren was reaching a stage where she felt that remaining silent might alter the facts. She was, after all, only twelve years old.

Spence was writing in his notebook when Ginger appeared at the table, managing a quick smile for her friends. He nodded at her, once, and half-rose as she took her seat.

He didn't sense her frantic, questioning gaze moving over his face. When he did, his rather leathery face twisted in surprise. "Are you aware of what I discovered? About the reduction of people—writers and their families—in the west wing?"

"Danny told me," Ginger said, keeping the explanation simple.

"Dan told you what?" April demanded, looking from Ginger to her husband and back again. She'd felt cold fingers moving on her spine. "Is something going on that I don't know about?"

Spence looked at her and took her hand. "We didn't want to alarm you gals any more than you already were."

April wrested her hand free, frowning at him. "You 'gals'? What is this unasked-for, unneeded male chauvinism, Spencer? That isn't like you—or Dan either!" Her pretty face was earnest but the addiction to scenes of high-drama remained, he believed; playing a scene was the way April played at life. "Look, my *dar*ling mate, we are all in this *together*—remember? If you've hit upon something to explain what's happening to us in this mausoleum, this Love*craft*ian crypt, *I* have a right to know!"

He glanced sideways at Ginger, saw her reluctant

nod. It wasn't just April's dramatic sense. With all her sterling qualities, her beauty, she had an unpredictable manner of handling sudden, stark disclosures which tended to unnerve her husband. Spence could never be quite sure how she'd take an unpleasant piece of news. Surrendering, however, he explained as briefly as he could how the number of writers and their families coming for breakfast had dropped, daily, since they all arrived.

"How m-many were left yesterday?" April asked shakily.

"I got seventy-six of the estimated, original one-hundred-and-fifty," he murmured. His gaze moved from April's newly-worried face to his daughter's and saw, for the first time, how drawn and pale she looked. He wanted to talk with her but he'd promised April a full explanation. "We *were* losing about twenty-five people a day. Now, understand, that original estimate Dan and I made may have been all wrong; we may have—"

"There's nowhere *near* seventy-six people in the dining room this morning," April whispered. She looked from empty table to empty table. And she saw, in the taut, conspiratorial faces and confidential whispers of those who remained, that others too had deduced what Spence had. "Nowhere *near* . . ."

"I counted." He looked at each of them, and nodded. "Looks like we lost a larger number than the average. I think they're accelerating it, probably because people are beginning to see what's happening." He closed his smoky eyes and, when he spoke, the courage had drained from his tone of voice. "Thirty-nine went, last night. Right now, there are—are *forty-five human beings remaining* in this room." He swallowed. "That is, including us."

"But—who *are* they?" April asked. Spence cheered for her, privately; her expression was honest, the way it was when they made love. *Used* to make love, he reminded himself. The artifice was wiped away. "What do they *want* with us?"

"Danny and Spence thought they might be from another planet." Ginger spoke, her colorless eyes intense. "Especially Dan. I—I have a confession to make. I've been psychic—a sensitive—for years now. Nobody knows about that but Danny." She saw their startled expressions and nodded. "I'm a very good one, actually, worse luck." She forced a smile. "And I've . . . *felt* their presence, with my mind. Spence, you're right. The manager and his wife—if that's what she is—*are* from a planet in another solar system. They're extraterrestrials."

"Dear God," April gasped.

Spence squirmed in his chair to face Lauren. "Honey, don't worry too much about all this. We've never let you down before, have we princess?" He gave her his most charming, natural smile because it was always easy to smile at Lauren. "We'll handle it some way. Everything will be okay."

"I don't think so, Daddy." Her young face was pasty, and grim. "I don't think it'll ever be the same again."

He studied her, deeply concerned. Lauren never called him "daddy" unless she was angry with him—or if she was seriously frightened. He didn't know what to say. He could only grip her small hand, tight, and stroke her long hair with his other hand.

Ginger leaned across the table to the child. "Lauren,

you've seen more than any of us. Haven't you?"

"How did you know, Aunt Ginger?" Lauren asked, startled.

"I told you. I can—*read minds*, sort of." She shrugged. "Now and then." She touched the girl's cheek. "Tell Aunt Ginger what's happened to you. Don't worry, honey, we'll all believe you now."

Slowly, dredging the recollections up from her memory, Lauren told them of the Hotel Girl, the way she had taunted her, always danced out of reach.

"Oh, baby, I'm sorry we didn't pay attention to you," April said, kissing her.

"And I," Spence said, meaning it. He frowned. "If I'd listened to you, our first day here, all this might not have happened."

The contact Ginger had, her fingertips light on Lauren's cheek, strengthened her impressions. She saw, suddenly, that her own dream about an Unidentified Flying Object was some kind of strange, altered reception of the little girl's genuine experience. "What happened last night, Lauren? Tell us about the UFO."

She did, under her breath, keeping her eyes on Ginger, drawing strength from the former tennis player. It was hard, so very difficult, confronting the terrifying events, especially since she had, at the start, believed she was only dreaming too. But little by little Lauren told them of the way the Hotel Girl led her, and Puck, up a short flight of steps to an old ballroom, and the incredible sight that awaited her.

"It was big," she whispered, "with all kinds of lights flashing on and off. And it made this *humming* noise that hurt my ears. And all the time, the Hotel Girl who looks like me was *calling* to me—her voice comin' from absolutely everywhere, the way people can't do." Abruptly, she shuddered and her voice raised in fear. "That's what I'm tryin' to tell you, that I don't think they're people *at all*—that they're sort-of like us, but weird, with all kinds of scary powers."

"It's a bit hard to swallow."

They turned to peer at April. She had drawn herself erect in her chair and was motioning to a waiter. At once Spence saw that she'd chosen to disbelieve Lauren because it was more than she could take in, and his heart went out to her. In the past, working on more mundane matters of corporate betrayal and dishonesty, he'd seen the faces of people who held to the trust that their employers were understanding leaders in the community. There were times when he'd presented them with unassailable, clear evidence and then watched them deny it.

When he realized how he could prove Lauren's story to April, he felt a surge of sadness move through him. "Princess," he began, "where's old Puck?"

That was when Lauren began to cry. "He's *dead!*" she sobbed, burying her face in her hands. "They turned him white—white *all over*—in their durned old UFO and then just threw him at me. *They scared him to death!*"

That did it. Crying, April put her arms around her daughter and hugged her close. People at nearby tables looked over, Spence saw, with haunted expressions, then looked back at their own survivors.

"What can they want to kill a child's pet for?" Ginger wondered, aloud, making a face. "Why are they concentrating this way on Lauren if they have some ulterior plan for you writers?"

196

"I think," Spence said between his teeth, "that on any planet they call it pure, damn meanness!" He waved a hand. "Or maybe this Hotel Girl of Lauren's is actually no more than a child, of sorts, and she has the typical cruel streak certain children seem to develop."

They paused to give their orders, largely toast and coffee, except for Lauren. *How badly can they ruin toast?* the redhead wondered sourly. But Dan, he remembered, Dan had *liked* the food! He was the only one of them who had, and for some crazy reason he'd found it delicious.

The realization broke on him almost at the same time Ginger saw it.

"Dan should have come down by now," she said very quietly, clenching her napkin in a fisted hand. Her voice broke. "He's never missed a breakfast in all our years of marriage. Even earlier in the week, when we stayed in our rooms, he sent down for breakfast."

Spence stared helplessly at her, his mind racing with anger and worry. "Dan was the one who liked the food here," he said levelly. "He's put it away here at the Holroyd like it was an expensive restaurant in New York." He saw Ginger's slow nod, her watching, frantic eyes. "And he hasn't really been—himself lately."

"Don't say it," Ginger said, tears leaping to her eyes. "Please, Spence. Don't put it into words."

He didn't have to. They all knew the truth, that moment.

Dan was never coming down for breakfast.

CHAPTER SIXTEEN

The hush that descended over the table in the hotel dining room was leaden until the food came. They felt, each of them, muzzled and gagged. There appeared to be no avenue of escape; there seemed, just then, to be nothing whatever to say or do. It was only a question of waiting for the pellets to fall beneath the chair, or for the knife of the guillotine to drop. The imprisonment mind-set that April had experienced, when they arrived in the hotel restaurant, was complete and now moved to a different mood. The mood of the condemned prisoner who knows a stay of execution will never come.

Then the waiter was placing plates, glasses, and cups around the table, his movements appearing sinuous, stealthy. It was easy as punch, Spence realized, to believe that this waiter was one of them, or certainly aware of what was happening; a paid human confederate, perhaps. For a moment, Spence was virtually convinced the man was part of the numbing, otherworldly plot and inched warily back into his chair, supernaturally fearful of even being touched by the waiter.

When the fellow bent slightly, however, to present Spence with his toast and jam, his inside-shirt pocket gapped enough for the redhead to see into it.

Two tickets to that night's professional basketball game poked incongruously up from the pocket.

Spence smiled, found he was beginning to relax. It was *that easy*, he realized, to turn truly paranoid; for the first time he understood how people under pressure could become convinced that lifelong friends were ganging-up to keep secrets.

Lifelong friends. The coffee in Dan's cup was steaming. His chair was still empty.

"I'll go get him," Ginger said, seeing where Spence looked.

"I'll go with you," he said swiftly, starting to rise.

"*No!*" She exclaimed the word, virtually snapped it at him. Then, tiny fine lines showing in her perfect outdoor complexion for the first time, she reached down to touch Spence's hand. Her gaze drifted to the faces of each of her companions. "It's my job. Danny's mine." The word sounded fierce, somehow; it spoke of her love, her worry. "You must stay with April and watch Lauren."

"Be careful, Aunt Ginger," the girl said fretting.

"I'll be back shortly," she said, and it might have been a prayer.

When Ginger was halfway across the room, a brave, dwindling figure, April caught Spence's attention. She gestured at the toast and coffee placed before her. "Do you think we even dare *eat* this crap?"

He'd thought about it for a couple of days, every chance he got. Whether he was manning the desk, or lying on his solitary bed upstairs, Henry Clurge was incapable of setting aside the wondrous idea he'd had.

Enormous literary success—admission to the fraternity of writers, respect from his peers and quick acceptance by editors from New York to Los Angeles—would surely be his when he wrote his book detailing the story of extraterrestrials at the Hotel Holroyd.

For awhile it had concerned the desk clerk that his own part in the invasion might be misinterpreted, that the earth people for whom he intended to write the book might consider him something of a sell-out for working so closely with Mr. and Mrs. Quince. After all, it was true that he'd handled the desk register and blotted-out the names of the writers in the west wing— every time Quince sent word down that so-and-so "never actually arrived for awards week," as the manager ubiquitously suggested it. And when Quince ordered him to devise an entirely new register, presumably because a decision had been reached about the order of authorial obliteration, Henry Clurge had moved with alacrity.

But that would only be a tragic misreading of the truth, Henry told himself, and one which he could certainly avoid with the brilliant new version of the facts his inventive mind concocted. The truth *was*, he had suspected what the Quinces were the moment he was interviewed for the job as desk clerk, and he had taken the position with uncommon courage. No one else would have possessed the imagination, the insight, to see that they were aliens, extraterrestrials, so it had clearly been his task as a respectable member of the human species to risk his own life. Scarcely giving a thought to it, his story went, he'd signed-on in order to be a firsthand observer, a dutiful recorder, in the hope that the manager and his woman could one day be apprehended and punished.

Viewed in that light, not only would his book become the greatest best seller of all time but Henry Clurge, himself, might be finally recognized for the uniquely foresightful and forthright, ultimately brave person he was.

Last night, however—Thursday night—Henry's busy mind had seen that something was missing, an element every nonfiction book needed for authenticity, for verisimilitude: Detail. Documentation, to be included in the photo section of his book where Henry himself would be smiling nobly out at his readers. It was even possible that the public wouldn't *believe* what happened at the Hotel Holroyd, without the reproduction of Quince's personal records.

Which was why, late this Friday evening, Henry Clurge was unlocking the glass-partitioned doors on the second floor landing, determined to search Peter Quince's office.

He'd found an old key that Smarty-pants Quince didn't know about, hidden beneath a stack of ancient papers in the hotel safe; and this moment Henry knew for a fact that the manager and the woman were upstairs in the ballroom where they kept their spacecraft. Quince's office would be vacated and, if Henry's memory continued to serve him well, there was a good photocopier right beside the manager's desk.

It took a moment for the rusted key to turn in the lock, and then Henry was into the brief hallway leading to the private office. It wasn't remarkable bravery that drove him down the corridor, his chest heaving with anxiety; it was overweening ambition and an adulthood of creative frustration. He didn't see the obese hotel maid staring after him, her favorite tune frozen on her lips. And he didn't hear the way she changed the song to a spiritual, the old hymn intended as a prayer for the desk clerk.

Outside the door, Henry read the pair of signs announcing the nature of the room and proclaiming that no one was admitted. A brow raised in near-amusement as he located the office key on his chain, and stooped to insert it in the lock. Everywhere he'd gone, all his life, he'd seen signs telling him—one way or the other—to keep out. He'd obeyed them all, every stupid one of them, right up to this moment; and what had his obedience, his law-abiding ways, ever got him? An ill-paying, utterly boring job in the employment of some homicidal madman from a distant galaxy! And if he didn't find proof—Henry knew, that instant, without a shadow of a doubt—*proof* of what had occurred, a publishing house would simply laugh at his valor.

It was high-time Henry Clurge looked after himself, whatever the minor infractions were that he had to commit from time to time. That was what all the really successful people did, after all—approach life with a hang-the-rules mentality. Henry Clurge was Number One—*numero uno*—a creative genius in the making, and now the world would know it too.

Still, he paused before turning the doorknob and entering, halted by the sounds that he heard from inside the office.

Peculiar, wholly unexpected sounds. Sounds of— *splashing*, as if someone were in there taking a bath!

But there was no running water in the office, never had been; Henry knew that. And there was no one inside, Henry thought he knew that, too; he'd stake his life on it.

Henry opened the door, stepped into the darkness, and staked his life.

The entire suite appeared to be empty. She called his name—"Dan, Danny, *please* answer me,"—repeatedly before she even began searching their rooms, and there was no reply.

Then Ginger had made herself conduct the search. Like the table in the dining room downstairs, it was preternaturally, uncommonly still here and she had to fight back a flood of fresh panic as she moved from room to room.

Dan's clothes were still scattered here and there, the way he'd always handled them—on chairs, in the closet, still in the suitcase. The only things missing were the garments he'd worn yesterday, she was fairly sure of that. But where could he have gone?

Standing in the bathroom door, she glanced nervously at the basin, the commode, the bathtub, paying no attention to the bare walls of the room themselves.

She even held back the vivid plastic shower curtains, half-anticipating that she would find Danny unconscious there or worse. But there was nothing amiss, and there was no clue to her husband's whereabouts.

Except—and fairskinned Ginger Lloyd stopped moving, gaping at what she'd finally discovered—*except a note*, clumsily affixed by one of her bobby pins to the mirror on the medicine cabinet.

It was nothing more than several sheets of toilet tissue, folded over and over to give it a necessary thickness; and the message scrawled there, in Danny's handwriting, was in her own eyebrow pencil.

For a moment she couldn't bear to pull it away from the mirror. But she couldn't make out what it said, so she snatched the bent bobby pin away and held the note under the light over the medicine cabinet.

"I let them take me. Now they won't hurt you or the Torrences. When it's over, when you're safe, get back to Porter and never tell a living soul about this. Babe, I love you and I always will."

It wasn't signed, but she knew it was written by Danny. Even with the uncharacteristic misspellings—"your" for "you're," "sole" for "soul"—her sweet teddybear of a husband had written it, and he'd surrendered himself for her sake. The idea of the mental tension he was clearly under—the obvious invasion of his fine mind, until he could no longer remember how to spell simple words—almost overcame her, and tears smarted in her eyes.

How could he have been so foolish as to believe they'd leave any witnesses to the dreadful things they'd done here? Surely, Ginger thought, they would never be so careless, so stupid. Danny, believing they would keep their word, when they'd kidnapped—or *murdered?*—nearly one-hundred people, was evidence of how they must already have penetrated his thoughts, perverted them.

—The communication hit her *then, making her blink. She knew.*

And a realization came to Ginger, too, that the only people she had for protection were downstairs in the dining room of the nightmare hotel—the damnable, incredible horror hotel—and she was as vulnerable to attack in her rooms as Danny himself had been. She stuck the tissue note in her purse, and ran for the door leading to the corridor with all the quickness of her athletic years.

Behind her, in the bathroom, the gasping walls of the Hotel Holroyd breathed again—once, twice, thrice. And then, as if they knew that the suite was empty, they shuddered a final time, and stopped moving.

CHAPTER SEVENTEEN

A single, alternating light was burning in the room, and that was the word for it, Henry Clurge decided quickly as he squinted his eyes against the glow and found his nose wrinkling: Burning. Because the manager's office of the Hotel Holroyd was suffused with an impossibly queer illumination that spread—in waves of steady beating, on/off, on/off in its rhythmic pulse—in hellish crimsons from corner to corner. It was bloody hypnotic, that damned light; but there was rather more to it than that, the desk clerk realized as he crept forward, *much* more.

The lighting in the office did not come from any kind of lamp made by man but issued in stunning silence from the two distant walls of the place.

It came . . . *creeping out*, he saw, like some kind of unbelievably disciplined campfire—or the flames of a well-organized, controlled Hades. It came from nowhere and everywhere as if the walls had pores, and were sweating blood. It was dispersed so that it drew within feet of the door where it dripped ugly, obsidian shadows on the faded carpeting, like pooling candle-wax.

And the illumination bore with it, the nearer Henry got to the peculiar walls, a vile stench that made him wish to spin away, or start to retch. It gagged the throat, twisted the stomach into knots, seeped offensively to the man's soul. For a second, he couldn't identify the stink, since it was not the kind that civilized man—even a man no more civilized than Henry Clurge—had frequent opportunities to smell.

But it was, he felt reasonably sure, reasonably panicked, the smell of flesh smouldering.

Okay, the desk clerk decided, standing up straight and wadding his hands into fists, jabbing the fists manfully into his slender sides; *okay then. It's part and parcel of the extraterrestrial's activity and I daren't fool with it. No need to get the wind up, though, or be spooked; it's meant for the* published *writers, those precious lucky buggers who see all their magical words in* print—*not for a poor struggling lad with more talent, more courage, in his pinkie finger than the whole lot of 'em have.*

All the same, replied Henry Clurge's curiosity, hearing him out and remaining completely unsated, what's *causing* the light and the reek?

Turning, he saw what he'd overlooked before. An aquarium set against the wall, one of the two that didn't light-up like a Christmas candle. And looking closer, half-bent to his curious task, Henry spotted the *connecting link*—a strange, tubular arrangement that disappeared into one of the scarlet walls and, at the other end, seemed to *dip* into the fish tank.

God, Henry wished he had a camera! Clearly, he thought, the world where the Quinces came from had some kind of goddamned *fish* that gave off energy, that gave it off in such monstrous-big quantities that it had to be harmlessly tapped-off into the structure of the building.

Energy, Henry breathed the word, half-aloud; *a new source of power.* For the first time in quite awhile the desk clerk's allegiance to the idea of making literary history slipped slightly and was instantly replaced with the wild, wondrous possibility of simply making a fortune. *If that fish tank contains a critter that produces cheap energy, and if it can be* bred *on good old Mother Earth, why Mother Clurge's young lad can solve the* whole energy crisis—*and make himself a justly-earned* trillion dollars *into the bargain!*

Suddenly it was clear to Henry Clurge why Peter Quince and his wife had come to this humble corner of the universe and decided to conquer the planet. *Power*—and all that went with it—was bound to be a draw anywhere in the cosmos. Since he was humanoid in shape, nobody would ask questions when Quince was ready to make his move. They'd simply start pitching contracts at him, and dollar bills with bunches of zeroes tagging after the number. Why, a man—or an extraterrestrial—could live like a *king* if he could supply the world with something to replace oil and coal! And in the last analysis, what the hell difference did it *make* whether you were on Arcturus or Andromeda or Earth, if it came down to *that* kind of power and influence!

Henry's mind tumbled over itself as he felt himself coming to a complete understanding. If a bright guy on Planet *A* saw that a lot of people who looked like him on Planet *B* would practically give their *souls* for what he could offer, well, business was business. For all Henry knew, there might be a huge market four-hundred light years away to the north for—for *ordure*, for plain old shit scooped out of the sewer; and to the west, five-hundred light years away, the natives might be creaming their jeans for old basketballs, or empty lipstick tubes, or used paperback books—*anything*. But if Henry couldn't know what they wanted, smart, modern people like the Quinces undoubtedly *did* know. They probably picked up television news, sat around in chairs made of Jell-O or old Diet Pepsi bottles just *waiting* until Ted Koppel or David Brinkley or Dan Rather gave the word, and then lit out of there in their fancy flying machines the way any sensible earthling would do—beating the suburbs to make a buck!

And if Quince and his wife wanted, they could sell their precious secret fish to the reds in Russia, or even China, without the slightest disloyalty. Which meant, Henry Clurge told himself assertively, moving toward the aquarium, that *he* had a duty to all of the free world to save the new energy source for the good guys! He'd be no less a hero, and a helluva lot richer, than if he

209

wrote a book exposing them. *Any* American would say he had more right to that incredible fortune, that boundless power, than a bunch of weirdo business types who were just lucky enough to live on a more advanced planet!

There was a covering on the tank. Henry ripped it off.

The Selector looked up at him with his baleful, unholy orbs, and the desk clerk knew where the splashing sound had come from.

It was the last thing he ever knew clearly at all.

Every thought that had passed Henry Clurge's mind had been read by the creature in the tank. Some of them meant nothing to him; all of them seemed more-or-less deranged, certainly ridiculous. Mostly, however, the Selector was maniacally frustrated by the pounding *emotions* of the earthling—the confused ideas, the naked greed, the absolute self-interest. In Henry Clurge there was no bewildering outpouring of the emotion called love, or the *caring* form it took. But the feelings experienced by the Selector were, in their own way, much more threatening. The avid lust *it* sensed reminded the thing in the tank of how the citizens of its own planet had lived, for millions of years; it felt plugged-in to something grossly atavistic, antediluvian, and all its modern, humming elements rebelled against such lurid, disjointed yearning. It was time travel of a kind the Selector had never desired to make, and more, the human's greed was just enough like the more-cultivated and self-deceptive intellectual planning of its own people to make *it* see how far its own world still had to go.

There was also the personal matter of vanity, and the

way this frail, human creature referred to *it* as a fish; although the Selector was nowhere near honest enough to confess that private annoyance to itself. Progress is never finished, never absolute; and the last improvements left to any species are those to be rendered in itself.

Without an ounce of warning, looking more bizarrely horrifying than anything Henry had seen before in his life, the Selector kicked out—thrust forward—and *sat up*.

Henry saw images of homely dolphins emerging from the ocean, dapper and eternally different; of divers in grotesque helmets, coming to the surface like fantastic Venuses rising from the sea; of the Loch Ness monster, and the "Creature from the Black Lagoon"—and then of concepts for which no description existed or was possible in the limited language of an earth person. When Henry shrieked his fright, sounded a note of how revulsed his senses were, and threw up his hands before his cringing face, the sound of his scream carried only a few meaningless feet and was swallowed up.

It was met by a barrage of returning telepathic powers which seemed, in Henry Clurge's closing mental meandering, like the shock waves from a thousand uranium bombs. Always piercing and painful to Peter Quince and his wife, the incoming beam of thought—uncoated by manners, consideration, or any other socially-poised sugar-pill—was fatal anathema to the desk clerk. Unable to disseminate or dispel the cannonading force of the Selector's mental hatred, Henry's brain was instantly overloaded, swollen, and burst.

Still standing, his skull shattered. Scraps and shards of it, with skin or hair adhering, shot into every corner of the office. It all occurred so quickly that the headless body continued to stand another moment, torrents of blood pumping geyser-like from the frayed butt of a neck. Something instinctive or otherwise biologically automatic brought Henry's hands up, the fingers reaching for the place where a face had been before clawing in last-second, soul-shredding discovery.

A slice of skullbone from the region of the late Henry Clurge's right temple landed in the aquarium. The Selector seized it, from where it floated redly on the surface, and settled on its back. For a moment it luxuriated in the absence of human feeling, of all sound, the computer function of its extraordinary intellect pumping messages by colored light into the distant walls and thence to the remaining rooms of the Holroyd where writers' wits blinked and went out. Then, its cosy smile blessedly unseen by any other creature, the Selector began munching on its midmorning snack. . . .

"He's gone," Ginger announced, dropping into her chair at the table in the dining room, her eyelids batting-back an onslaught of tears. "Danny's g-gone."

"That can't be," Spence argued, unwilling to believe it.

"What happened?" April asked; and "Where did he *go?*" asked Lauren Torrence.

"I d-don't know exactly," Ginger said in a voice that trembled. She poured lukewarm coffee into her cup and drank it noisily, gratefully. She seemed *so* pale, April thought with concern. "To save me—to save *all* of us— he surrendered to them."

"Can you be sure of that?" Spence blurted out. "How do you know?"

For an answer, Ginger retrieved the note Dan had scrawled on the toilet tissue and handed it wordlessly across the table to her husband's dearest friend.

"Sweet God," Spence muttered as he read it. He did not say "Shit and damnation;" what he said was a prayer. "Poor Dan."

April clutched his arm. "Perhaps they haven't hurt him, or any of the writers," she suggested, desperate to ease his despairing sadness. "He may be all right, wherever he is." She looked at Ginger. "If they're really extraterrestrials, genuinely *advanced* people, maybe they only want to analyze Dan's mind, his fine talent."

"Maybe they want to conduct *experiments*," Spence growled. "Use him for some kind of goddamned intergalactic lampshade, like a bunch of cosmic Nazis. Maybe they want to pick his brain apart, cell by cell, to learn how we creative types think. Maybe—"

"Stop it, Spence!" Ginger cried, close to slapping him. She'd never been so ghastly white before. "I know he was your friend but he was my husband."

"*Was*," Lauren said the word, hearing its connotations clearly, the way the young hear everything. She leaned forward on the table, her head beside her untasted milk, and began to cry. "Uncle Dan," she sobbed, "*was*."

"That much I must face," Ginger said bravely, raising her own chin and looking first at April and then Spence. "We'll never see my Danny again."

"We've never had this kind of difficulty before."

"Something about the way they think," replied the

woman, trying to fine-tune the intricate dial. "The Selector called it 'feelings.'"

"I am well aware of their primitive emotional state," said the man, coldly. He did not turn to look at her but continued listening, as best he could, to the interspersed, sporadic messages reaching them from the hotel dining room. "We were competently briefed on that topic before beginning this mission, you may recall. If the briefing was insufficient, it may be that these people are becoming *increasingly* emotional as a race or because of what is happening to the writers in particular." Then he did look at the woman and said the unthinkable. "Or perhaps the Selector did not properly evaluate them. Perhaps they are a kind the Selector has not encountered before."

She blanched, drew back from him. "It is a criminal offense to criticize the Selector. It is punishable."

For a moment the man did not respond. He glanced at where the young female was playing with the statis replicator in the recreation area of the gleaming spacecraft, thinking. His reply was accompanied by one of his very rare smiles. "I do not think we shall have to be concerned about being branded a segment of the criminal population," he said softly. "And there is very little punishment remaining which they can administer."

"Hold!" the woman called. "Their voices are coming in again."

He sighed, and tilted his head to listen.

"We absolutely *must* get out of this place!" April Torrence exclaimed. Her face was flushed and her dark hair looked wildly askew. "Surely that damned snow can't reach more than a few blocks!" She covered Spence's hand with hers. "If we could find some kind of heavy winter costume, and shovels, we'd have a chance. Can't we *try* to escape?"

"I don't think we can," Ginger answered when Spence simply looked down at his uneaten, cold toast. "You have no idea of the *depth* of the snow. I've seen outside, through our windows, and in some places it's as high as a man."

Spence shook his head. "Besides, honey, we can't leave the rest of the people—*our* kind, not only writers and their families, but *earth* people—to die. Perhaps, if Ginger proved to be wrong, we could talk to everybody, make a collective effort. But some of these writers are getting on, they're really old. And I don't think it would be right for some of us to leave and others to remain."

"You're just collecting material for some damned *book* you want to write!" April cried, pulling her hands away.

"You know better than that," he replied quietly, looking at her with sad eyes.

"I'm sorry," she said at once, abashed. "I know I didn't believe much of it before, but now I'm just so terrified. I never thought it could happen to Dan."

"Perhaps we could telephone the police," Ginger said. "I'll grant you, it would be hard to get them to belive it. They'd think we were stir-crazy from being kept in here this way. But it might be worth the effort."

"No." Spence sighed. "I tried to make an outside call before we left our room. They're smart, all right; goddamned clever. They have known *precisely* when to anticipate our next move, and then they've slammed

215

the door shut and bolted it."

"I still say we try to make it outside," April said with grim determination. She gathered her purse, ready to rise. "None of us is old. We're all in pretty good condition. I say we find something to dig with and walk right down the front steps and out the door!" She looked firmly at her husband. "I mean it, Spence, I'm going to try it. Our lives, and Lauren's, mean more to me than a bunch of strangers. Are you coming or not?"

"When you put it that way," he said, his voice gone suddenly old, "I have no other choice."

"We *can't* go." Ginger, staring at them both. She looked adamant, and courageous; she might have been looking the length of a tennis court at Tracy Austin on the bouncing verge of a service ace. "I didn't want to tell you, but when I was in our room, I tuned in—just for a moment—to what the extraterrestrials were thinking. And we dare not leave here."

"Why?" April asked defiantly, her cheeks pink with excitement and fear. "What did you hear?"

Ginger paused. "If we wait our turn, we'll be the last ones they take. But if we make any effort at all to leave"—she paused, clearing her throat, steadying her nerves—"We're *next*. And *we're dead!*"

CHAPTER EIGHTEEN

"But she *was here!*" Spence insisted, pounding his fist on the registration desk and reddening to the auburn roots of his flaming hair. "We spoke with her, we *discussed* things with her!"

"There is no Anita Simpson Lewis registered, sir," the middleaged woman replied frostily, glaring at him. "Obviously, there has been some mistake."

"Oh, there've been a few mistakes made, all right," Spence grumbled. "Look, the usual desk clerk who's on duty—what's his name, Clurge? Where's he? I'd like to ask him about the poet."

A beat. "I have been informed that Mr. Clurge is indisposed," she said steadily. "Customarily this isn't even my station. But I *can* read, Mr. Torrence, and Ms. Lewis is simply not visiting the Hotel Holroyd."

Spence took a deep breath and tried to get control of himself. When he spoke again it was in a gentler tone, intended only for the new desk clerk's ears. "My bet is that you're as human as I am, that you're helpless to do anything about the things that are going on in this place. Either they've bought you, body and soul, or you're as frightened as the guests. But I tell you plainly, madam, Anita Simpson Lewis—one of this nation's finest poets—is staying at the Holroyd. And I want to see her, I want to see her *now!*"

"I have no idea what you're talking about." The woman had paled; she looked drawn and glanced instinctively up at the horizontal mirroring on the second story. The one-way mirror fronting the managerial office of Mr. Peter Quince. Abruptly she spun the check-in book around to face Spence. "Why don't you see for yourself?"

He did, eagerly. While he had the chance—even with the desk clerk's angry eyes on him, even while he knew he might be observed by the extraterrestrial behind the ongoing mirror—Spence read the list of writers who were registered by the Holroyd.

It didn't take long and, despite himself, Spence gasped.

There were forty-four people staying in the west wing of the hotel, according to the book at his fingertips—and no more. The lovely lady poet's name was not among them. To any investigative third party, glancing at the register, there would be nothing to suggest that more than one-hundred people *had vanished.*

He paused, and stared up at the unblinking mirror on the second floor. "Bastard," he whispered, clenching his fists. "Murdering bastard!"

"I hardly think obscenity is called for," remarked the middleaged woman behind the desk. "Are you satisfied now, Mr. Torrence?"

"Not quite," he retorted, as the thought occurred to him. Again he scanned the lined columns of names, and when he'd finished, he felt his knees go weak and his vision marred by smarting tears.

Nowhere in the pages of the registry was the name of his dearest friend, Dan Lloyd. It was as if Danny had never existed. . . .

He went away from the desk and started walking, almost stiff-legged, back to the hotel restaurant. In the daylight the fading carpet beneath his feet seemed a mockery of modern comfort and living; everything in the lobby was bright, too bright, as if he'd moved somehow into a glaring spotlight. With each step Spence felt the familiar, old tingling warning of intentional falsehood—of severe risk—surging through his body. With each step he felt the eyes of unseen *watchers*, coldly following him, making sure they saw his every motion. By the time he was through the restaurant door and approaching the table where April, Lauren and Ginger were waiting, he was perspiring freely from every pore and felt more threatened, more in imminent danger, than he'd felt when he was handling a reporter's assignment in Iran. There, the Ayatollah's wild-eyed henchmen might have decided to turn on the press at any instant; but the worst that could have happened was his imprisonment, or his death.

Here, in the Hotel-Holroyd, Spence knew he was confronted by a more terrifying hazard. Because it was the *unknown* he faced. He did not know, even now, what the extraterrestrial Quince had in mind for him and the others. Perhaps it, too, was death; but as he sank into his chair at the table, avoiding the questioning gaze of the others, he was afraid that Quince and his female were after his immortal soul as well.

"Lord, Spence, I was so *worried* about you!" April cried, her fingertips touching his eagerly. "You said you were only going to the rest room and then you were gone so long."

"I was afraid," Ginger put in softly, and for a second she couldn't finish it. Her lightcolored eyes were moist. "—Afraid you'd gone where Danny went."

"Not yet," he said, forcing his old grin. "Shit and damnation, the old saying was always true. Where there's life there's hope."

It buoyed them a bit but he didn't know if he meant it. The atmosphere in the large room felt throttling, stultifying. April, he saw, was shivering again. Except for the couple of dozen writers and their families— Spence noticed that few of them had gone to their rooms, presumably feeling there might be safety in numbers—he found himself suspecting everyone and everything he saw. It might be paranoid, but after all, if the walls of a commonplace bathroom posed a severe risk, what *other* things of customary normality might the extraterrestrials have endowed with their special, advanced-world hazards?

. . . The *waiters.* They were leaning, arms folded and their eyes fixed upon the restaurant patrons, against a yellow railing outside the hotel kitchen, but they did not look relaxed, they did not really appear to rest. No one was ordering anything more to eat or drink but the waiters saw clearly that none of them had left his or her table. And so they lounged by the kitchen entrance, always watching, still as mourners in a funeral parlor, without a discernible emotion in any of their faces. Just for a moment Spence's gaze met that of the waiter who'd handled their own table and the fellow did not blink, or look away, or smile. He simply stared back at Spence until the redhead himself broke the connection. *Dear God*, Spence mused, *if one were to tour that kitchen, what would he find? Special herbs grown from crimson trees on a planet with two suns?*

Through the door to the outer corridor Spence could see the tiny giftshop. Inside it, a young woman with a bouffant hairstyle, or wig, did nothing at all. She too was leaning back with her arms folded, looking into empty space. *Is it my imagination*, he wondered, sweating, *or are they all just—waiting?*

"It's like a tryout," April said softly at his ear. Her dark eyes were huge. "You know, for some experimental drama playing out-of-town, or off Broadway. But it would never pack them in; it's too fantastic." She shook her head, some quality of her still incapable of fully accepting their plight. "Vanishing people, indeed!"

"A vast number of persons disappear annually," he told her. "More than you might think. I had to research it once, you know. The general attitude these days is that with the IRS, and social security cards, and credit, it's harder to disappear than it used to be. But it happens, April, at an *increasing number annually*." He glanced down at his trembling fingers. "For the first time I wonder how many of them are merely runaways—husbands tired of the bills, teenagers striking out on their own—and how many are . . . *taken*. Seized."

"They can't get away with it," April protested. "Not with people as wellknown as you, Dan, and the others. The hotel is full of prize winners!"

"Yes, they can get by with it quite easily," he contradicted her. "They have until now, haven't they?"

"He's right, I think," Ginger commented. "There'd be no obvious motive, not if they don't hold us all for ransom, and the police would simply place each of us in a file marked 'Missing Persons: unexplained.'"

"Daddy." It was Lauren, pale and frightened. "You promised me things would be all right."

"I know, princess."

"Well, can't we *do something?*" she wailed. With her face tilted to him, the long hair swept back from her forehead and flowing down her back, she'd never appeared more feminine or more helpless. "Do we just sit and *wait* for them?"

"I have an idea," Ginger remarked, "but it's probably full of holes. Each of us could circulate, meet two or three other guests, collect written data about them and where they're from—and then mail all the lists to police departments in their home cities."

"What then?" April asked, excited by the drama of it.

Ginger reflected. "Well, then we locate the manager of the Holroyd and *tell* him what we've done! If he knows all those police are investigating the disappearances, he won't *dare* harm the ones he's kidnapped—or kidnap any more of us!"

"I have a mental image of the Porter, New York, police department," Spence said slowly. "One old sheriff and two scroungy deputies about twenty-two years old. Why, they don't even have the resources to come here and check it out!"

"It's better than nothing," April objected, frowning at him.

"I don't think it is," he answered evenly. "For one thing, even the mail truck hasn't gotten through the snow to make a pick-up. For another, Dan and I discussed the possibility of Quince being an alien and he pointed out that any humanoids smart enough to get here would be incomparably powerful by our standards." He shrugged. "For all we know, if the mail were picked up at all Quince can zap the truck with some goddamned futuristic ray or blow up the whole post office."

"You're a big help," April muttered, lighting a rare cigarette and blowing smoke at him. "All you can do is shoot holes in our ideas."

She moved away from him, shivering, and her gaze met Ginger Lloyd's.

"Do you have a better idea, Spence?" she challenged him, apparently growing peevish herself. "If you do, please tell us. Quickly!"

"I think I'm getting one." Brows furrowed, he borrowed April's cigarette and inhaled deeply from it before returning it to the ashtray. He felt his daughter's loving, trusting eyes on him and tried to strengthen his argument while he talked. "Ginger, you've sort-of been in contact with them, almost seen them. Is that correct?"

"'Sort-of' is the word," she nodded. It was so difficult trying to get people without intuition to understand what happened to her. "I think it depends upon where they are, at the time. Occasionally, when I've tried to pick up their conversations or their thoughts, I can, but in spasmodic impulses like short-wave. Other times, I encounter some kind of immense obstruction and get nothing."

"What do they look like?" Lauren asked curiously. It was the most animated she had appeared all morning. "Tell me, Aunt Ginger! Are they buggy with weird antennae-things growing out of their heads? Or little-bitty guys with mummy skin and wrap-around eyes, the way they look in UFO movies?"

The athletic blonde laughed and squeezed the girl's small hand. "I've never been able to make out their faces, sugar. If I ever do, it's more likely to be in a vision than through telepathy, which is connected with the mind, what they're thinking." She looked back at the redhaired writer. "What did you have in mind, Spence. Openly challenging them?"

"I'm not that big a fool," he said. "But I was thinking about Lauren's look-alike, the one she calls the 'Hotel Girl.' Now, there is no way of knowing whether they're disguised or not. I'm not sure I believe an advanced science can actually influence us to see them the way they're not. So if the Hotel Girl *is* a child, even if she's a child who grows up in an incredibly progressive world, she'd *still* be a child with a child's physical weaknesses. I'd thought perhaps Ginger could contact her, psychically, and make her come to us."

"Then we can *capture* her!" April exclaimed, clapping her hands together as she understood. "Hold her, or something—try to make her weirdo parents a deal—a *swap!*"

"That's a trifle melodramatic," Spence replied, grinning. "But that's fundamentally the idea anyway.

224

What do you all think of it?"

"It could work," Ginger said. "Except for contacting her. I'd have no way of knowing my messages didn't reach her extraterrestrial parents too."

"Then let's go back to our rooms." Lauren suggested, eyes wide. "She usually finds me there, sooner or later."

Less than a minute later, April and Ginger nodded their agreement. No one could think of a better plan, and it was better than simply sitting—in effect, 'waiting for Godot.'

Spence, following the women and his daughter toward the restaurant door, felt the other humans in the dining room watching him. He knew they thought they'd never see any of them again. He prayed they were wrong.

And it occurred to him, by the time they stood alone at the elevator, what a tumbling assortment of contradictions went into the creation of the human species, what a topsy-turvy, egocentric and idiosyncratic collection of good and bad attributes described us all.

Until Lauren mentioned it, from her sweet vantage point of a child's fresh openness to fantasy, it had never occurred to him seriously that Peter Quince and his woman might look any different than he and his people. Arrogantly, we adults completely accepted the graceless belief that *ours* was the last evolutionary step, that *ours* was the Master Design, and that no one could conceivably have a more logical, well-functioning, attractive bodily style than the people of infantile Earth. Moreover, he saw, if we encountered something drastically different, we would think it absurd, ugly, inferior—the way we had always found races of a kind we'd never met before. Suddenly it became clear why no one from another planet would openly introduce

225

himself—or *itself*—to the human race.

Within months, we'd send missionaries to force our religions down their throats, to teach our politics and form of government, to thrust our styles and morals, and mores on them whether they had the slightest interest or not—and whether they'd been around ten-million years longer! An earthling's colony on Arcturus was bound to mean, sooner or later, an Arcturus run like Earth; because they might be smarter in a lot of ways, but Spence believed to his toes that no race anywhere in the cosmos had more effective salesmen and advertising agencies!

When the elevator doors closed, he tried to picture Mr. and Mrs. Peter Quince and thought: *If they are as different physically as their unscrupulous scientific trickery in the Hotel Holroyd, only Mad Avenue or the Moral Majority might possess the cunning to survive.*

CHAPTER NINETEEN

By the time the Torrences and Ginger Lloyd were ensconced in Spence's and April's suite in the west wing, it was nearly noon on Friday. While not exactly overjoyed or jubilant, each of them was happy to be doing something constructive toward protecting themselves and a feeling that they might somehow survive spread infectiously among them.

"Weapons," Spence said, standing in the front room, looking from side to side. "We each need some kind of weapon."

"They didn't exactly construct these rooms on the

basis of armament," April said, helping him search. "I can't *tell* you the last time I found a Thompson submachine gun in a hotel suite!"

"Well, they did a nice job of using what was here to attack the people," Ginger observed wryly. "Danny and the others must have been forced by *something*."

"Scientific gadgetry, I think," Spence growled, knocking over an end table and yanking at the wooden legs. Each one would make a serviceable club. "Probably some kind of updated hypnosis or mind-control through the panels in the walls. You know, match the pulse of the person touching it and then disrupt his system, slowly but surely, until he begins to believe what they want him to belive."

"What chance do we have against people like that?" Lauren asked, tugging at another leg of the end table. Her expression was one of awe. "If they can just 'zap' a mail truck, the way you said they could, Pop, they could do the same thing to us."

Sweating, he plunked down on his seat and gave her a reassuring grin. "Your Uncle Dan said people from a futuristic world would tend to be peaceable. Now, I'll grant you, princess, that kidnapping human beings isn't my idea of behaving in a law-abiding fashion. But we still don't know for sure that anyone has been harmed. And there's something else, too."

"What?" Lauren asked. April and Ginger were listening attentively as well.

"A lot of earth people have become overly well-bred, all the spunk and fight has been drained out of them by living the good, modern life." He paused. "I'm not advocating any kind of *macho* approach to life, but sedentary types—writers included—usually have about

228

as much physical strength as poor old Puck. And a good right hook to the jaw, or one of these table legs in the top of even an alien head, will probably be as effective as any of their scientific gobbledegook."

"Do you really think that's true?" April asked him from her perch on the edge of the bed.

"Shit and damnation, I sure do!" Spence retorted. "Wilt Chamberlain and Kareem Abdul-Jabbar are both mammoth men, well over seven feet and two-hundred pounds. But I remember Wilt protesting that the officials let other players gang up on him and that he pointed out how *his* eyes are as vulnerable as a midget's. And Kareem has worn goggles for years."

When three o'clock came, they were all tired of playing cards. "Fiddling while Rome burns," April said with a frown. "When is that damned Hotel Girl going to show up?"

When four o'clock came, all of them were hungry and none of them—including Lauren—suggested phoning down for food. Instead, Ginger was pacing the floor, her athletic resiliency making her restless, while April was taking a bath and Spence was seated near the door, keeping his eye on Lauren.

At six o'clock, the tenuous quantity of optimism that they had experienced when they arrived in their rooms was replaced by serious doubt that the look-alike girl would come at all.

Worse than the doubt, wintry darkness crept down the corridors outside the suite and the bizarre, early-April wind whistled sharply, beckoningly, at the windows. Each of the human beings felt fear building by the moment.

April, who was never the soul of tact, put their

feelings into words. If she sounded overly dramatic, none of the others was inclined to criticize her. "I know, somehow," she began, her gaze resting on the dozing Lauren's innocent face, "that if it becomes midnight and we haven't captured the Hotel Girl—or succeeded in making any kind of advance—it's all over. We'll never see morning, never again."

"*Look,*" Ginger said, so quietly they scarcely heard her.

She was pointing, her muscled arm aquiver, and they looked where she indicated.

It had stopped snowing. Nothing was drifting past the window. And suddenly, without the slightest indication that it was happening, the world—their *world, the world that had been manufactured for them at the Hotel Holroyd*—was filled with almost supernatural silence.

"At last," Spence said.

"What do you mean?" Ginger asked.

The redhead was peering out the window, giving them his warmest Irish smile. "I mean that if the snow has stopped, the snow can melt. Before long, we can get out of here—afoot, if it comes to that."

"You don't mean that at all." April sat on the edge of the bed, her black hair swinging dolefully forward. "You're just trying to cheer us up."

"You know what it really means, don't you?" asked Ginger.

He looked at her sadly, and nodded. *It means,* Spence thought, *that they're ready to make their final moves now. They don't* need *the snow any* longer. Aloud, he cleared his throat. "You were—psychically sweeping the hotel, weren't you, Ginger?" he asked. He and April saw the blonde nod. "What did you learn?"

She jumped up from her chair, unwilling to say it sitting down. Her back was to them, as she looked into a mirror, as she answered him. "The rest of us—are *gone*. I saw blackness, emptiness, nothingness. I'm sorry to tell you, but—"

"But we're the *last ones*, aren't we?" April finished it for her friend. "The very last human beings in the Holroyd?"

Ginger nodded.

Spence clutched his club, one of the legs from the end table, and got heavily to his feet. "That rips it, then. The period of patient waiting is ended."

"What are you going to do?" April asked with a gasp, frightened.

"What I should have done earlier, I guess," he answered her, grimacing. "Look, they must have done *something* with all those people. You can't just wave a wand and make more than a hundred people vanish into nothingness, however brilliant they are. If they killed them, some of the bodies must be left in their old rooms. It's just possible that I can save a few, arouse them to enlist their help in all this."

"I told you," Ginger reminded him, "the other rooms are empty."

"Well, then, I'll just collect evidence." He made a face. "You know, become a *recorder* of the tragedy. If we get out of this, I want to make sure nothing like it ever happens again." He kissed April and began walking toward the front door. "Perhaps I'll find some kind of clue to what's going on, or maybe I'll just run into Mr. Peter Quince and decide to part his miserable scalp with my shit-and-damnation goddamned *club!*"

"The rooms are probably locked," Ginger said softly. "How will you get in?"

Spence stopped. "I remember seeing an old black lady who's the maid for this wing. I doubt she's involved. But she's got the keys to all the rooms and I'll get 'em away from her."

"Be careful, sweetheart," April called. She looked beautiful to him, then, her paleness turning her fine complexion to an ivory that brought highlights to her black hair. "Please be careful."

"Oh, I will be!" he assured her, chuckling. "And when I get back, make damned well sure it's me. Ask me something only the two of us have the answers to. And don't let anybody else in, even if they—"

There was a knock at the door.

The question appeared in all their eyes, unvoiced. Spence looked numbly at the door, frozen where he was, devoid of motivation. When his mind began working again it told him, forcibly, that he'd never less wanted to open a door in his entire life. "Who is it?" he asked, but his voice came out small and inaudible. He cleared his throat and tried it again. "Who *is* it? What do you want?"

No reply. Not that instant. A moment later, however, the knocking sounded again.

"Don't answer it!" April mumbled, covering her mouth with her hands in terror.

Spence saw Lauren was awake, aware of the knock. "Maybe it's the Hotel Girl at last," she said. "It's our chance to catch her, Pop."

He grabbed a breath, nodded, and started for the door. The others were by his side quickly, gripping the legs from the end table. *Two women, a little girl, and a middle-aged man,* Spence thought grimly. *We look like the Israeli army.*

—Which hadn't done too badly at all, Spence remembered, setting his mouth in a grim line and reaching for the doorknob.

Before he could touch it, however, *the door began to open.*

April squealed. Lauren stared in astonishment. Ginger dropped her tableleg-club. Spencer Torrence simply looked at the figure filling the doorway.

Looking wan and exhausted, seeming even more rumpled than usual, but with a smouldering cigar tucked between the index and middle fingers of his right hand, *the missing Dan Lloyd gave them a broad smile and took two steps into the front room.*

CHAPTER TWENTY

"Danny, Danny, Danny!" Ginger shrieked with delight, going into his burly arms and clinging to him. Dan's likeable, homely mug hung over her shoulder wearing a huge grin. Spence pummeled his broad back, April was on the other side hugging him, and Lauren bounded around the whole group, making joyous Indian-style warwhoops.

"Gosh, it's good to be back," Dan said in his plain way, hugging Ginger. He held her cheeks between his meaty paws and kissed her repeatedly on the lips. Then he spread out his arms to include his friends, and wrung Spence's hand until the wrist ached.

"What *happened?*" Ginger squealed, drawing him further into the suite but refusing to let go of his arm.

"Where the hell did you go, Dan?" Spence echoed, trailing happily after them.

"Just let me rest my surplus poundage in a chair and I'll explain everything," the science writer said. It was true, Spence thought, he looked beat. Like he'd been through the wringer. Dan sighed and settled himself into the most comfortable-looking chair in the front room, running a wide palm over his bare scalp. "You got anything around here to drink?"

"Only water from the tap," April said quickly, looking as guilty as any homemaker caught unprepared. "Sorry."

"We were afraid to order anything from the kitchen," Spence explained, taking a seat on the couch beside his wife. Ginger had positioned herself on the arm of Dan's chair, as if making sure he never got out of her sight again. "Even bottled drinks."

"*Why?*"

Spence looked at his oldest friend with amazement. "Why? Well, because we didn't dare trust anything about the hotel. Especially after what happened to you."

Dan met his gaze, held it steadily. "Nothing bad happened to me. And there isn't anything so terrible about the hotel, either." He heard the silence of astonishment grow up around him. "Folks, I've met the enemy and he's not. That's the sum and substance of it. I was taken to meet Peter Quince and his wife, and they aren't so very different from us at all."

"What the hell are you talking about?" Spence

demanded, scowling. "They've been picking off the writers and their families one-by-one." He gestured to Ginger. "You even left a note saying you were 'letting them take you,' or something. And your wife says that all the rooms in the hotel are empty now. What do you mean, the Quinces aren't our enemy?"

"Precisely what I say, old buddy," Dan replied. He drew a cigar from his pocket, started to light it, and then rested it on the table near his chair. He glanced up at Ginger and hugged her around the waist. "You just didn't know where to look for them with your psychic powers, babe. Everybody's safe. Nothing's wrong at all."

Ginger's expression didn't change. Apparently, Spence thought, she was so glad Dan had returned she wasn't even hearing what he said. Her head was resting gratefully on his shoulder and her eyes were shut.

"Would you care to explain what the Quinces are up to?" April inquired coolly, frowning at Dan. "I think we need a little information before we can become *quite* so sanguine about this old barn."

The balding man gave her a broad smile. "Patience, April. And you, too, Spence. I think you'll like what I have to say."

Spence looked at the unwrapped, unlit cigar beside Dan and then at Dan himself, the wheels spinning. "I doubt that very much, Danny. Very much indeed."

"Well, to begin with, I was dead wrong about the rest of the universe caring nothing about this planet. Just as wrong as I was in claiming that it was nearly impossible for people from another galaxy to reach us." He hesitated, then rested his feet on the edge of the couch. "The fact is, the Quinces are an advance party looking into

236

the possibility of issuing Earth an invitation. An invitation to become a member of, well, a sort-of All-Galactic Society."

"They have a damned peculiar way of investigating a potential member," Spence commented. His gaze returned to the unlit cigar. "I've never really considered the act of spying the basis of a good social relationship."

Dan raised the chubby index finger of his left hand. "They had no other choice, pal. You see, we reached a point near the end of World War II when an invitation was imminent. But then we developed the means to blow ourselves to kingdom-come."

"The atomic bomb," April said.

"Precisely. At first, they didn't dare ask Earth because it was too early in our development, but it was against the rules of the Society to mingle in the affairs of a non-member world. Then we had the bomb—nuclear power—and they were amazed. That form of energy wasn't meant to be unleashed for another eight to nine-hundred years, on our planet, so suddenly we had the technology that was required but not the good manners to belong to the club. Savvy?"

"Oh, I follow you," Spence said wryly. "It's good manners, is it, to come to another planet and start *kidnapping* its people?"

"It was never a bellicose activity on their part." Dan looked serious. "It had to be covert, to talk with us one at a time, learn how we felt about things. Without influence from one another."

"Why writers?" Spence asked. "Why'd they start with us?"

"Because we're opinion makers, buddy," Dan said

easily. "Don't forget, every kind of writer is here this week. Novelists, journalists, TV people, playwrights, poets. By acquiring our cooperation, they feel that we can use our special sword—our command of the language—to prepare everybody else for the kind of peaceable outlook that will eventually guarantee our admission to the great Society."

"Seems to me I've heard of a Great Society before," April put in.

"They have everything planned out to the tiniest detail," Dan marveled. "By following their leadership, step by step, we can not only bring peace to our world but qualify it for the most important step human beings have ever taken." He dropped his feet to the floor and leaned forward, appealing to them. His hands were spread wide, palms-up, and his blue eyes twinkled. "Spence, you couldn't *believe* the marvelous things I've heard that they can do for us after we're members! The cure of every disease known to man! A form of government which is finally fair to *everyone!* And *longevity—* well, pal, they tell me human beings have always had the potential to live for at least two-hundred years. But *they* have a method involving vitamins produced on a member world which will guarantee *every human being* a minimum life expectancy of three-hundred-and-fifty years!"

"Isn't that wonderful," Spence said. It wasn't a question. His next remark was. "Would you light that cigar for me, Danny?"

The balding man blinked. He glanced down at the wrapped stogie without touching it. "That? You want me to smoke it? Why?"

"Because I don't think you can," Spence told him

238

flatly. "Because I think they've *altered* you, my dear old friend, and I don't think you're really Dan Lloyd anymore. I think something in that cigar would be very bad for you now or you'd have lit it the moment you came in here."

Dan shrugged. "I'm just not in the mood to smoke," he said offhandedly. His eyes glittered. Blue ice, Spence thought; chips of ice from the coldest part of the Arctic. "I resent what you've said. It isn't like you."

"*Nothing* about you is like Dan Lloyd, not really," Spence replied. "Shit and damnation, I *want* you to be my friend again—I *want* to believe what you're saying and we're all going to live happily ever after." He stood, slowly, feet from Dan. "But I think you've come here to fetch me—to get *all* of us—because, one way or the other, buddy, you've gone over to the other side. To the *extraterrestrial's* side."

"Bullshit," Dan said succinctly. He still hadn't touched the cigar.

"Then *prove* it, Danny," April urged him. "Why not just light up, the way you have a million times before?"

"*Because he doesn't dare.*" Ginger, sliding off the arm of Dan's chair, sidled toward Spence and April. She kept a watchful gaze on the heavyset man. "*I've looked inside him*, and he *isn't* Dan! Not *now!*"

Lauren, who had said nothing for minutes, spoke from beside her father. Her eyes were enormous as she gaped at her Uncle Dan. "When he spread out his hands," she said in a tight, anguished little voice, "*I saw it! The thing on his index finger!*"

Spence's hand shot out, caught Dan Lloyd's wrist. His motion was a surprise; he turned the wrist until Dan's hand was palm-up again.

239

On the tip of the index finger of the science writer's right hand something *had been implanted—something made of a strange metal, a button that* gleamed . . . and pulsed, *irregularly, as if in direct communication with an alien intellect.*

Dan came up from the chair in a single straight line, tearing his hand free as his head butted Spence in the chin and sent him tumbling deeper into the room. Lauren screamed. Dan charged forward after Spence, his big hands cupped and clawing, his expression so contorted in hatred it seemed impossible that any of them had believed him still to be the man they loved. Spence ducked, as nimbly as possible, and heard the *whish* as the thing-in-Dan's-body missed with a clutching right hand meant for Spence's throat. He hit the Dan-thing in the belly, hard, and heard the rewarding "oof!" But it didn't stop him, it only angered him.

I couldn't have defeated Dan when he was himself, he's too big, Spence thought desperately, staggering away from the attacking bulk. *Now I don't even think Dan's in there—if I hurt him, all I'll do is hurt Danny's body—not stop the extraterrestrial! Quince can't even feel it!*

The next blow thrown by the Dan-thing was like a ham hurled at Spence and it struck him along the side of the jaw, dropped him to his knees. When the creature kept coming, Spence scrambled back, crab-like, while he looked around for the table leg he'd planned to use as a weapon. *Shit and damnation, they've outsmarted us at every step! Maybe it's absolutely hopeless after all!*

The Dan-thing lurched for him again. Spence side-stepped, saw the heavy body fall to one knee, hammered

240

it in the back of the neck with both fists. But it shook off the blows and came erect again, its once-familiar face a dark burlesque of the gentle writer he'd known so long. *If he kills me*, Spence thought, gasping as he darted deeper into the suite, *April and Lauren are next! And God knows what he'll do to Ginger!*

Suddenly Spence saw that he was being driven into a corner: the open bathroom door yawned wide and, once he was inside, there'd be no escape from Dan—or Peter Quince. Standing his ground, he hit the Dan-thing full in the face with all his strength, and *the creature didn't even blink.* A moaning sound escaped Spence's lips, and he closed his eyes in the belief that he was doing it for a final time.

Danny!

Spence's lids shot open. The name had been utterly explosive, it *hurt*—Ginger, screaming it, he saw—but he hadn't heard it with his ears. He'd heard it in his *mind.* He saw the Dan-thing freeze, just for an instant, its eyes squinted in acute pain—

And Spence shoved him bodily into the bathroom. April, thinking quickly, had lit Dan's cigar and was rushing by Spence, stooping to place it just inside the room. Murky gray smoke raised into the air as Spence slammed the door shut. "Quick!" he shouted to the others. "The door locks from the inside and that cigar can't hold him forever. We'll have to barricade it!"

Stumbling, thrashing noises from beneath the bath-room door, then the sounds of a heavy body slamming against the far wall. The outraged, furious shout ripped from the throat of Dan Lloyd did not belong to Dan. It belonged to nothing human.

Together, Spence and the others upended the double

bed and jammed it against the door. Lauren ran for chairs, handed them to her Pop, and Spence piled them atop each other as best he could. The Dan-thing—or the extraterrestrial using Dan's body—had seen the smoking cigar. Pounding footsteps made it clear to the humans that the creature was trying to figure out how to circle it.

Spence added the television set, other tables, Lauren's cot. But a glimpse told him the barricade could not hold for long. Soon, he knew, the cigar would simply go out. . . .

"We have to make our next move fast," he told them as he whirled. Sweat seeped into the creases of his face. "Ginger, can you—"

Spence was interrupted. His mouth dropped open. They all stared into the front room, incapable of motion.

Someone—or something *else—had rapped, softly, on the door.*

TRANSCRIPTION FOUR

"WILD PLACES"

"The universe is not hostile, nor yet is it friendly. It is simply indifferent."
—John H. Holmes

"The *wild places* are where we began. When they end, so do *we*."
—David Brower

"There is clearly something entirely wrong with our conception of time . . . One mind can extract pictures of what appear to be memories from some level in the mind of another person. *Many* of these memories are of events which *have not yet come to pass* in our earthly time scale. They are *future* memories."
—T. C. Lethbridge,
Ghost and Ghoul

work of the Almighty. He marvels, that father, at the fair, splendid, feminine creature who is part of his own sturdy masculine self. He stares at her when she is an infant, helpless in her crib, there to be molded, and when she takes her first hesitant steps. He hears her describe her first days at school, and, when she hands him her report card, his eyes will scan her apprehensive features in order to memorize each one. There is a very good chance that she will be quite special to him, in brief; and by the time she is entering puberty, beginning to become a woman like her mother, he knows the unique setting of her eyes, the particular tilt of her nose, the infinite variety of her smiles and scowls better than he knows his own right hand.

Before Spence she stood: Long-haired, slight of build, pretty in her way, eyes swimming behind lenses as thick as bottle-bottoms; and the flashback played through the writer's mind: "Pop, I just can't *read* my history book, the letters are too tiny and blurry"/Sharp Pang/"April, we'd better get this punkin to an optometrist." At first glimpse the Hotel Girl seemed to *be* his Lauren, and Spence found it unavoidable to refrain from turning to see again his genuine daughter, who was pressed against April. April and Ginger gasped in astonishment; both of them looked down at Lauren I.

But in the second it took for Spence to look back, the old, familiar recollections of his daughter twisted in disagreement. Lauren never looked malicious, or cunning; Lauren never stared insolently at him; and Lauren did not have incomprehensible flecks of scarlet in her pupils that gave her the demeanor of something evil, something inhumanly Satanic. Lauren looked like a human girl.

By the time he had dropped the homemade club and

246

was shooting his arm toward the Hotel Girl, trying to seize and hold her the way they had planned to do, Spence was much too late. With a shrill, high-pitched giggle that set his teeth on edge, she spun away from him and darted several quick yards down the black corridor. With one step taken, Spence saw the way the girl had stopped, clearly taunting him, just as clearly waiting for him to follow. And something finely-trained and experienced *shrieked* in his brain as the ice-water tingling sensation careened down his spine, "Don't *do* it! Don't go *after* her—*it's a trap!*"

Then April and Ginger Lloyd, doggedly striving to put action to their plan, were brushing past him and scurrying after the Lauren look-alike. For a moment he stared after them, numb except for the admiring realization of how *fast* the extraterrestrials made their moves, how *swiftly* they recovered from a setback and anticipated his every idea. *How can we hope to best them when they're that fast, that smart? It's as if they know me better than I know myself, understand my own reactions before I do!*

Then there was nothing to do but follow, chase after them—unquestionably the way Mr. and Mrs. Peter Quince *knew* he would do; because he could never let his wife confront such an unguessably terrifying situation on her own. Filled with a clear sense of doom, Spence broke away from the door and charged after them.

He did not observe that Lauren herself had lagged behind, too, in the hotel room, that she was only now tagging reluctantly after him and the other adults. He didn't know that she was trying to decide whether to shout at them her special knowledge, the incredible discovery she'd made with her own eyes—that the Hotel Girl did not *need* to flee from them; because Lauren, days before, had seen her merely *disappear!* If the girl wanted to get away, Lauren realized as she rushed after her beloved Pop, all she had to do was *will* it and she'd be gone! But the adults were spread out single-file ahead of her due to their different running abilities, their different positions at the outset; and when Lauren decided to raise her voice in an attempt to scream her vital information, *again* the words traveled only twelve inches or so from her mouth before being swallowed up by the otherworldly atmosphere of the Holroyd. She could not stop, remain by herself; the only thing in the world she could do was run to her doom.

Most of the illumination in the west wing hallway was dimmed, now, or completely shut off. Lauren knew it was no economy gesture. Gaunt gray walls leaped to the ceiling at their sides as they ran, appearing to be impenetrable mountain slabs imprisoning them in the valley of futility—yet Lauren saw, as well, the fleeting glimpse of grinning, macabre faces staring down at her from pictures that weren't there before; and she saw the way the hotel walls *swelled, exhaled, inhaled,* scenting each of their fatal steps.

Ahead of them all the Hotel Girl sped, turning a corner. She was waiting for them as they manuevered around it, each of the humans gasping for air. Her *running,* Spence thought with awe, passing April, her running looked unimaginably *effortless;* she seemed nearly to flow along the empty corridors and at times to float like some youthful spectre above the carpeted floor. It was such a nightmare; he felt that he was speeding down some subterranean tunnel to a destination no sane man would ever choose.

Ginger was nearest the look-alike, padding nimbly after the alien with the quickness and economic grace of the athlete she'd been. But everytime it looked like the tennis player would close the gap, and seize the Hotel Girl, another fantastic burst of jetlike speed shot her forward—almost as if the child *materialized* another yard farther on.

It's hopeless, absurd; we're totally outmanned, Spence realized. "It's a trap. she *wants* us to follow her!" he screamed at Ginger Lloyd, the breath virtually wrenched from his aching lungs; but his warning went unheard, his mortal sounds instantly devoured by the altered atmosphere of this familiar world turned into an alleyway of some futuristic hell.

Light. Bright, pink light ahead of them, just before the corridor turned again—flowing around the edges of a narrow door. Spence broke his pace, slowed to gape at it; but Ginger was closing-in again on the extraterrestrial child, who was stepping into a doorway that hadn't *been* there a second before—the door itself had vanished—and blonde Ginger was darting through it too! *God* help *us*, Spence prayed, accelerating, his red hair wet with perspiration and his smoky eyes blinking as he drew nearer the glaring pink light; *if* we're *made in your image, please remember it!*

His feet pounded up a brief flight of stairs scarcely wide enough to admit him. He heard April following him inside, then Lauren, and they were dashing after Ginger—and the Hotel Girl—across a *dance floor*—sliding once, recovering balance—

And standing mere yards from something *few people of Earth had ever seen.*

249

A tiered, gleaming, multilit spacecraft filled most of the deserted ballroom, more genuinely and finally a fact of the Quinces' outer space origins than anything else they had seen or experienced during their week at the Hotel Holroyd.

Protecting his vision with his bent hand, heart thudding rapidly, Spence stopped walking at once. He would no more have considered striding right up to it than he would have reached for the hand of the President, or a towering religious figure—not really because of fear, although that was present too, but from some instinctual, queer respect he felt immediately for the creation. There was nothing about the UFO that reminded him of the craft used in the American space race; there were no flags, no emblems, and the design itself—though capable of description with human words—gave the aura-like impression of titanic, foreign intellect well beyond the range of understanding given to earthlings at this point in Spence's existence. April and Lauren joined him, speechless on either side as they all looked up at it; and Spence reflected, *Well, it's no longer an* unidentified *flying object. They may deride me for seeing it, if we get out of this—they may claim I was hypnotized, or had a vision or something; but no power on earth could convince me this was anything but a space craft from another, technologically-superior planet.*

He saw that it was almost two stories high, crammed snugly into the immense ballroom, but for a moment he couldn't detect its color. He finally decided it might be the color of glowing sand. The bright lights, constantly changing hue, made it hard to tell but he suspected that was not for disguise but was somehow involved with the craft's energy. There were peculiar windows, or portholes, which seemed to circle it above the glittering seam uniting the two halves of the well-publicized pieplate design. But like the one-way mirror overlooking the hotel lobby, it was impossible to see through the windows at the marvels within. Powerful tripod legs held it off the floor and, for a second, Spence thought it was under full power and ready to take off. There was, he realized, an ungodly *humming* sound that was certainly mesmeric—a *drone,* part of it buzzing into the upper registers at periodic intervals, then leaking-over into a range he could not hear. His nerves, more than his ears, caught a sense of vibration that made him tremble with fright when he identified it. *A human electrical engineer could happily spend the rest of his life trying to understand this.* April's moist hand fumbled for his, and he held it, gladly; the two of them and their daughter gaped another moment at the spaceship with the eyes of simple island natives seeing their first airplane, or cigarette lighter.

For it was not tomorrow they were seeing, but a day at least one-million years into the future.

A door appeared! It wasn't there, and then it was, in the midsection of the spaceship. Lauren's look-alike was there, at a distance nothing but a pubescent child; and she was casting her gaze in several directions, obviously troubled.

Spence blinked, remembering. *Where was Ginger?* Apparently the Hotel Girl had run directly into the craft and, when she turned, her immediate pursuer was no longer in sight.

"Shit and damnation!" exclaimed Spence, starting forward. He knew he'd let his friend's wife down, then; he knew what he should have realized; and he knew that if he stopped to think about striding right up to the alien female and tried to get *inside*, he would not have the courage. But he had just remembered how much Ginger adored her Danny, and how brave and competitive she was.

Ginger Lloyd hadn't headed the pursuit of the Hotel Girl in the hope of gaining her freedom. She intended *vengeance* upon the extraterrestrials who had ruined her beloved husband.

He saw her only after beginning to jog toward the ship. She came up from a crouch, at the curving bottom of the craft, and she still had the makeshift club Spence had given her! She was *swinging* it, he saw, toward Lauren's look-alike, valiantly and foolishly striving to take control of the incredible flying machine!

He caught a glimpse of the startled Hotel Girl's face—snow-white in the ambient glare of the UFO as its color faded to a lighter hue—and then saw, with amazement and horror, the *diabolical swiftness* with which the alien race reacted.

Because an invisible forcefield of some miraculous kind seemed to have formed around the young creature, the full swing of Ginger's club stopped *inches* from the Hotel Girl and appeared to become ensnared. April shrieked; Spence winced. *A zigzag line of something electrical ran from the tip of the tableleg, through it, and into a Ginger who was gripped in place and who, when the power hit her hands clutched at the end of the club, turned an intense violet, and screamed with an agony that Spence knew he would never forget.*

For a moment Ginger's entire body was outlined in electrical dashes. It *shook*, violently. Her mouth was twisted out of shape; the whites of her eyes rolled into view; the veins in her arms and legs showed *purple*, as if

252

her bloodstream had been charged with an other-worldly magnetism.

"Aunt Ginger!" Little Lauren cried, unable to look away.

Then there was nothing to see anyway. Ginger Lloyd had vanished.

"*Bitch!*" Spence growled, and started running toward the spacecraft at full speed. *"Don't!"* April called frantically, beseechingly.

But she needn't have worried. There were other plans for the Torrences. The Hotel Girl no longer stood in the doorway of the magnificent ship; she was several yards away, bouncing on the balls of her feet; and when Spence veered in her new direction, she darted toward a distant door. *"Killer!"* he shouted. She paused and, to his maddened astonishment, made a tongue-out, eye-popping face at him the way any impudent human child might have taunted him.

Knowing full well his efforts were futile, but knowing he had to try, Spence ran after her with April and Lauren at his heels. At the distant wall a quite-ordinary door opened and he and the others followed the fleeing child-thing without hesitation. It slammed behind them; they heard dials spin, locking the space-ship away from prying eyes—

And found themselves in an unfamiliar corridor of the Holroyd. The hellish girl was ahead of them, giggling joyfully, jiggling. Spence realized then that they had entered the hallway he'd seen before, on the second story—but from the *other end*.

The manager's office was halfway down the hall.

At last, he realized, they were going to meet Mr. and Mrs. Peter Quince.

CHAPTER TWENTY-TWO

The Hotel Girl did not enter the manager's office.

Instead, after glancing back to make certain they were coming, she opened a door several feet shy of the office—unmarked, its secrets unforeseeable, the door had surely been locked but swung back with the look-alike's touch—and jumped lightly inside. There was a giggle that reached them and it seemed to the redhaired writer that the child, alien or not, genuinely believed she was engaged in a game. He did not doubt that she really *was* a child, regardless of the horrendous parentage that might be hers.

But more than a hundred men and women whom he had respected, and loved, were victims of the game and someone had to pay for it—if that was even earthly conceivable.

Spence, April and Lauren approached the door and it slid slowly, concealingly to, stopping only an inch or two before closing. It was neither inviting nor menacing in itself; it was noncommittal, perhaps nothing more than a door. But what lay on the other side was beyond the imagination of man, woman, or child.

He looked at his brunette wife whom he had adored so long he could not even recall accurately the time before her, did not want to; and she met his steady gaze with a mixture of tenderness and terror showing in her dark eyes. Each of them knew there was nowhere to run, nothing else to do but enter. Without uttering another word, Spence reached for April, drew her against him, and gently kissed her. Her body tremored. The bare skin of her slender, earthling's arms were cold to the touch. But she didn't flinch or try to flee. She merely let him make the next move. Both of them bent to hug their daughter.

Grabbing a breath, he stretched out his arm and gave the door a push.

Creaking faintly, the hinges requiring oil, it slipped back. Plain electric light pooled down on the carpeting outside, in the corridor. Oddly, Spence thought, there was the odor of something that had been *cooked*. Held securely in the clenching palm of fear, Spencer and his loved ones stepped inside.

At first the most extraordinary thing about the extraterrestrials' suite was nothing more than how ordinary it looked. Here, there were no flashing lights of every color, no obvious or overt marvels of an advanced science. Staring nervously at the floor, their wary gazes drifted up to take in the customary features of a hotel suite's front room. A fireplace was going, in one corner, the flames almost merry and taking off the chill.

Yet ahead of them, just behind a jut-out which marked the entrance to the dining room, *people*—humanoids, at least—sat peacefully before a table. In that instant the normality of the sight was stunning. Worse, there was the quiet sound of silverware clicking, as if some ordinary American family sat at dinner. If you listened, intently, the way the Torrences were doing, you could also hear the murmur of affable voices—and the surprising realization came to them that the voices sounded familiar.

Spence closed the door after them, and glanced to the left. April saw where he was staring then—frozen in place—and made a small, shrieking noise of astonishment.

The front room had looked ordinary only at first glance. There was very little ordinary about it. The wall, to the left as the Torrences entered the suite, had been knocked out. The purpose behind it was hideously transparent. Someone had wanted to provide ample room.

Ample room for dozens of folding chairs which were neatly lined-up and squared off, and in which—men and women and children—dozens of human bodies were sitting in total passivity. Unmoving, silent, giving the impression that they'd been propped-up in the chairs, they were the celebrated, prize-winning writers of the United States of America, and their families; and

Spence Torrence said, with an ugly catch in his throat, "They're all dead. Dear Lord, every one of them has been killed." He turned away, shocked. Saddened.

April, however, continued to regard them and Spence, seeing her, wondered if she had gone into shock.

"I don't think so," she murmured, moving toward the nearest rank of bodies. "I don't think they're dead—exactly."

"What the hell does that mean?" he grunted, finding the sight of his wife putting out a hand to touch the corpses unbearable. "They aren't dead 'exactly?'"

"They look the way I've seen actors look, on stage, when they were making their debuts or forgot lines and simply froze until a prompter or another actor jolted them out of it."

"There's Anita, the poet," Spence said under his breath. "You would have liked her; she was quite a lady." He pointed, gasping. "Oh God, there's the great Harry Werlin—and that screenwriter, Alistair Cummings!" Despite himself, he ignored the "family" waiting for them in the dining room and glanced over the columns of unmoving people. He had the feeling some old men have, when they visit a late friend in a cemetery and know, deep in cringing bones, that they're next. "They even took 'Pop' Cormach, the wittiest playwright of our times."

He was aghast with horror and knew that Lauren, silent by his side, shared his feelings. Here he saw the lanky political columnist who also wrote best selling novels, his graying hair ivy league-lank on his wide forehead; there, the bespectacled champion of horror writing, clad in a letter-sweater and faded jeans; over

257

there, an aging and kindly Hebrew novelist—a sharp-eyed and tongued woman writer of commercial exposés—a tall, Irish joke writer. He wished Lauren didn't have to see this.

"Spence, dammit, come here." April, incredibly, had brought her purse even as they'd rushed from their suite. He hadn't noticed before and, despite himself, he almost smiled at her womanly practicality. She fumbled inside it and produced a mirror. "Watch."

"What are you—cosmetician to the corpses? You aren't going to make them *up?*"

She ignored him and held the mirror before the lips of the reclusive genius, Harry Werlin. A massive, heavyset woman's body was propped beside his and even with her face fixed in its death-mask, Bernadine managed to look disapproving and sour. April glanced up, excited; incongruously happy. "See?"

For a moment Spence didn't get it. Instead, he was looking at Harry Werlin's fingertips. And on the index he discovered a tiny, metallic button like that which the converted Danny Lloyd had worn when he attacked them! Abruptly, he did notice what April was doing and took a closer look. She moved down the front row of chairs, repeating her experiment over and over, wreathed in smiles.

April's mirror clouded *as she placed it in front of each person's lips.* Something *had turned them into vegetables, but all of them were indisputably* alive!

"You're right!" Spence cried with relief. "Thank God! But if they aren't dead, what the hell *is* going on?"

"Perhaps we can clear all the mystery away for you, Mr. Torrence—if you'd be good enough to join us here in the dining room? And your charming family as well, of course. I understand you're an investigative writer who appreciates facts, so you may be a stripe above your predecessors in terms of dinner conversation." There was a pause; but still, the extraterrestrials' "guests" had not budged. "Come, come," he said, a trifle louder. "There's no reason to be quite that afraid of us."

"'No reason?'" Lauren repeated beneath her breath. The remark seemed to give her anger and, with it, a measure of fresh resolve. "You killed my cat Puck and my Aunt Ginger and—and *ruined* my Uncle Dan!"

April and Spence had whirled when they heard the being call to them. The voice didn't sound threatening in any fashion. It didn't sound unnaturally high, or abnormally low; it wasn't metallic of quality nor did it function on a computer-like, even line of unaccented sound. Again, however, all three of them—particularly April—believed the humanoid's voice was peculiarly feminine.

Fleetingly, Spence considered flight. That second he did not *wish* to investigate the extraterrestrials, or learn any otherworldly secrets. He only desired to escape, to go home to Porter with his family, and he felt they might that moment have the advantage of surprise.

But a look behind him told Spence that a flesh-colored, thin tissue like that of human flesh had crept stealthily up the front door and settled in the seams, effectively sealing them in. The famous writers sat like zombies, unable—or unwilling—to help. He turned back, his face grim and his mind made up. If they were to get out of there, and escape the Hotel Holroyd once and for all, they would have to confront the extraterrestrials who dared perch languidly at a dining room table in a ghastly parody of the human commonplace.

Forming a chain, hands linked, the three of them walked slowly through the front room and stopped, at last, just at the threshold of the dining room.

Three *other* "people" were seated at the table on which were placed platters, bowls, and tureens of food. Each plate contained the remnants of their meal, which seemed at an end. The tablecloth was snowy, pristine. The food smelled delicious. In the center of the table an ornate candelabra sheathed a single golden candle and gave off the only illumination in the dining room. There was a door, at the rear of the room, presumably leading to the manager's office itself. Shadows were cast, and played over the humanoid shapes; and for a moment the Torrences could see just the face of the Hotel Girl—the Lauren look-alike—who faced them from the far side of the table. Her young face was bright with animation, the way Lauren's became when they'd expected interesting company, and she'd tucked a white napkin in the bodice of her dress. The stains on it looked like blood. She smiled at them as they approached, but the ferocious flecks of uncanny red in the eyes behind the thick lenses stripped away all genuine signs of greeting and gave her a slightly demonic appearance.

Then the male at the head of the table slowly turned his head, to face his guests. He'd affixed to his thin lips the cruel parody of a welcoming smirk. "Join us!" he cried. "Your conversation shall be our dessert!"

Spence, April and Lauren were rendered speechless. Their amazement overshadowed everything that had already occurred and there seemed to be nothing left to say—and simultaneously, *all* things.

Mr. and Mrs. Peter Quince had the precise features—the duplicated faces—of Spence and April Torrence. It was like looking in a mirror.

admitted to herself, *I suppose you do. . . .*

"It will be pleasing to speak with your kind," said April-II, her gaze fixed clearly on April. Her dark eyes gleamed with appraisal, with curiosity. She was polite, but there was, despite her resemblance, the slightest taint of a superior air, as if some unguessable difference in social class set her apart. "For a change. We've had no opportunity to converse with—the others."

The male extraterrestrial with Spence's face, running a wide palm over his red hair, gestured to six chairs grouped nearby in a circle. They had *expected* it to be this way; they'd *planned* for this meeting. He gave them all another humorless, unaffectionate smile. His manner was that of a corporate president who was obliged to be host to the mail boy's family and wanted to get it over with as soon as possible. "Let's adjourn to a more comfortable seating arrangement. It would be rude for us to let you stand."

As the fellow rounded them up, even clapped Spence on the back as he led them to the easy chairs, Spence tried to consider their position. All right, the extraterrestrials—if that was truly what they were—had not taken the lives of the other wordsmiths at the Hotel Holroyd; but they had obviously done something to turn them all into vegetables and worse, automatons like Dan, who could be forced to attack their closest friends. That kind of power was awesome. The people of earth were inclined to mete out the harshest legal penalties to those who took human life. But when you considered the genius—the awesome, creative variety of the visiting writers at the time they'd arrived here at the Hotel Holroyd—wasn't this kind of dehumanizing mind-control at least as bad as actual murder? Spence let himself be led to a chair, but he surveyed it carefully before sinking into it, wary of traps. At the first instant they produced the tiny metallic button, or tried to implant them in his index finger, he vowed to fight back in some manner.

While April-II poured coffee, he began his own close appraisal of the male who looked like him. All Spence's investigative training as a writer was put into his evaluation and he found it fascinating despite his ongoing anxiety. Surfacely, he admitted, there was no obvious distinction between the two of them. It seemed foolish to think of the fellow as "humanoid" when he seemed so obviously human. There was the identically-colored hair, combed straight back; the same hue, shape and setting of the keen, smoky eyes; the same middle-sized structure. The alien did not lurch like a robot; he spoke normally, if in a rather more stiff and formal fashion than Spence.

Yet there *were* distinctions between them, the writer saw. And between both April and Lauren and their duplicates. Part of it was the superior attitude, a feeling of condescension; but underlying that was a clear impression of different origins. A human being, after all, was rather more than face, hair, and build. He grew up and emerged as an individual with the moods, the environment, the education, the life-experience intrinsically special to him coloring the way he spoke, gestured, moved. Surely that held true on any planet in the cosmos, even that of the extraterrestrials. And just as a bright, shrewd person can often detect a different national origin on the part of someone who speaks flawlessly yet comes from somewhere in Europe or Asia, Spence recognized in Spence-II the unique traces of the fellow's home-base.

When he did—when he realized that Spence-II

possessed few if any emotions, when he discerned the fundamental *heartlessness* of the extraterrestrial and his family—his terror was renewed and redoubled. This fellow would not hesitate to kill them all at once; it would mean nothing to him. And why *did* he and the others resemble the Torrences? What was going on?

"I'm sure you are full of questions," April-II remarked, sipping her coffee and peering over the cup at them. "There's no harm in answering them, is there, husband?"

"None whatever." The humanoid's absolute confidence that he was in charge of the situation and completely free of risk was unnerving. His smile was frosty. "Begin your queries anywhere you desire."

Lauren's hand shot into the air, a clear gesture of confessed inferiority. She was a child taking part in a class exercise and she didn't see her father's annoyance. Her question was direct, blunt: "Where are you from?"

"We come from a planet in a distant galaxy," Spence-II began. "The name would mean nothing to you. Your astronomers have not yet located the galaxy in question. What will interest you is that, in many ways, it is a *sister* planet to your Earth. We are, or have been, very much like the people of Earth."

"What does that mean?" Spence demanded. "You 'are, or have been,' like us?"

"Our civilization has progressed almost precisely the way civilizations of Earth have progressed. We, too, had our period in which two massive nations were locked in a cold war because they were the first to develop nuclear power, energy, intercontinental ballistic missiles, and all that. We had our presidents and premiers, our Congress and our Presidium—a ghastly age of terrible wars and more ghastly genocide preceding them, and of course that period when a threat of nuclear annihilation hung like a dark cloud over our planet."

"You *had* those things," April murmured. "But in your past?"

Her look-alike nodded. "In our very distant past. It is a period of history which our students must study although, to them, it appears to be longer ago than dinosaurs and the Ice Age appear to Earth people."

"How long ago w-was it?" April inquired.

"*All* the events with which you are now involved, *all* the dangers which your people confront," replied Spence-II, "occurred nearly *four-million years ago,* on our world." He sipped his coffee and gazed sardonically at the Torrences. "*You,*" he said deliberately, "are going to be *us*—in another four million years."

"Dear God," April whispered. "It's staggering."

"So long as you are fully restricted to the time-stream which you naturally experience," the male said with lofty superiority, "and associate that with the sum and substance of all reality, such a quantity of years will, in truth, appear staggering. Unfortunately, few of your scientists have yet apprehended the multiplicity of reality. Even while you know that time aboard a speeding spacecraft is different from that experienced simultaneously on earth, you have virtually no knowledge of the applications suggested by such a paradox."

"Then you're here to teach us?" asked Spence. For a moment he felt hope filling his heart, a willingness to believe these beings were the kindly, uplifting "space brothers" at which he had scoffed for years. "You plan to help us make a quantum jump in our development?"

The smoky blue eyes that were almost, but not quite,

his own turned to ice. *"Scarcely."* Spence-II murmured. "Scarcely that."

"Well, if you know what life on earth will be like in the future—*our* future," April began afresh, "because it duplicates the events of your world, can't you tell us what happened? How do we solve our major problems? Is there a way to escape nuclear war?"

Her living replica raised her chin and laughed. In the sound was an echo of April's own dramatic sense. "Oh, my dears, of *course* there is a way to escape it!" She glanced at the male with bright, teasing eyes, engaging his amusement. "Clearly enough, even with the most rudimentary logic, you know that the people of your world will not be wiped from the map—not *all* of them. If that were not true, how could we be sitting with you *now?*"

"You've said enough!" the husband snapped, warning her with his frigid gaze. He looked back at Spence. "There are ways in which we are not permitted to interfere with your planet and its development. I think you can appreciate that."

"I can appreciate," Spence retorted, "that you just confessed there are ways in which you *can* interfere with us. What are they?"

"Grand, grand, grand!" His look-alike brought his hands together, fingertip-to-fingertip and heel-to-heel, in a pattering of earnest applause. "You *do* have a modicum of alertness as well as logic, after all!"

"Thanks a bunch," Spence said dryly. "Will you answer my question?"

"Why not?" The extraterrestrial shrugged elaborately. "We are permitted to interfere in the lives of

266

individuals but are denied any form of *collective* reconstruction. That is not to say you and your other writers are devoid of importance in your scheme of things. Quite the contrary. Which is why, dear Mr. Torrence, we could not actually take your lives." His eyes glittered. "Why we were allowed only to—make certain *improvements* in your outlooks."

"Such smugness, such arrogance." The writer risked a frown. "There is not really so much difference between our civilizations, I think. Shit and damnation, we've suffered meddlers like you before. Brainwashing is nothing new."

For a moment Spence-II's face contorted in an angry grimace and he looked nothing at all like Spence. For the duration of that moment, Spence believed he had gone too far. Then the icy composure settled again in the lines of the fellow's face. "You shall not force me to precipitate action. I am confident in the superiority of our civilization, even if we cannot return to enjoy it. Consider this little fact, Mr. Torrence: All our people have perished of natural causes for hundreds of decades." He drew himself erect in his chair. His pride was evident. "No one has been *killed* for some two-million years—*no one!* Not in battle or private conflict."

"*Why* can't you return to your place?" Lauren asked, and felt the alien's chilly glance swerve to stare at her. Her lower lip trembled. "Well, you *said* we could ask questions, and you just *said* you weren't allowed to go home!"

"My daughter asks an interesting question, Mr. 'Peter Quince,'" Spence noted mildly. Suddenly he wanted very much to know the rest of it, to learn what the extraterrestrials were trying to accomplish on earth. "Would you mind answering it?" He paused. "Are you . . . undesirables?" He remembered his own early reflections. "Are you—*criminals?*"

The male with his face permitted himself a slight smirk. "I am proud to say, sir, that we are the ultimate *desirables*—the most preferred beings to be born on our world."

"But they don't want you back?" April asked, confused.

He ignored her. "We are like the sailors and the hunters of your own past, the adventurers and explorers. Like them, we are constantly engaged in a valorous quest, in a pursuit of our duty."

The female nodded. She rested her coffee cup on the floor beside her chair and folded her arms across her bosom. "Our planet, as we said is incomparably advanced. But it is also . . . *blood-thin*. Drained of certain fundamental drives that contribute to the discovery and development of new worlds. Only a few of us, from time to time, are born with the age-old lusts still beating in our hearts."

"Blood lusts, then," Spence said softly, carefully. "Atavistic throwbacks to a time when aggression was a necessity. Am I right?"

"Call it that if you wish," replied Spence-II, a trifle arch, even defensive. "We remain soldiers of spirit, foragers, pioneers if you will."

"And our efforts serve many valuable purposes," injected April-II. "Our major activities are filmed and recorded. We provide graphic images of the things we achieve and they are sent back home. There, they become the major means of entertainment for our kind."

"I think I understand," said the redhaired writer. Again his heart was thudding in his chest, because he was beginning to understand a part of it and learning that the aliens might be more dangerous even than he'd thought. "The people on your planet—whom you say will be *us*, in a very long time—are so disciplined, so *controlled*, that they are full of repressed instincts and desires. I assume that they must be kept that way by your government. And so, they live vicariously on the bloody thrills *you* provide for them."

His look-alike arose, glaring down at Spence. "I have perceived your implication and touched your brain telepathically. *You* think that *we* are *insane!*" His cheeks, *Spence's* cheeks, turned red with growing anger. "*You* believe that we are nothing more than—than paid assassins, *madmen!* Homicidal maniacs!"

"Oh, no," Spence answered him quickly. Frightened badly, he tried to clear his mind. "I didn't say that at all. I *wouldn't* say that!"

"You—you prehistoric *nothing!*" the extraterrestrial flared. "How *dare* you think down on your betters!"

April was pale with terror. "I'm sure he didn't mean to imply such things, Mr. Quince. He—"

"Very well, Torrences," the redhaired duplicate said, his gaze sweeping all three of them, "consider certain facts. Even here and now, on your precious Earth, insanity is generally defined as that which does not correspond to the norm. The madman is he who is socially unacceptable, a continuing irritation to the great majority. Isn't that correct?"

"I suppose it is," Spence agreed. "What's your point?"

"My point is that your definition of criminal insanity has already been a major problem for you and you are scarcely aware that it is. My point is that it will be a *growing* problem for you in your future. Reflect, dear Mr. Torrence, on the fact that in the society of your Adolf Hitler, it was entirely acceptable to slay certain types of people—socially acceptable, and therefore in no sense an act of either criminality or madness."

"Yet today," April-II put in, "you claim the Nazi society was insane as well as criminal. It *was*, of course." Her dramatic voice rose. "But don't you see, a judgment of that kind comes much too late? What good does it do . . . the victims?"

Spence-II spread his legs and rested his balled fists on his hips. "So long as you earthlings must judge insanity on the basis on that which is not the norm, you must *remain subject* to such costly errors of judgment and the killing may continue. You will always risk inhabiting a world in which things are done that, customarily—in earlier days, *or* in days yet to come—would be regarded as abominable, atrocious. And so, my dear Torrences, if *we* are psychotics in the minds of certain people on our world today, it is nothing more than a question of *who* happens to be in control—in power, in authority—at any given moment!"

"Because it is against our ultimate law to take a life," April-II picked up the thread, "our people could not kill us."

Her mate smiled sardonically. "All they could find to do was a way to use our special talents and aptitudes, our unique gifts of agression. And they certainly found a

270

way." For the first time his smoky eyes revealed the flecks of red that were so evident in those of his daughter, and the Torrences realized that—by any sensible or useful definition, on any world—the "Quinces" were stark, staring mad. The male chortled. "A way that would benefit *our* civilization quite marvelously—and at a relatively small cost to your own. I think you'll find the explanation rather interesting. . . ."

CHAPTER TWENTY-FOUR

The only living thing in the manager's office adjoining the hotel suite of Mr. and Mrs. Peter Quince, the Selector turned lethargically, almost feebly in its life-sustaining chemical soup like some ugly chunk of meat-bone coming to life. For a brief moment, *it* did not know where it was, and the realization of that was incredibly shocking.

The realization should have sent its special, intricate brain on a rapid search for an answer. *It* should have made contact with the home planet, run cross-reference checks of its complex circuitry, tested to see if something else living had instigated an attack.

But the only thing of interest *it* could see through the aquarium wall was the mouldering corpse of the desk clerk, Henry Clurge. Headless, the leaking from the neck had ceased and the shoulders of the human being were drenched in a brownish stain the Selector identified as blood. There was no regret whatsoever that it had killed Henry Clurge, since people of this planet were of no conceivable interest to it except as the sentient elements of the vast puzzle the Selector was there to govern. But it rather wished its companions, Mr. and Mrs. Quince, would collect the body, get it out of there. Or slice it down, for meat.

Deciding to demand precisely that attention, the Selector focussed and sent one of its piercing telepathic orders across the office, toward the manager and his woman. That is, it *tried* to dispatch the message. In point of fact, nothing happened except the formulation of a series of peptic bubbles that took shape and then popped along the surface of its liquid.

Curious. Clearly, *it* must recapitulate, review what had happened to limit its customary abilities. Where it had been, mentally, it was not certain; but it had the impression of being absent from its body in some meaningful manner. For the first time in the creature's existence, it experienced anxiety and considerable indecision. If it had been intellectually absent, was it the result of the experience they referred to as one's mind "wandering," or was it even worse than that—had it actually been *asleep?"*

There was no record of it in its memory banks; not a clue. The Selector kicked, more in concern than anger, although it very much wished to kill someone or something at that instant. This situation was intolerable and apparently growing worse by the moment. In its uncharacteristic ire and worry, it even lost sight of one of its primary instructions—to contact its originating planet in the event of emergency. Unbelievably even to the Selector's remaining grip on machine-like detachment, it found itself mired in a *self-interest* that was almost humanoid of kind and proportion. It was too anxious about its own problems to remember the key imperatives, or act upon them.

But as the minutes passed and the Selector analyzed the situation—its plight—to the best of its ability, it finally came to a realization of *what* was destroying the usefulness which was the sole reason for its existence. It saw that it should have identified the source immediately, since that source had been troubling the Selector since the four of them arrived on this planet:

Earthlings. The *people* of this world.

Yes, yes, there was no doubt about it. The headless being called Clurge, dead on the floor near the tank, had been only a more heedless and direct representative of these *people* with their detestable "emotions."

Now the Selector saw that it was the *proximity* of people *en masse* that had become the source of its dysfunction, its miserable loss of telepathic command. Why, the humanoid Quinces in their adjoining suite had gathered an *army* of the confounding species—more than one-hundred of their confusing ilk—and then compounded their calamitous act by bringing the "people" named Torrence into their very dining room!

So irrational, so murderous, had the Selector become that it was incapable of facing the fact that the Quinces had acted exclusively and in every instance on its *own* orders. Inexperienced in facing its own errors of judgment, because it had never made any of which it was aware before, the Selector behaved in a singularly human manner: It placed the blame on others instead of accepting the responsibility for its own decisions.

But there was time. There was a way to retaliate, to regain command of the situation—to repay the bewildering, emotional earth "people" for the discomfort and disorientation it was feeling. Sooner or later, either Mr. or Mrs. Quince would come to the office to feed it. Eventually they would lean over the container, close enough for the Selector to discharge its telepathic instructions in its old, hurtful style.

And when that time came, it knew, without a doubt, what its instructions would be. It did not need to contact home; it did not require further orders and it certainly would not seek them.

Merely thinking about the time when the Quinces came brought a measure of solace to the terrifying mind-creature in the tank. Because it would simply tell them to put every human being they could find, inside or outside of the Hotel Holroyd, immediately *to death*—by the most inventively hideous means they could conceive.

Spencer Torrence tried to look casual, but he held on to the arms of the easy chair tightly, needing to know the answer to his question but fearful, at last, of asking it.

"Tell us," he said softly. "*Why* did you come to our world?"

April, beside him, straightened and he could see that she, too, was readying herself for the explanation. On his other side, Lauren reached for her Pop's big hand and held on for dear life.

"What is the expression you use?" asked the extraterrestrial male. Then he snapped his fingers. "'Damnation and shit,' it is difficult to decide where to begin."

"Tell them," April-II urged him, "that *everyone on Earth has an exact* duplicate *on our planet.*"

The alien nodded. "That is precisely the case, in the physical sense. You recall I mentioned that we are sister planets? And that it is against all our most sacred laws—however ridiculous my family and I consider it—to take a life . . . even the life of an enemy?"

"Then you *have* enemies?" Spence remarked. "There are those who oppose you."

"Certainly!" Spence-II snapped, irritated. "I told you we were in advance of your world by millions of years and so we have a completely free electoral process by which our government is chosen. There are no speeches, no campaign promises, since we have the capability of reading the minds of one another and, with the utilization of certain scientific devices you would not comprehend, the intent of an individual who seeks political office is made accessible to every voter—the total, *truthful* intent."

"Perhaps you are more advanced than we," April confessed.

"After election to the federal government, however," said her look-alike, "there is the question of internal security to bear in mind. While an official is in office, consequently, his or her thoughts are *blocked* by another clever device—so that those who might illegally benefit from secrets at the highest level are no longer able to know what the leaders are thinking."

A thought occurred to Spence. Something about nature, human or otherwise, which he felt might pertain anywhere in the universe. "How long has your present government served?"

Spence-II saw that he understood and smiled evilly. "For an exceedingly long period of time. By virtue of being the only persons in our world whose thoughts are not available to all, our government officials have a remarkable advantage over their political adversaries. *Secrets* may, again, be kept."

"But do not think our government falls short of magnificence," said the female extraterrestrial. "Consider: There is no killing, no war, no execution for crimes of any kind, no abortion, no elimination of the elders."

Spence frowned, perplexed. "No elimination of your elders?"

"I forgot," April-II said, "that you have not yet reached the point in your development where your old people are—banished. It lies ahead of you still."

"Despite our advances, of course, we have problems. Two of them, to be exact." Spence-II finished his coffee and replaced the cup in the saucer. None of the Torrences had dared drink theirs. "The first, overpopulation. Candidly, we have learned that there are billions more persons than we require for optimum living. But as we pointed out, it is against our law to remove them. Second, our present government is faced by mounting political opposition which seeks to *return* our world to yesteryear—to a reactionary society in which lawbreakers, even people such as we, are executed in order to lower the population. Clearly, our government fears defeat but knows it must prevent the opposition from gaining control. If it does not, lives there will again be taken. Executive orders will eliminate not only the undesirables but all varieties of person who fail to serve a useful, productive existence."

"Do you see?" asked the female, her eyes appealing to them. "It is a terrible stalemate. If our present government is sustained, over-population will press every male and female into such limited space that the quality of life will drastically diminish. But if the opposition wins, millions will be slain."

"Including us," said the Spence-duplicate, spreading his hands. "There seemed to be no solution to the problem until certain geniuses within the government determined that we—individuals like us; ruthless, pioneering explorers—could not be regarded as being subject to our laws. Because we can never set foot on our world again, because we are always light-years away from home."

"And Earth, you say, is your sister planet," Spence mused, thinking, the mystery increasingly clearing for him—"where you have an exact replica of every individual in your society."

"Excellent. You begin to perceive the nature of our ingenious, ultimate solution, and I begin to wonder if I've underestimated your primitive intelligence. A pity there isn't a way to continue this dialogue indefinitely." He paused, sighing. "You see, by changing the way a man or woman on your planet thinks, why, upon *our* world there is instantly *one less enemy* of our government! It is an admirable solution, is it not?"

"It's horrible," Spence growled under his breath, knowing they did not hear him; "it's the ultimate Watergate."

But April-II nodded her delight for her husband's comments. "We can direct the opinions and therefore the decisions and actions of the opposing party, at home," she went on, "by altering the views and deeds of

278

his *duplicate* here. That keeps the ruling leaders in power"—she beamed happily upon the Torrences, the way April had looked when applause rolled-up from an audience—*"indefinitely."*

"It's certainly ingenious," the real April murmured, awed. Spence watched her with pride, detecting that she was acting, now, stalling for time. "Then you do not mean to kill any of us, correct? It's enough for you to gain control of certain earthlings' minds—right?"

"Ah, in point of truth, madam," replied the male, taking his seat afresh and neatly pinching the knees of his trousers in turn, "it *is*—now and then—necessary for us to . . . *remove* one of you. Fully. Some of our enemies enjoy such powerful influence that only by death may they lose it. Of course, it also trims the population, by consequence serving *two* useful purposes. The taking of such rudimentary life-forms as we find here, as I've indicated, in no way abrogates the law in our society." He gave them a generous, forebearing smile.

"Killing a handful of writers can scarcely do much toward reducing your, ah, 'surplus population,' as a man named Dickens put it a long while ago," Spence observed. "Of course, since I write I object to my peers being harmed. But there aren't all that many top writers on the planet."

"Oh, my dear sir, *your* people aren't the first!"

Spence hadn't expected that. His shoulders sagged and he gaped at his look-alike in open shock.

"My, no," said the extraterrestrial, "we've visited *other* major groups of human beings quite often in the past. You writers are merely . . . *next.*"

"Monstrous," the redhead declared, no longer able to choke back the words. "This is incalculably evil by anyone's standards!"

"Oh, come, let's not become so hypocritical." His replica scoffed, his features twisted in a sneer. "After all, killing isn't universally objectionable at this stage in your world's development—admit it! You still fight senseless wars and police actions, 'brushfires'; political foes are still removed around this globe by means of assassination. Even religious leaders become targets. Rioters and terrorists may strike anytime, anywhere. Even your police sometimes fire at mobs of your people without hesitation. So what are a few more deaths on Earth?"

"Death," April whispered, "is personal. You killed my friend Ginger."

"Did we?" The alien actually looked surprised. "Are you quite sure of that?" He saw them nod. With a frown he turned to peer at his daughter, Lauren's look-alike. "Child, do you know anything about this person called Ginger?"

For a second she didn't reply. Then she nodded. avoiding his gaze. "Yes, father, I know a lot."

"Hm-m." Spence-II sighed, mildly embarrassed. "I wasn't informed."

"It gets out of hand, doesn't it?" Spence demanded, his brows raising. In his lap his fists clenched and unclenched as he tried to swallow the fury. "Don't you see that when you begin toying with a people's God-given right to a secure life, it gets away from you? That all your planning, all your brilliant gadgetry, can't prevent you from making tragic errors?"

"Well, what of it?" Spence-II glared at him. "We can't be held accountable for anything we do in this backwards of the cosmos. You're a writer, Torrence. You appreciate inventiveness, cleverness! Think of the beauty in what we've described to you." He looked at the ceiling, rather dreamily. "The very finest members of our government—without lifting a finger—eliminate their reactionary enemies and the population is reduced by us—and *no law* at all is broken!" He lowered his red-haired head, nearly bowing to unheard applause. "Candidly, I suggest it is the ultimate logical morality."

CHAPTER TWENTY-FIVE

For a long while—which is to say, an internal realization that her own private time-clock was ticking away the minutes and hours—there was nothing at all but an optical sensation of seeing an infinite number of shrinking stars in the night sky, twinkling miniature points of blazing light above her, below her, everywhere she looked. Although there was no feeling of motion, a residual part of her that thought knew she was rocketing through some alternate space; for the points of light plunged past her, quickly vanishing, only to be instantly replaced by more of their myriad kind.

It was, in a way, the perilously closest that a believer in the Creator could come to literal nothingness. If she existed at all, it was of no matter; surely she could not be reached in this lifeless canopy of unchanging night, surely she could not—in any sense—be brought back. While she had a dull, far-away awareness of who she was and what had happened to her, there was removed from her being any emotional connection to her former identity as well as any desire to recover or reestablish it. Actually, she did not care about anything at all other than a rudimentary embryonic urge to touch-down somewhere on something real, and solid—to end the nightmare sameness of a universe that should, in her condition, be seen only by a Divinity who understood it because He had *made* it. In time, or what passed for time since that was exclusively her distant property now, she sensed that she would lose even this remnant of useless awareness, not so much because she had gone mad with the abject loneliness of it but because, from sheer pointlessness, she would perish from boredom.

What's this? The spirit of Ginger Lloyd discerned, across unfathomable depths of twittering night, a certain strange *narrowing*. She seemed to have entered a kind-of tunnel—*no, a funnel*—and instead of rushing directionlessly through the cosmos, she had the dim realization that she was starting to *plummet*. Stimulated, her fragmented thoughts groped for unison, perceived that in order to plummet—to fall; to drop—there must be a direction, one at least. *Down.* With the knowledge she experienced the complexity, the heaviness, the connectiveness that a child who must be born experiences. While they were yet shadows, she knew there was *more* to her than the swiftly-regathering assembly of her ideas and beliefs; there were . . . *parts* belonging to her, substantial chunks of a substance she felt to be flesh and bone.

And with that knowledge, a world caroomed *up* toward her, she realized she must crash into it, and she *willed* herself not to see the collision. . . .

And sat up on the floor, reborn, dazed, uncomprehending—but otherwise unharmed. She was not even aware of the incredible assortment of data flowing back into her mind; she could not even appreciate the miracle that every scrap of data—memory; knowledge; emotion—had returned to her intact.

The fact that she was Ginger Lloyd, Mrs. Daniel Lloyd, female human being, a person of a certain age and a certain race and of a certain inconsequential microsecond of cosmic time, no longer seemed to be of much importance. She took it all for granted, the way every member of her species always had, and peered around the room.

She saw two desks and two chairs. The fact that she identified them easily and at once did not seem miraculous. She saw file cabinets, no windows—how *perfect*, how *special* it was that her brain made the synoptic jump to appreciate not only what she *could* see but what she could *not* see; it was a level of thinking quite beyond the capacity of nine-tenths of the living things on her planet—and a door.

Feeling beneath her, she experienced the texture and particular warmth of manmade carpeting, then let her fingers trail along her own shapely legs and feet, testing the condition of her physical well-being. When she *remembered*, at last, that she had tried to strike an extraterrestrial—when she saw in her memory's eye the instant when she had felt the shock of electrocution, and the numb nothingness that her disintegration had brought her—Ginger shut her almost colorless eyes, bowed her head, and whispered her gratitude that she had survived it all. She knew, now, how close she had come to dying; and with the knowledge that she was perfectly sound, perfectly well, Ginger came complete.

Slipping her hands beneath her, she forced herself to her knees, preparing to rise. *This must be the manager's office,* she thought, starting to straighten but still looking around the room. *But where are April, Spence, and Lauren?*

That was the instant she felt herself being—*scrutinized. Stared at; watched.*

Her questioning gaze swept to a container shaped like a tank, or aquarium—

And met, only a few feet away, the cold, probing eyes of the ugliest and most terrifying creature she'd ever seen in her life.

The Selector looked *at her*—*and Ginger felt the clammy internal touch of its telepathic thoughts, wriggling to* invade *her mind.*

"If my friend Dan Lloyd were here, and himself," Spence said as he formulated his thoughts, "I think he might ask you who selects the people to be brainwashed or murdered. Since you claim to operate on such a high moral plane, I'll return the compliment and suggest that it would be sheer hypocrisy for your own people to make the choices."

"I quite agree," said the extraterrestrial. "Your reasoning is admirable, Mr. Torrence. We employ an objective third party called the *Selector.* It accompanied

285

us on our journey."

"*It?*" Lauren asked, shuddering.

"The Selector," replied April-II, "is an ideal blending of man, animal, and computer. It is—what is that phrase of yours—'neither fish nor fowl,' but consists of the most pragmatic and subtle ingredients of each species."

"Of course, there are *many* Selectors." The male alien let the news drop among them like a hand grenade. "For the simple reason that yours is not our *only* sister planet. There are many and, as a consequence, many Selectors." His eyes glittered. "As well as many teams of specially-trained explorers such as we. Obviously, dear Torrences, for the lowering of our population to be genuinely beneficial—a problem you cited yourself, Mr. Torrence—there must be many alterations, many assassinations. If there were *too many* on earth, your people might come to notice it. But spread across a number of planets, the loss is negligible and the changes of mind on the part of your influential citizens seems merely to be a natural shift of opinion."

"If this is your idea of progress," Spence snapped, "I want no part of it."

"But you shall *have* to become a small part of it," said the extraterrestrial's woman, without any special malice, "before the day is over."

"You said we were not the first people of earth your Selector chose. Writers and their families." April was, Spence saw, back to playing her role, stalling for all she was worth. He hoped he was the only one who detected the headdress of perspiration beading her forehead. "Who else have you . . . influenced?"

"Ah, there were so *many* to choose between!" cried Spence's duplicate, chuckling. "Several levels of govern-

286

ment, the military, big business, labor leaders, persons in education—all the rest. Happily, the Selector was able to choose two groups prior to your literary bunch." He jabbed a finger in Spence's direction. "Surely you have seen the way life is changing on your planet, Mr. Torrence? Growing incidence of murder and assassination, the acceleration of crime, a speedy breakdown in common morality?"

"You *wanted* your opposition on your world to become violent?" Spence asked.

"You do not understand the nature of a sister planet," replied the male alien. "The *precise opposite* occurs at home, because ours is a mirroring existence." When he smiled, his teeth shone brightly. "Our enemies are becoming exceedingly docile, even timid. They lack the will to mount any kind of convincing opposition."

"Then that's the story," said Spence with a huge sigh.

"Not quite." The redhaired extraterrestrial lifted a warning index finger. "Your sanctimonious attitude toward our clearly-superior grasp of morality annoys me. Would you be surprised to know that there is a small, exceptionally-elect group of your *own* people—*earth* people—who are doing precisely the same thing *we* are doing? Elsewhere?"

"That's a damned lie!" Spence snorted.

"We wouldn't have the technology to do such terrible things," April supported him, "even if we were murderous enough to do it!"

"*Think*," said the Spence look-alike, leaning his head back in his chair. A small shiver of a smile moved on his thin lips. "*Consider.* When next a person of prominence here *vanishes* into thin air—when his death is clouded in mystery, or when he is assassinated and there appears to be *no understandable reason* for it—don't just let it drop. Remember there is a reason for everything, and investigate. You shall learn, my dear Torrences, that your own little conspiratorial group of men and women from the planet Earth are brothers under the skin of my wife and me—because *they* are doing what *we* are doing, but in another corner of the cosmos, on another sister planet of Earth." The extraterrestrial laughed. "Of course, you *could* blame us for providing them both with the useful idea—*and* the means of transportation."

"The means of transportation?" asked April, wide-eyed.

Her duplicate grinned. "What else did you think UFOs were *used* for?" she asked with an arched brow. "*Do* let me refill your cups, that coffee must be ice-cold by now."

CHAPTER TWENTY-SIX

"I'm sorry, my wife," began Spence's double, rising slowly and stealthily from his easy chair, "But I do not think there is any time left for more coffee. Or for more polite social conversation." He put his hand into the pocket of his sports jacket and, when he withdrew it, a trio of small, silver metallic objects gleamed in the light from the chandelier above the dining room table. The Torrences recognized, at once, the buttons implanted in the index fingers of the others. "Nor, I fear, is there any time left for our interesting guests." His smile vanished and his eyes became hard as marbles. "Not, at least, as they are presently constituted and motivated."

"Damn you, your tricks won't work against us!" Spence retorted, jumping to his feet. "We'll know, from here on out, that anything we see must be an illusion—and none of us will fall for it." He groped for April's and Lauren's hands, without taking his eyes off the other male, and forced them to stand behind him. "Shit and damnation, friend, I think it's safe to say we're a pretty even match!"

"An 'even match?'" inquired their host. "Explain, please."

Spence doubled his fists, took a step forward. "I mean we're exactly the same size and weight. And I don't intend to let you take us over the way you did poor Danny Lloyd without a fight!"

"A *fight?*" The extraterrestrial offered him a grand, open sneer. "My, my, you *are* primitive, aren't you. There's been nothing like hand-to-hand combat on our world in over a million years!"

"Well, we still know how on good old uncivilized earth!" Spence snapped, only feet from his look-alike now. His heart was thundering in his chest and he knew the risk he took but there seemed to be no other way. His eyes were locked with the alien's, and he hoped April was watching her replica closely.

The male extraterrestrial lifted the hand which he hadn't slipped into his pocket. Something lean, tubular, gleaming rested in his palm and it pointed at Spence. "Such antiquated defensive techniques," he whispered, "will have no effect at all on *this* . . ."

Ginger crouched over the aquarium, looking inside, her head hurting painfully. She didn't know why she'd approached the ineffably ugly thing in the tank. In a way, she felt drawn to it, she supposed. Undoubtedly curious. What in the name of God *was* the slimy thing, she wondered; and immediately she doubted that the Selector existed in the name of any kind of Deity.

Floating on its back, filled with a sudden urge to be stroked, the Selector stared up at the female human being. Only once before, in the presence of the desk clerk called Henry Clurge, had it been this near to an earth species. Data concerning the woman named Ginger Lloyd filtered steadily into its intricate, unfeeling brain as it touched the soft center of her own brain. Superficially, of course, she was constructed on the same lines as the female entitled Mrs. Peter Quince; but near the Ginger-Lloyd—*this* close to her—the Selector began to perceive a wide range of differences.

Foremost among them, it realized, was a positive *geyser* of emotions, those senseless, nearly anti-intellectual things it had sensed before. *Control,* it told itself firmly: *Seek and maintain control over inferior species.*

The segment of Ginger's mind which remained liberated wanted, that moment, to spin away from the creature and rush pellmell from the office—to find her friends the Torrences, to enjoy normality once more. But there seemed to be something . . . *compelling* . . . about this small, strange being in the tank. Partly, she had the notion there was something about *it* that she should know, that she *must* know. But also, she realized, there was in the monster a driving, single minded aggressiveness not wholly unlike the competitiveness she had used in playing winning tennis. Here, however—in the case of the thing beneath her—that aggression had been reduced to an elemental level of open *murderousness.* Unlike

Ginger, unlike all the athletes she had met on tennis courts around the world, *this* devil's invention would do whatever it took to be entirely in control; to win at all costs.

On that shaky, slender strand of understanding Ginger's own half-forgotten psychic sensitivity rushed out and encountered, with a shock that was acutely painful, the horrid, complex, futuristic and consciously-designed brain of the Selector. Telepathy brought her into the closest conceivable proximity with the creepy thing; and when it saw that she was present in its brain—when it *reacted* in the most personal of ways—there was a lightning instant of complete recognition on both their parts.

This ugly monstrosity ordered *what happened to my Danny! This ghastly creature was the one who* chose *Danny, who* made him *attack us!*

Inwardly, the Selector acknowledged that she was right. It seemed pleased with itself. Unbelievably, it *smirked* at her. *Stroke me*, it commanded, lolling lazily on its pimply backside, blowing bubbles; *oh*, stroke *me!*

Staring down at it, Ginger put her hand into the tank.

"Why, you goddamned fool," Spence shouted, "you *can't* do anything to us or our minds—you *don't dare* kill us!"

The extraterrestrial's eyelids quivered. His lips turned up at the corners. "Why ever not, Mr. Torrence?"

Spence was undaunted. He had been waiting for this moment and, for the first time in a very long while, he laughed. "Are you so crazy, so psychotic, that you can't see it? Are you people so 'advanced' you cannot recognize the most *obvious* truth when it's right in front of you?" He reached out and hugged April and Lauren, delighted by the expression of perplexity spreading across all three alien faces. "The fact that we're replicas of persons on your world works *both ways*, pal. You people are *our* duplicates, too. And specifically, *each* of you three . . . is a *duplicate of us Torrences!*"

The male extraterrestrial shot a frantic, questioning glance to April-II. Both of them gaped openly at the redhead. Now they understood it, he realized. But he wanted to rub it in.

"That's right! If you alter the way *we* think, why, that means you'll be changing your *own* minds!" Spence grinned from ear-to-ear. "And if you *murder* us, all three of you will drop dead that second!"

"The Selector," mumbled his look-alike, half turning to leave. "Must consult the Selector . . ."

"That thing can't help you now, brother." Spence chuckled. "But I suspect it knows the truth, all right, because it's clear as glass. They've tricked *you* this time, decided they've had enough of your kind—which is the first genuinely progressive thing I've seen 'em do. Don't you get it, pal? The same law against life-taking you've admired so much won't permit them to influence your brain or to take your lives—but they mean for *you* to do it for them! Undoubtedly we were supposed to meet, this way. You were supposed to use your handy-dandy little gadgets to wipe us out and, in the process, you'd have been changed as well. Or *dead!*" He saw April smile happily at him in understanding and he bent down to kiss the top of Lauren's head. "That progressive society on your splendid new world isn't any better than the politicians here on your sister planet, *Mr.* Quince. They can't *afford* to leave the three of you as you are, because you can identify the people in the opposition party who were altered or killed. It's the old sweet story, buddy—you *know* too much! So put your pistol in your pocket. It's all over!"

For a moment the being called "Peter Quince" did not speak. Across the room, when Lauren looked out the window, she saw that the snow had melted and the sidewalks and streets were clear. Yet Quince drew himself erect and put his shoulders back with determination. To the amazement of all the Torrences, he slowly raised his hand. Again, he aimed the weapon at them. "In a modern society, Mr. Torrence," he said on a note of regret, the sound of sorrow heavy in his identical voice, "a part of the peaceable atmosphere stems from the fact of obedience to one's betters. Loyalty to our superiors is second nature to us."

"I should have seen that," Spence said softly, staring at the glittering weapon. "You're so repressed I should have known real individuality was dead in your future world."

"I must confess that you have astounded me with your observation," Quince continued. "It is a pity, I suppose, that I have learned this late that your people are not as intellectually backward as we'd been told. And I certainly have no desire to lose my identity. But really, you know," he centered his silver weapon on Spence's forehead, the metallic button ready in his other hand, "we have no other choice."

The door leading to the manager's office smashed against the wall. "Ginger!" April cried, staring with disbelief and joy at her friend.

In three swift steps the blonde athlete was beside them. She didn't bother even to glance at the extraterrestrials because she had scanned the Selector's mind and knew what to expect. *Something* was gripped tightly in her arms, something that writhed helplessly and sought to escape.

"Oh, Pop," moaned Lauren, seeing that "something" and turning away. April took a single look and covered her mouth.

Spence looked down at the ugly creature wriggling in Ginger's arms, and caught his breath.

"*The Selector!*" The male extraterrestrial blanched, started forward. "You must *not* remove the Selector from its tank. This is sacrilege!"

It seemed to weigh no more than twelve pounds or so, Spence realized. At a glance it appeared to be a three-foot length of greenish slime with pale yellow protuberances that puckered, like pustules, up and down its form. It was fishlike of body except for the impossible head. Mammoth for its size, cradled in Ginger's arm, the skull was utterly hairless. Pulsing red veins ran from one side of the head to the other. Within it lived a brain of pure mentality, taken from the human embryo created by brilliant parentage, but then altered and "improved" with the hardware of an advanced computer. On either side three wires and a leathery black cord extended from the head, over the ears, but Ginger had unplugged them. Still it survived. Its features, baby-pink of hue, were remotely human and its popping fish eyes were even now analyzing the situation with an otherworldly cunning that narrowed its pupils and made them glow the color of emeralds.

"Take it," Ginger said simply, and slipped the monster into Spence's arms.

Which was when the Selector managed to communicate, telepathically. Its words were seared into all their heads. *"Them!"* came the electrical squeal, like finger-nails on a blackboard. *"They* are *next!* I have chosen! *Kill them!"*

Spence saw his look-alike pause and gave the humanoid a grim smile. "Okay. You wanted prehistoric passion, buddy, I'll *show* you prehistoric passion," he grunted, ignoring the scaly feel of the thing in his hands. "You wanted killing so I'll *show* you killing!" He raised the squirming Selector above his head. His voice raised in outrage. *"I'll* show you your past—and for all I know, Quince, your damnable *future* as well!"

In a single motion he slammed the creature to the hotel floor, raised his foot, and ground it into the monster's head. There was a crunching sound, a certain *popping;* yet Spence went on grinding his heel into the ruined Selector until the only thing left on the carpeting of the Hotel Holroyd suite was a green stain flecked with red, and a stench like that of a thousand-year-old, very dead fish. . . .

"Spence!" April cried and pointed.

He looked where the Quince family had been and saw instead a shimmering of sunbeams—a trillion-trillion microscopic stars raining through a beautiful lace curtain of gold. At the heart of it the three look-alikes stood, hand-in-hand, as they began to fade, to go. Only one message was uttered before they were gone: *"Wait and see,"* came the voice of Spence-II, sepulchral and darkly ominous, like an eerie communication from a world halfway across the teeming universe; *"wait and see what happens now."*

The curtain and the shower of sunbeams lifted like reversed lightning from the floor, acquired a certain apex, and—vanished.

Gasping their relief, Spence and April hugged Lauren first, and then Ginger. From the front room of the suite, they heard the sounds of people—human beings—shifting, standing, making muttering noises of clear amazement.

"What in the name of all that's holy," demanded prize-winning Harry Werlin, stepping into the dining room and plucking a shining metal button from his index finger, "is going *on* in this madhouse?" The elegant, heavyset woman behind him bobbed her head in agreement. "Don't you people realize I'm a man who values his *privacy?*"

Spence laughed aloud. There would be a lot to explain; there would be many books written, he knew, and the world—*their* world—would be forewarned in case a team like the Quinces ever returned.

Then he touched his friend Ginger's arm and, when he spoke, saw her pretty face break into a delightful smile. "Let's go get old Dan out of the bathroom," he told her, "and tell him the whole story. You know, he must be dying for a cigar by now!"

EPILOGUE

Halting days of limping recovery passed, and difficult efforts toward resuming normal lives were made, all around the nation.

During midsummer in Porter, New York, the natives sweltered in the merciless, relentless heat. But a few of the residents, at least, had sworn they would never complain again about a summer, and kept their word. From time to time they still experienced unexpected chills in their remembering bones—icy shivers that darted up and down their spines until they gulped down hot coffee, good brandy, or fell into one another's arms.

They supposed, these natives of Porter, that it might be years before they could place the events of late March and early April into a more comforting perspective.

Or stop awakening in the middle of the night, screaming.

Books had been written about their ordeal with the extraterrestrials, but not until many of the writers— including Spence Torrence and Dan Lloyd—formed a loosely-organized group and went to their publishers *en masse*. Only then would the people who hadn't been there admit, even grudgingly, that their writers' new work was not fictitious. And privately, among themselves, editors at the publishing houses discussed the strange possibility that the most celebrated authors in the land had gone collectively mad simultaneously. No other explanation seemed to fit the bill.

Eventually, too, there was a motion picture made for television. Produced in the somewhat stilted style of a docudrama, it was nevertheless advertised and promoted—despite the protests of all the wordsmiths who'd suffered through the invasion by extraterrestrials—as science-fiction. The film drew a Neilsen rating which placed it fifth from the bottom for its particular week, a number of scathingly skeptical and insulting reviews, and a single proposal—from a producer who should have known better—that the controversial story be turned into a weekly series.

In time, winter came to Porter despite a number of prayers that it would not. When an early snow storm drifted into town in the dark of night, Ginger Lloyd sat up in bed, shook her husband until he opened his eyes, and begged him to take her to Florida. She was terrified that it might snow forever; the possibility of being imprisoned, once more, was more than she could take.

A few days after that, Dan Lloyd was leaving the office of a travel agent, pounding his bare hands together to keep them warm, when he saw a familiar figure ahead of him. Shuffling through the foot-deep snow that impeded his progress, he clapped Spence Torrence on the shoulder and called his name.

"Dan, you old war-horse!" Spence exclaimed, shaking his friend's hand. "Glad to see you!"

"Well, it'll be the last time until spring." Dan stuck a cigar between his lips and puffed to get it going. "Ginger can't stand the idea of winter just yet." His softly affable eyes flickered at Spence above the flame. "Too many bad memories. How's April taking it? And Lauren?"

"Surprisingly well, I'd say." The redhead, his hair freckled by the descending snow, gave the other man a somewhat rueful grin. "April wants to go back on the stage when the weather breaks." He patted his gloved hands together thoughtfully. "She got a good deal of publicity out of—well, *you* know—and it seems there's a demand for her. She's even talking about writing a play."

The science writer grunted. "Look, we haven't had a chance to rap for ages." He gestured to a small restaurant up the block. McROBERTS PLACE, proclaimed a neon sign in the window. "Let me buy you a cup of coffee and a sandwich?"

"Well, I'm a little involved in something right now."

"Come on, pal," Dan urged. "All work and no play."

Spence grinned. "Shit and damnation, why not?"

They hung up their coats and took their seats at a wooden table draped with a red-and-white checkered cloth. Dan accepted his menu and ran his gaze along the familiar columns. Both he and Spence had eaten there often, over the years; reading the menu was nothing more than routine. He put it on the table, puffed on his cigar before it could go out, and noticed how warm it seemed in McROBERTS PLACE.

He noticed, as well, that Spence was still scanning his menu and still wearing his gloves.

"What are you going to have?" Dan inquired.

The redhead paused. "What do you recommend?" he asked without looking at Dan.

Dan blinked. *Now, what the hell kind of question was that?* "You always used to like Number 4."

Spence looked at him. He smiled. "Number 4, of course. Shit and damnation, how could I have forgotten a thing like that?" There was a sound, deep in his throat. He rested the menu atop Dan's, made a face. He put his gloved hand over his mouth, and coughed. It was a racking, agonized noise that made his shoulders shake. "Would you mind putting that stogie out, pal? It's getting to me."

For a second Dan did not reply. Finally he nodded, and did it. "Of course," he said carefully. He inclined his balding head in the direction of his old friend's hands. "Why don't you take off your gloves, Spence?"

Without a word, Spence dropped his hands beneath the table. Out of sight. He grinned at Dan, and shrugged. His eyes were watery, presumably from the cigar smoke. They looked red to Dan. Spence opened his mouth to say something, perhaps to explain; but nothing came out.

"I asked you a question," Dan said slowly, persistently. The panic welled up in him, and he realized he was being rude but somehow didn't care. On impulse, he put out his strong, meaty hands to grasp Spence's arm and drag his hand into view. "I asked: *Why don't you take off your gloves?"*

Spence looked down at the fingers locked on his wrist and his expression changed. Dan was tugging with all his might but it was no problem to keep his hands beneath the table. The redhead glanced up at his oldest friend and what Dan saw in the glacial set of his face made him yank his own hand away quickly.

"Shit and damnation, old buddy," Spence said, quite softly, the flecks of scarlet in his pupils hard like frozen blood—"you *know* why . . ."

". . . We are forced to deal now not in facts, but in possibilities. Nobody in quantum mechanics talks about impossibilities any more. They have developed a kind of statistical *mysticism*, and physics becomes very hard to distinguish from *metaphysics*."
　　　　　　　　　　　—Dr. Lyall Watson

"The universe is supposed to contain *everything*, by its very definition: it is better, therefore, to talk about many '*worlds*'. We imagine the universe branching into infinitely many worlds, only one of which we experience. There are closed worlds and open worlds; initially uniform worlds and initially chaotic worlds; high entropy worlds and low entropy worlds. In most worlds, life never evolves; in some worlds, life evolves but is scarce; and in relatively few worlds, *life is abundant*."
　　　　　　　　　　　—Dr. Martin Clutton-Brock